The Waiting Game

The Waiting Game

Elizabeth Cadell

William Morrow and Company, Inc.
New York

Library of Congress Catalog Card Number: 84-62590

ISBN: 0-688-04198-1

Printed in the United States of America

3 4 5 6 7 8 9 10

To
Barbara Waterson
with thanks for
tidying it up

1

Mrs Mirren finished her breakfast of tea and toast, walked to the kitchen window and wiped the mist from a pane of glass in order to get a view of the snow-covered garden.

Very un-English, she decided. More like Switzerland. No; too flat for Switzerland. Throw in a range of mountains and a tent or two and it could be a Himalayan base camp. Never in the twenty-five years in which she had lived in this cottage had she seen the lawn under so deep a covering of snow, or the trees looking as though they had been transported from a Russian forest. At the end of the path, the wicker gate seemed to have sunk to half its height. No snow was falling, but the gloomy, greyish light left no doubt that there was more to come.

She turned back to the cheerful warmth of the kitchen. It was a large room with a wide arch opening on to a living room of similar size. Both were served by a two-way fire, considered by visitors to be unnecessary in a moderate-sized cottage which had adequate central heating. There were three well-filled bookshelves in the living room, but not much furniture; what there was was comfortable but shabby. Glancing now at the faded chair-covers and the curtains which years of sun had rendered colourless, she told herself, as she had done countless times before, that she must exert herself and go up to London and choose new material. But there was no hurry. She had got used to those subdued tones and thought the pale colours suited to these homely rooms.

Her father had for many years been vicar of this feature-less, straggling, overgrown village of Downpass. He had built this cottage for his retirement, but his retirement had been to the grave, and after the funeral Laura – not as yet

7

Mrs Mirren – had come to live in it. She had been twenty-one, pretty, shy, with a fund of quiet humour, and totally untrained in anything outside the domestic sphere. It was fortunate that she had inherited enough money to meet her needs.

She removed her breakfast things and laid a place for her stepson. Her dog, mild in temper and lazy by temperament, had retreated to his basket by the fire. The cat, who had an uncatlike nature, scorned the warmth of the house, and spent most of his time seated on one of the supports of the gate, sneering contemptuously at passers-by. There were not many to sneer at except at weekends. The cottage stood in a narrow, isolated lane and would have been little used if it had not been a short-cut from the main street of the village to the church and the playing fields beyond. On weekdays, few people went by, but on Sundays there were church-goers to inspect, and on Saturdays there were groups of cricketers or footballers, according to season, and then the cat might, with luck, get in a vicious scratch or two on hands that had the temerity to try and stroke him.

There would be a very thin congregation this morning, Laura thought. Snow had blocked the lane; the vicar – a confirmed bachelor who had succeeded her father – would have nobody to preach to but the verger and half a dozen old women who kept the church tidy and polished the plate. Those who normally attended the Sunday morning services – a very small proportion of the residents – would today, the last Sunday before Christmas, make the weather an excuse for staying at home. It was certainly not a morning – the thought raised Laura's spirits – on which Beatrice Risdon would be in church. There was therefore no risk of her dropping into the cottage on her way home, as she did on most Sundays, to drink coffee and have what she called a little chat. There was no danger of her coming in to discuss what Laura guessed most of the village would soon be or were already discussing . . .

She went into the hall and looked across the garden to the miniature chalet erected four years ago by her stepson, Ross, to accommodate him on his occasional weekend visits. He had telephoned yesterday afternoon to say he was coming to spend the Christmas week with her, but added that road conditions would delay him – she was not to prepare dinner for him. She saw that he had arrived, for he had forgotten to turn off the outside light of the chalet.

It was beginning to snow heavily, but she thought the sky looked slightly clearer. She would have liked to go out and clear the path to the gate, but she knew Ross would be annoyed if she did not leave the task to him. If he slept as late as he usually did on his visits, he would have to carve his way out of the chalet.

It was just after ten when he woke, stretched, sat up in bed and stared in disbelief at the depth of snow outside. It must have been coming down in buckets all night, he thought. Thank God he had left his car at the garage in the village – he would have had to dig it out. And snow was still coming down, so he'd better get up and clear the path to the gate before it became a job for a snow-plough.

He put ski pants over his pyjamas, struggled into a sweater and put on his anorak and ski boots. Then he went outside, turning up the hood of his anorak, and got a spade from the woodshed. He could see the lighted kitchen and his stepmother moving about inside, and thought it looked the kind of cosy domestic scene pictured on Christmas cards as a change from angels.

Watched by the cat, he began to dig, musing that if snow conditions were like this in England, there should be plenty on the slopes in Italy, where he would shortly be bound. A great relief, as he usually skied in February and had wondered, when agreeing to go so soon after Christmas, whether he had been wise. But this weather looked safe enough: five days to Christmas and two after it – if there wasn't a sudden thaw, conditions would be perfect.

He banked the snow on either side of the path, dug out the lower part of the gate and had turned to scrape the path clear when a voice – familiar and unwelcome – came to his ears.

"Hi, Mr Mirren."

9

He glanced over his shoulder. Yes, there she was, or so he presumed – there was so much woolly cap and enveloping coat and outsize boots that she was all but lost to sight. The small area of face left exposed to view and to the elements was scarlet with cold, and her small, pointed nose looked like a red arrow. Like him, she was in snowproof trousers.

"Hi," he said, and resumed his scraping. If humans had tails, he reflected morosely, this would be his – hanging behind, firmly fixed, going wherever he went. Away from this village, he was a reasonably free man. When he came on visits to his stepmother, which were of necessity only at weekends, the school was closed and he was tracked down and trapped. As now.

Her name was Jasmine. She was eight, the only, and greatly indulged, child of the landlord of the village inn – the Coach and Four. Disliking her name, she had turned it into Jass, and would now answer to no other. She was small for her age, thin, and as cunning as the monkeys she resembled. She was given to showing off, except in the presence of Ross, when she became almost cringing. Jass had attached herself to him three years ago; since then he had found it impossible to shake her off, and had finally arrived at resignation.

"I knew you were here," she piped. "My Dad told me. He saw you last night."

"Does he know you're hanging about in this blizzard?"

"Yes. I told him I wanted to come and help you, because you'd have to dig the snow off the path."

"Thank you. But I don't need help. So you can run home and get warm and eat a nice big breakfast, as I'm going to do in a few minutes."

His stepmother rapped on a window-pane, and he shouted in response.

"Five more minutes, Laura."

"You don't call her Mum, do you?" Jass commented. "Why not?"

"Because I like her name better."

"I've got a stepmother too, but she likes me to call her Mum."

10

"Then go on doing it. Did you have breakfast before you came out?"

"Yes, lots. With my Dad. He comes down early every morning because of clearing up the bar."

She was longing to be asked into the garden. Inch by inch the gate was opening, but she knew that if she showed any sign of trespassing, he would order her home.

"You going to be here on Christmas Day?" she enquired.

"Yes."

"Then will you come and see our tree?"

"Depends where it is."

"It's going to be in the window of the bar, so's people can see it when they go past. It's got lovely lights."

"I should know. I fixed them myself a couple of years ago."

"These aren't those ones. These are new. My Dad bought them when he went to London. They cost a terrible lot, but he said they was worth it."

"Good. Why don't you go home before you freeze?"

"I'm lovely and warm," she lied. With the back of her hand, she wiped the drips from her nose. "Shall I shake the tree branches to make the snow fall off?"

"No."

There was an interval during which she jumped energetically up and down – in order, he presumed, to restore her circulation. Then she resumed the conversation.

"I got the music prize at school."

"Congratulations."

"And I sang solo at the carol service. I didn't go flat, not once."

"Good."

"I asked Mrs Mirren if you was coming, and she said, yes, but only for a few days. So I looked out for you. My Dad says I'm too young to go skiing. But I'm not, am I?"

"No."

"Would you ever take me with you?"

"No."

"I didn't think you would. You haven't often come here for Christmas before, have you?"

11

"No."

"My Mum says it's funny you coming on the same day as Mr Hargreaves. My Dad said so too. They said you must have a reason, but they didn't say what."

For a few moments, shock halted the movement of the spade. Then he recovered and in an access of fury attacked the ice that was forming on the flagstones. He shouldn't have been surprised, he told himself. It had been the main topic of discussion when he entered the Coach and Four last night, and he had heard a good deal before someone recognised him beneath his thick woollen scarf and with nudges and winks and warning coughs alerted the company to the fact that he was present. So he already knew that news of James Hargreaves' return had set tongues wagging. Jass' casual remark merely confirmed his suspicion that the village was buzzing with rumours. How much, he wondered, had his stepmother heard?

He came out of his reverie to find Jass beside him. She must have asked permission to enter and he must have given it. It was a pity, he thought, that he could not ask her what else her parents had said about James Hargreaves – but caution held him back. She was a sharp child, and she would undoubtedly sense his interest.

He placed the spade against the wall of the cottage and decided to go indoors to breakfast. His stepmother would expect him to ask Jass into the house, but as he hesitated the church bell began its cracked summons, and to his relief she turned and hurried to the gate.

"I gotta go, Mr Mirren," she called over her shoulder. "My Dad said I could go up to the belfry. See you later." She paused. "You'll come to the children's party and give away the presents tomorrow, won't you?"

"No."

But opening the front door, he knew that he would be at the party and he would hand out the presents and perform any other service the village required of him during his visits to his stepmother. How many cricket matches had he umpired? How many times had he pounded up and down sodden fields refereeing football games? How many bicycle

12

tours had he sponsored? At how many dog shows had he acted as one of the judges?

He entered the hall. On his heels came the cat, his expression one of frustration at having been deprived of his Sunday morning inspection. His fur left a trail of snow on the tiled floor.

Laura came out of the kitchen and greeted him.

"Good morning, Ross. Thanks for doing all that clearing. Why didn't you ask Jass to come in?"

"She went on a trip to the belfry, thank God. Any porridge on the menu?"

He was getting out of his boots and sweater and pants. In socks and pyjamas, he entered the warm, glowing kitchen and with a happy sigh of anticipation surveyed the preparations for his usual mammoth breakfast. Porridge, which he never dreamed of eating anywhere else, eggs, bacon, two fat, sizzling sausages, hot toast, homemade marmalade, aromatic coffee and a large jug of hot milk.

"I love you, Laura," he said contentedly as he drew up a chair to the table.

"I know you do," she said. "Every meal-time."

He had spoken lightly, but what he said was the truth. His father had been a widower when he married her. After his death, which took place two years later, when Ross was eleven, he had been under his stepmother's care. She had watched him through school and through Oxford and through his numerous love affairs and his brief, impulsive marriage at the age of twenty-one. Now he was thirty-two, an architect working with his father's old partners in London, but he still found time for weekend visits, and the affection between them remained warm and steady.

Sprinkling salt on his porridge, he wondered whether she would broach the topic that was uppermost in his mind. She did not often speak of herself. The matter he wanted to discuss had never been raised between them; he knew only a few details and had not been interested in learning more. It was part of her past, the eventless life she had led before she met his father. The departure of James Hargreaves had taken place – when? – more than twenty years ago. If Ross

13

had ever heard him mentioned by his stepmother's friends, it had been a casual reference and no undue interest had been shown in the subject.

But now he wanted to know more.

She was at the stove, and spoke without turning.

"What time did you get here last night?"

"I got to the garage about nine. I left the car there – I knew the lane would be blocked. Then I went along to the pub and had – guess what – mulled wine. It did a wonderful central heating job."

"When do you have to leave for Italy?"

"Monday. I'm driving to Folkestone and leaving the car there. Dave Forrest is meeting me and we're crossing together. Did I tell you he's bringing his girlfriend?"

"You said she might join you. Won't three be an awkward number?"

"We won't be three for long. I made a sort of tentative date with that Swiss girl who turned up at Zermatt last year."

"But you're not going to Zermatt."

"No. Cortina. She said she'd be there."

And if she wasn't, Laura reflected, deftly cracking eggs and sliding them into the frying pan, some other girl would be, and they would pair up and part at the end of the two weeks with no undue regrets. It was today's way and she had got used to it, but she still wondered at times what her father's reactions would have been.

He spoke as she put his plate before him.

"I don't suppose anyone's managed to get to church on a morning like this. Not even bossy Beatrice."

"She doesn't often miss a Sunday. The lane's impassable but she could go round the long way."

"Don't you ever get tired of having her dropping in Sunday after Sunday on her way home?"

"It's the only time she visits me."

"And as she never invites anybody to her house, you can't visit her." He speared a piece of bacon on to his fork. "How long, exactly, have you known her?"

She paused to do the sum. It took her some time, not

14

because it was difficult, but because the simplest problem involving figures became, as she struggled to master it, as complicated as a Chinese puzzle. He had long ago given up the attempt to clear up the mysteries of her account book.

"I'm not quite sure," she said at last. "Her father and her two brothers were here for some time on their own."

"Where was she?"

"Married and living up in Warwickshire. That's where the family originally came from. Old Jasper Hargreaves built the house here. The three who lived here in my father's time – Beatrice and James and Walter – are his grand-children. When their mother died, the father and the two boys went on living here alone. Then the father died, and Beatrice made his death the excuse to come back and keep house for her two brothers."

"Uninvited?"

"Yes. They were both – and even their father, I think – afraid of her. She was the eldest of the three children, and she'd bullied her brothers all their lives. They must have been surprised, as well as relieved, when she married – she was too forbidding to attract men."

"What became of her husband?"

"He retired early and went to live in the Bahamas. He died there."

"And brother James – did he take off for the Bahamas too?"

She was at his shoulder. He could not see her expression, but he knew that for a moment or two there was a slight air of tension.

"No," she said. "James' firm had branches on the Continent – France, Italy – and he used to visit them about twice a year."

"To supervise the branches, or to get away from Beatrice?"

"I don't know." She poured more milk into the jug. "People don't give her much credit. Of course she's a bully, and nobody can bear it, but by the time she came back to live here, her brothers had let the house get into a pretty bad

15

state. They couldn't get resident servants and they couldn't keep dailies because they expected to go on living as they'd done when they were young – suits cleaned and pressed, shoes polished, meals served with ceremony. The dailies departed and the house deteriorated. Beatrice came back and pulled things together."

"Why didn't her brothers get married and leave the house to her?"

"Walter, her younger brother, hardly notices his surroundings. He spends all his time – "

"Yes, I know. Books on Buddhism. He came to lecture once when I was up at Oxford. Bad platform manner but a good lecture. And the other brother, James?"

"He married in France. In Nice."

"Married who?"

"A girl he'd known since her childhood – her father had a job in the Nice office. After their marriage, they went to live in Biarritz. He never came back to Downpass."

"Until now."

She met his glance, and nodded.

"Yes. Until now."

"With a daughter, so they said in the pub."

"Yes, he's brought his daughter. He only had one child. She was born in Biarritz."

"Where's his wife?"

"She died about six years ago. There was a notice in *The Times*."

He got up, fetched a second cup from the dresser, filled it with coffee and handed it to her.

"Drink that," he ordered. "It'll give you strength."

"Strength what for?"

"To tell me the whole story. Gossip was busy in the pub last night."

"Gossip?"

"That's right. The villagers were on to an interesting piece of news and they were making the most of it. They weren't, for once, watching television; they were standing in groups exchanging views on the topic of the evening. Anywhere but in Downpass, one could have said that there

16

were animated discussions – but there's nothing animated about this place, which is one of the reasons I come here."

"I thought you came to see me."

"That, as the French say, doesn't have to be said. This is the only place I know, barring Antarctic wastes or Saharan solitudes, where there's peace. It's a backwater. It's like a sluggish river. No cinema, no bingo hall, no community spirit, no nothing. Nothing here for the motorbike brigades. Nobody here but children, and greybeards returned after a life spent in the big world outside. So when I noticed the unusual liveliness in the pub last night, I began to listen to what they were saying – and out of their talk and the smoke and the fumes of mulled wine came certain revelations which I found interesting."

"You needn't call them revelations. There was never anything secret about any of this."

"There was nothing out in the open, either. Or perhaps I wasn't interested and didn't ask. For me, you began when you married my father. What happened before that was, I thought, unimportant – to me, that is. But James Hargreaves is back, a widower with a daughter of, I gathered, twenty-two, and the general opinion was that he shouldn't have returned. And why not? Because when he went on that last business trip to his office in Nice, he was engaged to you. Right?"

She drew a chair to the table, sat down and spoke quietly.

"Quite right," she said.

"And then you got a letter saying, 'Dear Laura, I hate to tell you this, but the fact is that I've jilted you.' Jilted," he repeated, his eyes on her. "That was the word being used in the pub last night."

Her response to this was reassuring – a laugh that began as a gurgle and went on to become a peal of pure, unaffected amusement. Relief flooded his mind, and an answering smile appeared on his lips.

"Jilted?" She was still laughing. "Did they really say that?"

"They did. And you were."

With an effort, she became serious.

17

"Well yes," she admitted. "I suppose I was. But whether it was an unconscious determination to avoid the word or not, I never thought of it as jilting. Didn't that expression go out in the twenties?"

"According to the spokesman at the pub, no. Or if it did, James Hargreaves revived it. I felt there was a strong anti-James party being formed in the village, to convey to him without words their conviction that having done so dirty a deed, he should have stayed out of sight and never returned, especially toting a daughter."

She smiled.

"It's difficult to think of James as a villain," she said. "Or as a father," she added.

He pushed aside his empty cup, put his elbows on the table and studied her.

"You know something? I was worried," he said.

"About James?"

"Don't be silly. I was worried about you. I wanted to find out how you felt about his coming back."

"You needn't have worried." She got up and began to clear the table. "I told you there was nothing secret about the affair. There was only one thing people didn't know and which I never told anyone."

"What was that?"

"When I got the last letter he sent me – which wasn't as brief or as direct as your version – I only felt one emotion."

"Anger?"

"No."

"Humiliation?"

Again came her laugh.

"No. All I felt was relief. Deep, deep relief."

"You'd fallen out of love?"

"I'd never fallen in." She stood still, gazing into the fire. "You know, I haven't really thought about this for . . . oh, twenty years. But when I used to turn it over in my mind, I came to the conclusion that what made me say I'd marry him was a mixture of pity because he was so miserable in that cheerless house under Beatrice's thumb, and an inability to form the words: 'I like you, but I don't want to

18

marry you.' Nobody had ever asked me to marry. I felt very grateful to James."

"You were very pretty. Why no suitors?"

"Because Downpass was almost as full of greybeards then as it is today. The retired, the old, the away-from-it-alls. My father was vicar here for over thirty years, but I don't think he ever brought a young man to the vicarage. I left school, came back here, settled down with him, kept house for him, and was as happy as any girl could be. It's impossible – I've told you this many times before – it's quite impossible for young, energetic, restless people like you to imagine life in a quiet, comfortable home with a steady and unchanging routine. No, not routine; rhythm. The Craigs, next-door, think I've missed everything that makes life worth living. When they're in their house, which isn't often, they need all the modern playthings: colour television, video, the latest hi-fi equipment, his chess computer, her gymnastic machine, a steady stream of visitors from the outside world. I like the Craigs, but I think I'd rather live in a circus than with them. Life with my father, life with your father, life with you during your younger days, life by myself . . . no, it hasn't been dull."

"Didn't you ever think about marriage?"

"When I did, which wasn't often, I decided that there were certain aspects of it I was willing to do without."

"Sex, for example?"

"Yes. No man will ever believe that any normal woman can live happily without it, so it's no use trying to convince them."

"I'll refer them to you. Dull or not, I consider you a bad case of escapism. How did you fill in your time when you lived at the vicarage?"

"I cooked, I did some work for the church, I rode four mornings a week with my father on hired horses, I made my own dresses, I visited sick people and read a lot of books. My father built this cottage for his retirement, but as it turned out, I came here alone. I remember thinking on my first evening here: 'This is where I belong, where I want to stay; please God let this always be my home.' I suppose

19

it was that feeling that made me hesitate when James Hargreaves asked me to marry him. The thought of leaving this cottage and going to live in that house – with Beatrice in it too, because nothing was said about her moving out – made my blood run cold."

"When this happened, how old were you?"

Once again she had difficulty in doing the sum.

"Let me see . . . I'm forty-six. When James went away that last time, it was the year the Craigs moved into the house next-door. That was in . . . I can't remember exactly, but I'd only been living in the cottage for two years, and I was twenty-one when my father died and I had to leave the vicarage and –"

"Two years living here. Two added to the twenty-one when you moved in makes . . . let's see if you can do it. Twenty-one plus two equals?"

"Don't be silly. As if I can't add up a simple –"

"Equals?"

"Twenty-one and two make twenty-three. I'm not quite an idiot."

"Not quite. Only when you're confronted with figures. So you were twenty-three when you were – let's familiarise ourselves with the word – jilted."

"That's right; twenty-three. I remember now, because James was just the opposite – thirty-two. The same age as you are now. It was just a year later that your father came to Downpass to design an extension to the Craigs' house and he couldn't make anyone hear when he knocked, so he walked next-door to ask me if I knew where they were. And I've told you before that we didn't fall in love, but we liked each other and went on liking each other more and more. I met you when you were nine and I thought you were a nice boy. I didn't know you'd turn out so badly."

"Thank you. Now shall we –"

"He was so sweet, your father. So quiet, so gentle, so kind."

"And a first-class architect withal."

"He used to carry house designs in his head all the time, the way I suppose a composer carries concertos. When we went out to a meal, he used to ruin the menus by drawing sketches of arches and mouldings and shafts and cornices. He used to – "

"Quite so. Now shall we return to the subject we were discussing – namely, your engagement to James Hargreaves, which took place when you were twenty-three. Twenty-three from forty-six leaves – ?"

"You work it out."

"It leaves twenty-three. So he absented himself from this village for twenty-three years. Did Beatrice approve of the engagement?"

"She must have done. All I know is that she thought he could have done better – she's always had rather too high an opinion of her family's position in society. That's one reason she never made friends here – she thought nobody was good enough."

"And when James married, how did she feel?"

"He didn't tell her he was married. He told me, but all he said in the letter he wrote her was that he had decided not to return to England, but would be marrying and settling in France. I only heard that later, when she and Walter came back from Devonshire, where they'd tactfully placed themselves for a time. It was just before Easter, and she sent me a postcard from Honiton. When they came back, she dropped in after Morning Service and told me she thought James had behaved disgracefully. I didn't tell her he was already married. She only learned that a year or so later, when he wrote to her to say he had a daughter. After that, he wrote to her about once a year."

"He didn't write to you again?"

"No. I kept his letters, not from sentiment but because they made a story. I got snippets of news about him from Beatrice now and then; she kept up the habit of dropping in on Sunday mornings – but she never asked me to the house again. This blizzard was the answer to a prayer – I was dreading her arrival after the service."

"But you think she'll still come?"

"Yes. And then the whole thing will be raked up again."

"How did you learn that James was back?"

21

"How does one learn anything in this place? The milkman and the baker both made a point of knocking to tell me that the price of milk and bread was going up – which I knew already – and added that Mr Hargreaves was coming back on the twentieth and bringing his daughter. Did you hear anything in the pub last night about how Walter felt about his brother's return?"

"No. There was speculation as to whether Beatrice would move out of the house if James was going to settle in it. If she did move out, where would she go?"

"She owns a large house in Warwick, left to her by her husband. When she came back to Downpass, she let it on a long lease. James once had rooms in London, but he gave them up and used his club when he went up. If he or Walter wanted to invite anyone to a meal, it had to be in a restaurant or at the club – Beatrice made it plain from the beginning that she would run the house and do the cooking, but she wouldn't entertain her brothers' friends."

"Didn't they ever invite anybody to the house?"

"Not after Beatrice came back and took charge."

"Didn't it occur to her that if they couldn't have any fun at home, they'd look for it elsewhere?"

"I don't know. I think she considers that men are like cats – feed them and warm them, and they'll settle."

"James didn't." He paused. "You're odd in some ways," he went on. "Most women would be standing with their noses flattened against the window, looking out for Beatrice to come walking up the path bringing news. Don't you want to know what's going on?"

"Yes, I do. I'd like to sit down and have a nice, cosy chat about it. But all I'll get from Beatrice Risdon will be bare bones of fact without any meat on them."

"Don't you want to see James again?"

"Not particularly. I'd like to see what his daughter's like. James said her mother was beautiful."

"A tactless thing to put into a jilt letter." He rose reluctantly. "I suppose I'd better go and get some clothes on. What time is lunch?"

"Whenever you want it. Cheese and salad."

"Wouldn't some nice hot steak and kidney pudding be more suitable on a day like this? With hot mince pies?"

"After the breakfast you've just got through? You'll get a nice hot dinner tonight – but no mince pies."

"Why no mince pies?"

"Not before Christmas Day. Remember to put out that outside light."

2

Downpass had been discovered in the early years of the century by Jasper Hargreaves, a wealthy merchant whose fortune had been made in tea. Planning retirement, he searched for a site on which to erect a family mansion. He wanted it to be within reasonable distance of London, but in rural surroundings; he had begun life on a farm and in his leisure moments dreamed of himself as a country squire.

When he found Downpass, it had been a hamlet of some eighty inhabitants who lived on smallholdings round the church which, though half-ruined, had a genuine Norman tower. Behind the church was an extensive area of open heath known as the Common. At one end of the single, narrow, rutted road was a duckpond; at the other end was an ancient inn with a faded, crudely painted sign depicting a coach and four horses. Access from this secluded retreat to London was by a winding, tree-shaded lane which, after wandering for some miles, came as though by accident upon a road which led to the capital.

Pleased with his discovery, Jasper began by shrewdly buying up large areas of land round the hamlet. The squire's house he had dreamed of was in time erected on the border of extensive woods owned by an absentee Berkshire land-lord. With the aid of Hargreaves money, the fabric of the church was restored and a vicarage built near-by.

The first settlers began to arrive; soon there were a few villas, a small school, a large garage and, opposite the duckpond, two or three modest shops offering a multiplicity of goods. When Jasper brought his wife and son to his newly built mansion, he was confident that Downpass was almost on the map – an expanding village, almost a town, but also a haven of peace, a retreat for the discriminating.

At this point, unfortunately, the planning authorities decided to construct a motorway. Despite a deputation from the residents of Downpass, the new roadway was placed along the edge of the common. This effectively ended Downpass' hopes of peace and seclusion.

The duckpond remained; so also did the vicarage and the villas and the shops. London was even more accessible, and the road that led from the village still ran in gentle curves under sheltering trees, but the traffic along it dropped to a trickle; it was used only by tradesmen's vans and a dozen or so modest cars belonging to the residents. And these, for the most part, had become a community of the elderly, for the village offered nothing for the young – no amusements, and no hope of lucrative work. A number of the residents, seeing no future in so stagnant a place, sold their villas at considerably less than they had cost to build, and departed. There remained the parents of the children who attended the local primary school, but these, too, left when the children were old enough to go to the state schools in the neighbouring town of Upleigh.

The Hargreaves remained. Their house was spacious and comfortable, and if they wanted amusements, they could go up to London. There were now three of the family living in the house: Jasper's grandsons, James and Walter, and their sister Beatrice, who, after an unsatisfactory marriage to a stockbroker in Warwickshire, returned to Downpass and became housekeeper to her two bachelor brothers. She was the eldest of the three, and domineering by nature; under her rigid and parsimonious rule, the house lost its easy-going atmosphere and became a bleak place.

Walter, the younger brother, scarcely noticed the change, since he passed most of his days in the library, immersed in the study of Buddhism, a subject which had occupied him since his Oxford days and on which he had written several books. But James, the elder, though almost as quiet and as meek as his brother, chafed under his sister's bullying. He had an outlet, however, in his daily visits to his office in London; another means of escape were the annual journeys he made to his firm's branches on the Continent.

The three had little or no contact with anybody in the village. Beatrice performed the civic duties which she felt devolved on her in her self-appointed role as leader of the community, but the only social contacts she had were with the vicar and his daughter Laura. James paid frequent visits to the cottage into which Laura moved on the death of her father, but he went alone, never in the company of his sister. In Laura's humorous, undemanding company he could relax and enjoy a drink or two before returning to the austerities of his own home. He ended by asking Laura to marry him, and after much hesitation she agreed. They became engaged when he was on the point of leaving for his office in Nice. He would be away for two months, and she felt that this interval would give her time to make a final decision on the matter.

The letters he wrote were detailed, but dull; he had no powers of description, and the places and people he mentioned formed no picture in her mind. Shortly before he was to return to England, he went down with a bad attack of influenza and was treated in hospital. There was a brief gap in his correspondence which Laura thought was caused by his illness, but his next – his last – letter to her brought the news that he was not returning to England. He was going to live in Biarritz and he was not going to live alone; he had married the daughter of a Frenchman who worked in the office – a girl who had often figured in his letters, as he had known and liked her since her childhood. Laura, folding the letter and putting it away with the previous ones, felt thankfully that she had been saved from making a serious mistake.

The effect of the news on his sister Beatrice was far more shattering. This lapse on the part of a brother who for most of his life had done nothing without her permission, who had never before shown any signs of rebellion, whose engagement to Laura she had sanctioned, brought out all the latent vindictiveness of her nature. Perhaps he had been aware of her probable reaction, for he had told her merely that he had decided to live permanently in Biarritz, and had said nothing about his marriage. But his desertion of his home and his fiancée were enough; her letter in reply to his news was vitriolic, and contained a refusal to have any further communication with him. From the brief letters he continued to write to her, she learned in time of the marriage and the birth of a daughter. This was all that Downpass knew of him until he wrote at the beginning of December to say he was returning before Christmas.

During the intervening years, Beatrice had continued to nurse her resentment. But when it was certain that he would not be returning to England, she realised that although running the house single-handed for two men had hitherto been enough to fill her days, there now remained only Walter, who spent his time with his books and who accepted uncomplainingly the tasteless food she served, too absorbed in Buddha to react to her bullying. He filled the gap left by James by forming a friendship with the vicar, whose interest in Buddha was, in spite of his calling, almost as great as Walter's. The two men met frequently at the vicarage to discuss their subject, and Beatrice had to look for new outlets for her energy.

She turned her attention to the village and began by attempting to instil into the lethargic inhabitants some spark of enthusiasm for civic or political life. She formed committees to battle for women's rights, nuclear disarmament, anti-terrorism, higher pensions for the aged and lower profits for capitalists, but the initial sparse attendance at meetings was soon followed by wholesale resignations under her domineering chairmanship.

Having failed to rouse Downpass, she began to visit London three times a week to seek response in more fruitful fields. She had no clear idea which campaigns she wished to ally herself to, but being by nature warlike, joined groups of the more aggressive type and took part in several demonstrations of a violent nature. She had torn down many a poster and torn up many opponents' banners, but had not yet succeeded in finding a cause to which she could give herself wholeheartedly. A further disappointment had been that in spite of numerous encounters with the police and her success in depriving several of them of their helmets, she had not as yet achieved her ambition to be taken into custody.

She went to see Laura on the Sunday afternoon following James' return to Downpass. She left her car at the garage in the main street and walked to the cottage. Laura, admitting her, helped her off with her coat and, familiar as she was with Beatrice's unnecessary economies, saw without surprise that her suit had been turned, and was now grey-green instead of green-grey. Her close-fitting hat had seen innumerable winters and her boots were of the type worn by intrepid women of the last century when walking in the Alps.

Ross had taken the dog for a walk. The morning's heavy skies had been succeeded by pallid sunshine, and a thaw was beginning. Laura hoped the visit would end before Ross' return, for he and Beatrice detested one another.

The visitor's first comment was the usual one: the living room was far too warm. The next remark, after a glance at the dog and cat baskets near the fire, was also familiar: domestic pets should be kept out of doors.

Laura placed a chair for her as far from the fire as possible, and seated herself at the other end of the room. It was a pity, she thought, looking across at Beatrice, that all three Hargreaves might have been called handsome but for some marring feature: Beatrice's thin lips and small, mean-looking eyes, James' jutting chin, Walter's receding one.

"I don't believe in leading up to a subject that has to be discussed," Beatrice began. "I shall simply say that you must have heard these rumours circulating about James' return?"

"Yes. I'd heard he – "

"They're not rumours." She waved aside Laura's offer of tea. "He has, in fact, returned. He wrote at the beginning of the month to tell me he intended to come, bringing his daughter with him. As I heard no more, I concluded he had changed his mind and so I said nothing about it to you. He was always a mind-changer, as you found out."

"Is that all he said in his letter?"

"Yes. All, that is, except the usual meaningless enquiries about my health. There was just the bare fact that he was returning. I didn't expect any more. He was always a secretive boy and he grew up into a secretive man. He has given me little or no news of himself all these years. He told me – long after the event – that he was married, and he mentioned a daughter, but he said not one word about the death of his wife six years ago. If I hadn't seen the notice in *The Times*, as you did too, we should have known nothing of it. I've been left in total ignorance of everything concerning him. The postmarks on his letters told me where he was, but lately he seemed to have taken to wandering, never staying long in any one place. And now he is here."

"He and his daughter?"

"No. He came alone. The daughter arrives tomorrow. I understood him to say she'd be coming by car with a French friend, whether male or female was not stated. He is as evasive as he always was. When I began to question him, and learned how much he had kept from me all these years, I became more and more angry – but what enraged me most of all was the information that his daughter was actually here, here in England, for three years, at an English university." Two spots of colour appeared on her cheeks. "Three years, and not one word, not a single word to me. And not a word to the girl telling her that she had relations in this country. It was only after James made up his mind to come home . . . believe it or not, those were his words: come home. Home! After twenty-three years of absence, to come home. Fantastic! It was only then that he told the girl she had an uncle and an aunt in England. Her name, incidentally, is Gianna. It seems she had an Italian grandmother or godmother or something of that sort. Godmother; that was it."

"Did he say he intended to stay?"

"Yes, he did. You see, don't you, what an impossible position this puts me in? To say nothing of Walter. The house belongs to James. What does he expect us to do – move out? I made it quite clear that if *that* was what he had in mind, I should certainly not agree. I've looked after the house and kept it in good order and repair ever since he left it. I've installed modern equipment – a washing machine, a roller iron, new curtains, new chair-covers – I can't begin to add up the cost. So I should certainly not dream of going away. And if I did, where would I go? My house in Warwick has just been relet on a long lease. Some consideration, I told James, must be shown to Walter and to me. His rooms are as he left them. The girl can have the room he used to occupy as a study; I don't think she'll need it for long. In fact, she'll be leaving shortly after Christmas – she's enrolled herself in a London institution – post-graduate studies, computer programming or something of the kind. James said she was going to look for a flat in London. When she finds one, he said she would probably stay up there during the week and come home – there's that word again – come home for weekends. However, she'll probably find this place too dull, and get out as fast as she can. I daresay she'll marry a Frenchman and go back to live in France. And the sooner the better, in my view."

"If she leaves, surely James will leave too? He'll want to be near her."

"I doubt it. You didn't see the look on his face when he set foot in the house yesterday. I'm not given to exaggerated descriptions, but he looked to me like a thirsty desert traveller who had just sighted water."

The water, Laura thought, would prove to be a mirage. He must have forgotten what life in that house had been like before he left.

As though she had guessed this thought, Beatrice spoke in a bitter tone.

"I know perfectly well," she said, "what the people in this village have thought of me ever since I came back to live here. I've been regarded, I'm still regarded, as a hard woman who kept her brothers on a leash. Well, I am, and I did. But there are two sides to every coin, and nobody has ever troubled to look at my side. I shall tell you now, while we're speaking frankly, that there are people – in this case, men – who go to pieces unless they're under the care, the dominance if you prefer the word, of a strong-minded

30

woman. I made that discovery when I was a child. My two brothers were like some of the soft toys I owned; left without support, they sagged. And it had to be stiff support. Throughout my childhood I supplied it, at first without realising what I was doing and later because I understood I was the only strong member of a weak family."

"As we're talking frankly," Laura ventured, "couldn't one say that they might in time have learned to stand alone? If—"

"If I hadn't provided the support, you mean? No. It's said the child is father to the man, and James and Walter remained, as adults, what they had been as children. You're going to tell me that people can't help their natures. Perhaps you're right. My nature was to keep a grasp on things, to be clean, to be tidy, to keep my surroundings decent and habitable. Every time I came home for school holidays, the house—we had servants in those days—looked impeccable. When there were no more servants, my brothers soon reduced the place to shoddiness. They expected some invisible agent to pick up the garments they left on the floor, remove the mud their shoes scattered over the carpets, and clean up after their guinea-pigs and hamsters and white mice. People said they were nice children, nice boys, nice young men – well-mannered and well-behaved. But the people who said that didn't have to live with them."

"Your father—"

" – was the same. When he and my brothers were living here alone and I was married and living up in Warwick, I used to wonder how they were getting on with only a daily woman to do the work. I could imagine the disorder, the mess . . ."

She paused for so long that Laura thought she was not going to resume. Presently, however, she went on, "When my father died, I decided to come back here and run the house. I found more than disorder. The details are not interesting; I'll only say it took me weeks to make the house look once more like the home of civilised, cultured people. When your father was alive, he and you used to pay frequent visits – you saw it, you saw its cleanliness, its order: regular

31

meals cooked by myself, shining floors and furniture. A gracious home."

Laura said nothing. Cleanliness and order and glossy furniture and life regulated by the clock, cold meals for those who appeared late at table, lists apportioning daily duties, no relaxation, no revelry and no laughter.

Beatrice's lips were set in a thin, hard line.

"I made clear to James on his arrival yesterday," she said, "that not only was I not going to leave the house, but I was also going to see it remained as orderly as I have made it."

"Young people – " Laura began.

"There is only one young person in question: this daughter."

"Haven't they any home abroad?"

"No. He sold their house in Biarritz when his wife died. Since then, he and the girl have been living in hotels or apartments. When his daughter finished her education, she and James set out on what sounded to me a kind of Continental tour. James always detested rushing from one place to another, but that is what they seem to have been doing lately. I can't imagine why he allowed himself to be dragged round for so long. I'm convinced – "

Laura did not learn what the conviction was. There was the sound of cheerful whistling, followed by the scraping of shoes outside the front door. Then it burst open and the dog, snow-covered, bounded in and threw himself on to Laura's lap. From the hall Ross, shaking the damp from his anorak, shouted to Laura, "I'll make the tea if you'll release the mince pies. No sign, thank God, of – "

He was in the doorway, and seeing the visitor, fortunately pulled himself up on the point of finishing the sentence.

"Good afternoon," said Beatrice.

Her tone was glacial, and his was not much warmer as he greeted her.

"Good afternoon, Mrs Risdon."

He had once, once only, addressed her experimentally as Beatrice. She had made it clear that he was not to do so again.

32

Since that time, he had spoken to her with exaggerated deference.

She rose.

"I must be going, Laura."

Ross hastened to help her on with her coat.

"Not staying to tea?" he enquired with a good imitation of disappointment.

"Your stepmother offered me tea. I refused."

"I didn't see your car outside. Mine's at the garage, or I could have run you home."

"My car, too, is at the garage. I do not need a lift home, thank you. Goodbye, Laura."

"Goodbye, Beatrice. It was nice of you to drop in."

"I have no doubt James will be round to see you and give you his news."

She paused at the door, which Ross was holding open.

"I wonder," she asked him, "if you would do something for me?"

He looked surprised and then suspicious, but soon changed his expression to one of polite expectancy.

"Anything within my power . . ."

"I give a Christmas tree each year to the village school. The gardener has been ill and can't be asked to do any heavy work. Not that this is heavy work; it's simply to dig up a tree I've donated. It's in the wood at the back of the house. I shall leave a label on it so you'll know which one it is. If you will kindly put it into a wheelbarrow and wheel it the few hundred yards to the school, I shall be grateful."

"Any deadline?"

"Deadline?"

"I mean, does it have to get there at any special time?"

"I promised that it would be there tomorrow before midday."

"Tomorrow before midday. Right."

"I shall remove the padlock from the back gate. Please replace it when you've finished."

"I will."

He opened the door wider, but she was not yet ready to leave.

"As you're going to be here over Christmas," she said, "I hope you will manage to fit in one or two engagements like those you've undertaken in the past. There's the inspection of the Junior Band – they are going to parade and they are also going to play some pieces. There's also the Junior Gymnastic display – it shouldn't take more than two hours. I shall give away the prizes but I would like you to say a few words about the value of body-building. And I should like you to look in on the Senior Citizens' Handiwork exhibition; they would welcome a visit. They will, of course, hope that you will buy some of the things they have made. I think that's all. Please don't forget to replace the padlock on the gate."

He saw her out and returned to supervise the preparation of tea.

"Nice technique she's got," he commented. "Treats me like a serf and then asks favours."

"She doesn't think of them as favours. She regards them as your duty as a semi-resident of Downpass."

"Ex-resident. The last time I bought a firescreen from the Senior Citizens' exhibition, it fell to pieces as I was carrying it out to the car. All Beatrice said was that I handled it roughly – d'you remember?"

"Yes. But it gives them pleasure to have someone taking an interest in what they're doing."

"You think everyone ought to do Good Works, don't you?"

"I wouldn't go as far as that. I just think people ought to look outside themselves now and then."

"That's why you go to the sewing meetings and sit there wasting your time. They'd sew just as much and just as well if you weren't there."

"No, they wouldn't. Incidentally, that tree Beatrice has picked out for you to dig up might be quite large."

"Then I shall remove the label and tie it on to a small tree. The wood's full of them – I've seen them through the prison bars."

He was referring to the tall iron gate which opened on to the back entrance of Hargreaves House. It was of plain

34

design – long, straight bars which could be said to resemble those of a prison.

"What did Beatrice talk about?" he enquired.

She gave him a brief account of the conversation

"I feel sorry for her," she ended.

"Sorry for her? *Sorry?*" he echoed in amazement. "You mean you're sorry for her victims, don't you?"

"I suppose so. But her, too."

"How her brother James can walk straight back into the trap beats me. I bet he'll decide to leave again before he's got through his unpacking."

"Beatrice thinks he's here to stay. Not the daughter."

"The daughter'll take one look at Beatrice and depart. Aren't there any mince pies?"

"I told you – not until Christmas Day."

"They might go bad or something."

"They won't go bad."

"Why not until Christmas Day? Is it a tradition, or are you just being mean, like Beatrice?"

"They make Christmas more Christmassy." She paused in front of the tea caddies. "Indian or China?"

"China for a change. It'll make Christmas more Christmassy. What does Beatrice donate to the village besides a tree?"

"She lends the grounds of the house for the church bazaar. You didn't mean what you said about changing the label on the tree she asked you to dig up, did you?"

"If she's chosen a specimen that would look well in Trafalgar Square, I shall most certainly change the label. I'm not a lumberjack. Do you want me to injure myself?"

"Sometimes, yes," she said.

3

Ross was up early on the following morning, and began the day by putting himself through a course of physical jerks – a somewhat cramped performance, as he was a large man and it was a small room. But the walk with the dog on the previous day had revealed a disquieting lack of fitness, and he was anxious to get himself into form during the short time remaining before he left for Italy. Keeping up with the girl in Zermatt last year, he recalled uneasily, had taken some doing; in retrospect, she seemed to him to have had the stamina of an ox. If she joined him in Cortina, as he was almost certain she would, he didn't want to find himself lagging in the rear.

After a shower and a hearty breakfast, he set off for Hargreaves House. It stood in extensive, wooded grounds on the edge of the village, with only the school, some distance away, separating it from the wide, unpicturesque expanse of heath that bordered the river. It was not yet eleven o'clock; plenty of time to dig up the tree and deliver it to its destination.

He was not surprised, shortly after leaving the cottage, to hear a familiar call behind him. He did not turn. Jass caught him up and slowed her pace to a series of skips.

"Hi, Mr Mirren. I went to your house, but Mrs Mirren said you'd gone to dig up the Christmas tree for the school."

"If you'd rather do it, you're welcome."

"Me? I couldn't dig up a tree, not a tree as big as the one you're going to dig."

"Oh, it's large, is it?"

"It's hooge." She jumped as high as she could, one arm raised to give him an idea of the tree's height. "It's going to look lov'ly. I don't know how you're going to get it to the school all by yourself."

"In a wheelbarrow."

"You should've asked Mrs Risdon to let you use their tractor. Then you could've driven it, if you could've got the tree in."

"I presume you're going to help me."

"Me? I can't. I've got to go to the school and we're going to fix all the decorations and candles. Six of us were chosen to go – me and the Murray twins, and Ron Wright and his sister. And Marian Grove, but all she does is stand and watch. And you know what lights we're putting on? Those ones you did for our tree at home before my Dad bought new ones. We gave the old lights to the school for this tree you're going to dig up, only they won't be enough, it's so hooge. Wait till you see."

They parted before he saw. She climbed a fence and took a short-cut to the school, while he walked beside the high wall bordering the Hargreaves property until he came to the gate which he had likened to prison bars.

It was a day on which to enjoy being active. The sunshine was pale but steady. Underfoot, the thaw had turned the snow to slush, but the sky was clear and there was an invigorating breeze blowing. He felt equal to cutting down an entire forest.

It was some time before he could get the gate open. Beatrice Risdon had removed the rusty padlock, and left it hanging on one of the bars, to be replaced when he left the grounds. But this entrance was seldom used, and a thick layer of melting ice had formed round the foot of the gate and was preventing it from opening. When it had resisted all his efforts to effect an entrance, he broke a stout branch from a tree beside the road, thrust it through the bars and broke up the ice. He was then able to open one side of the gate – and that, he decided, was as much as he needed to do; there was space enough to get the wheelbarrow through. He lifted one of the heavy iron bars, hooked at one end, and fitted it into iron staples in the ground that held the side of the gate open.

He had no difficulty in finding the tree he was to dig out. It was as large as Jass had stated, larger than any of the other young trees. His eye fell on the label and he unhesitatingly removed it and tied it to a tree whose removal did not require such undue exertion. Nobody but a slave-driver like Beatrice Risdon, he thought, would have expected one man to tackle a job like that.

He walked to the tool shed. Here, too, the padlock had been removed ready for his arrival. He picked up a spade, threw it into a large wheelbarrow and wheeled it back to the wood. He had chosen a small, well-shaped tree. Digging it up was hard work, but exercise was what he needed, and this was a good way of getting it.

There was no sound from the house. He did not expect that anyone would come out to see what he was doing. He dug deep, put aside the spade and pulled until the roots left the damp earth. He lifted the tree into the wheelbarrow and pushed it to the gate – and then remembered that he had not replaced the spade. He left the wheelbarrow balanced somewhat unsteadily against the unopened side of the gate while he went back to the wood, retrieved the spade and returned it to the shed.

When he walked back to the gate, he saw that a new element had entered the scene. In the road stood a car – an expensive scarlet sports model with a left-hand drive. Its elegance was somewhat marred by a deep dent in one of the door panels. Outside the gate was a girl, bent double, pushing with all her force the side of the gate he had left closed. As he drew near, she succeeded in moving it. It reached and overturned the wheelbarrow, and the tree which he had dug up with so much labour fell under the wheel, its branches broken as it was dragged along the gravel.

"Hey, what d'you think you're doing?" he shouted angrily.

She straightened and looked at him through the bars. Enraged though he was, he registered certain details – dark hair under a green woollen cap, dark eyes, clear olive skin. When she spoke, it was with a slight French accent.

"I'm glad you've come," she told him. "One side was open, but I couldn't get the car in."

Her tone was calm, her manner untroubled. She was entirely free from self-consciousness.

"Do you realise you've ruined a tree that was to be presented to the school?" he demanded.

She waved a careless hand towards the wood.

"Over there are many more trees," she pointed out.

"I dug this one out," he informed her. "I spent a lot of time and energy digging up this particular – "

"If I had known there was someone here, I would have waited, and not pushed all by myself. I'm Gianna Hargreaves. Who are you?"

Curiosity cooled his wrath.

"You're James Hargreaves' daughter?"

"Yes. And you?"

"My name's Ross Mirren and I'm here on a short visit to my stepmother. Why didn't you drive to the front gate instead of coming to this one?"

"I went to the front gate. I drove up to the house and I got out of the car and knocked, and knocked. No answer. I tried to open the door – locked. Where have they gone? My father, at least, knew I was coming."

Her tone remained matter-of-fact. His impression by now was that she was endowed with a fund of calm common sense.

"I daresay your aunt Beatrice went shopping," he said. "Your uncle Walter's probably shut up with his books, deaf to knocks. Perhaps your father went with your aunt."

"He shouldn't have gone. I told him I would come on the morning ferry."

"There are two morning ferries. You must have come on the earlier one. The next is two hours later."

"He said he would come and meet me, but I told him no, because I was coming with Pierre in his car. Pierre is a friend of mine, but very forgetful. He's a musician. His two sisters live in London – they were at school with me and now they have an apartment and Pierre and I are going to stay with them after Christmas. They asked if Pierre could travel with me and stay with me in Downpass for a few days as they were going to be away. So he and I came together, but he had let his passport run out, and the police at Calais said he couldn't go on, so I had to leave him. He had also forgotten to book a place for the car on the ferry, but a man put it on for me – he drove it on because he saw the dent in the door and thought I had done it, but it was Pierre. What I want to do now is drive the car inside."

"You could leave it on the road. There's not much danger of anything being taken – people will be going up and down to the school today."

"Then I must arrange the things in another way. There are some expensive articles that can be seen."

She dived into the car and reappeared holding a large cardboard box. As well as being large, it was, as he discovered when she thrust it unceremoniously into his arms, extremely heavy. On to it, after another dive, she placed some records and on them, a camera. The next load, some thick sweaters, she pushed under his arm. She then took out some camping gear and rested it against his legs. Having arranged the remainder of the car's contents to her satisfaction, she relieved Ross of his burdens, replaced the things in the car and locked it.

He spoke coldly.

"If you've quite finished fixing things as you want them, you'll excuse me if I go and dig up another tree."

"Why another?" she asked in surprise. "We have only to pick this one up and straighten out the branches and put it into the barrow. When they have put on all the candles, nobody will see any damage. I'll go with you to the school. Perhaps after that, my father will be here. Or my aunt. Do you know that it was only a little while ago I knew I had English relations? My mother and my father never told me about them. Only when my father decided to come back and live here, he said to me: 'You have an uncle and aunt in England.' I was sorry he hadn't told me before, because for three years I was at a university in England and I could have come here for the vacations. Let's lift up the tree."

Replaced in the wheelbarrow, its branches rearranged in

something like their former shape, the tree looked, she said, like new. Ross wheeled the barrow on to the road and came back to close the gate. He wondered what the people at the school would make of her clothes – green ski pants, a scarlet anorak, fur boots of a Norwegian design, bright yellow leather gloves. She matched, he thought, the millionaire-class car.

They closed one side of the gate. The other – the half-opened side – remained immovable.

"We shall leave it as it is," she announced, after they had pushed in vain.

"No. I was asked – told; your aunt Beatrice does more ordering than asking – to lock it when I left."

"What were you going to do with the barrow?"

"Leave it at the school. Look, if you hang on to the bars of the gate, I'll go inside and move that iron hook. It's pretty heavy, and I think it's the cause of the trouble. I'll lift it. When I say shove, give the gate a hard push."

"But you'll get trapped inside."

"No, I won't. Once the gate has moved, I'll be able to get outside again."

"You really think it's a good idea?"

"Can you think of a better one?"

"No."

"Then let's stick to mine."

He had considerable difficulty in moving the bar. She stood grasping the gate, waiting for the word of command, watching him without impatience and also, he thought, without much interest.

"Now shove," he ordered.

She gave the gate a strong push. His hold on the bar was not firm; as the gate moved towards him, he took a step backwards and felt himself slipping. Having been given the order to push, she continued to do so. The bar fell from his grasp and the next moment had hit the ground. As it fell, the hook on the end of it ploughed a deep furrow in his shin.

He gave a yell of pain. She released her hold on the gate and watched him as he bent and clutched his leg.

"Something is wrong?" she enquired.

"Nothing at all." He spoke through clenched teeth. "I've just been crippled for life, that's all."

She came to stand beside him.

"The hook has torn your trouser leg," she said.

"The hook has torn my leg."

He had parted the long rent in his trouser leg and was trying to assess the damage. He thought he could see bone, but blood was flowing freely and had already soaked his woollen sock. The pain was almost more than he could bear.

"In the car, I've got a first-aid set," she said. "Would you like me to attend to the cut?"

"Cut? Is that all you think it is – a cut?"

"How do I know if you don't show it to me?"

He hopped on one leg into the road, closed the gate and put on the padlock. His shin felt as though it was on fire.

"If you'll drive me to the garage in the village," he said, "I'll get my car and go over to the hospital in Upleigh."

"Hospital?"

"There's a doctor three miles away, but his surgery closes at midday. It's now twenty to one."

"You think your leg is so bad?"

"I want to get it attended to, that's all. I don't want to die of rust poisoning and I don't want my ski trip messed up."

"Will you leave the tree here?"

"Yes. Somebody'll be along soon to find out why it hasn't arrived."

"How far is the hospital?"

"Four miles. I can get there if you'll take me to the garage."

She took the car keys out of her pocket, walked to the car, opened the doors and walked round to help him in. He was sweating, not only with pain but also with anxiety. This was no superficial wound – was it going to ruin his skiing holiday?

She took her place at the wheel and put the car into gear.

"Hold on a moment," he said. "Someone from the school."

42

He had never before been glad to see Jass. With her were two boys. He leaned out and spoke to her.

"Get the wheelbarrow to the school and leave it there until it's called for."

"Aren't you coming?"

It was one of the boys who put the question. Jass seemed to have been struck dumb. Her eyes were fixed on Gianna, and the expression in them told Ross that her hero-worship was undergoing a sex change.

"Let's go," he said to Gianna.

They drove away, leaving the boys to shake Jass out of her dazed condition. It was at once clear to Ross that Gianna was an expert driver – but a driver, he saw, who assumed other drivers to be equally skilled and aware of what they were doing.

"You turn right here," he directed.

"I'll take you to the hospital."

"There's no need . . ."

He did not finish the sentence; he was holding his breath. She had skimmed past a milk float, brushed two wheels against a sack of potatoes which a greengrocer had just lifted out of a van, and with the other two took the Upleigh turning. He wondered how he would have felt if his mind had not been occupied with the pain in his leg. He decided he would be fortunate if he reached the hospital with only one limb out of action.

He had visited the hospital a few times when his step-mother had been brought in with two broken ribs after her attempt to descend a ladder without using the rungs. He remembered large, bright rooms, sunny corridors and urbane physicians. The out-patients' department, however, proved to be nothing but a bare room with benches round the walls and a central table on which were tattered magazines many years out of date.

He telephoned Laura and said merely that he had hurt his leg and thought it wise to have it seen to at the hospital. Twice he asked Gianna to leave him – he could, he told her, return to Downpass in a taxi and did not want her to waste her morning waiting for him – but she refused to leave, and sat contentedly watching the other waiting patients.

"Why should I go? It's interesting here," she said. "I like looking at these other people and wondering if they've been fighting with gates, like you. I've never been in a hospital. Have you?"

"Only as a visitor."

They said no more; he did not feel in a mood for talking. And when he eventually went into the doctor's room, he found him not at all urbane. To Ross' question, put at the end of the session of examination and wound-dressing and injections, as to the possibility of his going skiing, the answer was terse.

"Out of the question."

He rejoined Gianna, sunk in gloom, and in silence followed her out to the car. If she made any remarks, he did not hear them. She helped him into the car and resumed her place at the wheel.

"You'll have to tell me the way back," she said.

He sat beside her, hunched in misery and self-pity. She allowed some time to pass, and then asked a question.

"When are they going to amputate?"

The tone, rather than the words, made him cringe. He turned to look at her. She was gazing straight ahead.

"I'm sorry," she said after a time.

"That's all right. I deserved it." Then he remembered the manner in which she had spent the morning, and groaned. "Oh my God, you've had no lunch."

"I didn't notice. I had a big, a very big breakfast on the ferry with this nice Englishman – no, Scotsman – who was alone, like me. I had croissants with honey poured over them – do you ever eat those?"

"Without the honey, yes. If you drop me at the garage, I can make my way home and you can go and meet your father."

"A man from the garage will take your car to your house if you telephone. I want to take you home and meet your stepmother, and then I will go back to my aunt's house. I didn't like it from outside – it was too square, too ugly, and

44

no balconies to go out on to when there is sun. And no view. If I had all that money to build such a big house, I would have built it in a better situation."

"So would I. Turn down this lane."

He stopped her outside the wicker gate. She switched off the engine and sat for a few moments gazing at the cottage.

"*That*," she said, "is a house I would like to live in. When I was in England before, I used to go on my bicycle looking for cottages like this, but I never found one. Are you here only on a visit?"

"Yes. I used to spend my school holidays here. I built that chalet a few years ago so's I could bring my friends down without going in and out of the cottage at all hours and disturbing my stepmother."

He was getting out of the car. The front door opened and Laura appeared on the doorstep, the anxiety on her face deepening as he limped up the path beside Gianna.

"It's all right," he reassured her. "It hurts, but it'll heal. This is Gianna Hargreaves, who arrived to find nobody at home. She hasn't had any lunch, and if she goes back to the house, Beatrice certainly won't offer her a meal. Perhaps you can feed us both?"

They were in the hall. Ross looked down at the thick bandages round his shin.

"If they slip," he said, "it'll look a bad case of gout."

He limped into the living room and lowered himself gingerly into a chair.

"Should I give you a strong drink?" Laura asked.

"No thanks. Incidentally, skiing's off. I'll give Dave a ring later today. He might put off his trip, but I doubt it. I've got to stay here and do some more trips to the hospital to have this leg dressed."

Gianna had taken off her anorak and a sweater, and had removed her woollen cap. Her hair was very dark, thick and glossy; it was smoothed back and tied with a length of narrow green ribbon.

"If you will allow me," she said to Laura, "I will make something to eat."

45

"Good heavens, no! Sit down and watch me do it," Laura directed. "We don't have more than bread and cheese and salad as a rule, but there's some – "

She broke off. Gianna had gone through the archway into the kitchen and was opening cupboards and selecting the things she needed.

"I am going to make a little lunch," she announced. "You will sit there and look. This is what my father liked to do – sit and watch me preparing our meals when we lived in apartments."

"Look, Gianna," Laura protested. "I'm used to – "

"Please." It was a plea but it sounded more like an order. "You will sit, I will cook, Ross and I will eat, you will taste and then you will award me a *cordon bleu*." She had opened the door of the refrigerator. "These mushrooms – I can use them?"

In the circumstances Laura felt that it would be churlish to say they were intended as part of the chicken and mushroom pie she had planned for dinner. To the mushrooms were added and assembled on the kitchen table eggs, garlic, salt and pepper, oil and vinegar, two large bowls and a frying pan.

"If you want, Laura – I may call you Laura? – while I make the omelettes, you could make coffee."

Ross called to say that he would have coffee, but wanted nothing to eat.

"If you don't eat," Gianna called back, "you will get weak and your second leg will not support you, so you will have to go in a chair with wheels. After we eat, I will go home and you can go to sleep on the sofa. But wait until you taste my omelette. It will be de-li-cious."

Her way of pronouncing the word seemed to summon up visions of perfect meals. Nor was hers an idle boast, for soon there issued from the stove an odour so tempting that Ross stood up and came limping to the archway.

"That smells like more than an omelette," he remarked.

"It is an omelette *plus*. The plus can be many things; today it is mushrooms and a little of this and that to be company for them." She removed two hot plates from the

46

oven, put them on the table and with a swift movement halved the omelette in the pan and rolled the halves on to the plates.

"You must eat *now*," she directed. "Like when you eat a soufflé – you must not delay for a single instant. Sit down and begin."

He began. She sat opposite, and while they ate, Laura poured out three cups of coffee. The sparse morsel of food which Ross begrudgingly allowed her to taste confirmed her in the view that this girl was a superb cook. Perhaps all skilled cooks, she mused, needed assistants and underlings to clear up after them. The counter near the stove was littered with peelings from mushrooms and garlic cloves. The bowls were in the sink, where the empty plates soon followed them. Through the doorway into the hall she could see the anorak left on the floor, the cap dropped beside it, the sweater slipping from a hook on the hall stand. Ross, on entering the house, had made some attempt to wipe the melted snow and mud from his boots, but Gianna's tracks passed across the hall on to the living room carpet. Laura thought of Beatrice Risdon's immaculate kitchen, with its gleaming equipment and polished floor. She thought of the Hargreaves House hall, with its unblemished tiles, coats in neat array on a rack. She measured the perfection of the meal against the resulting debris and remembered that Ross, emerging from his chalet looking perfectly groomed, left behind chaos that took hours of the daily woman's time to clear up.

He had gone back to the sofa, looking a good deal better than he had done on his return from the hospital. They drank coffee seated round the living room fire, Gianna on the hearth-rug, the dog beside her, his head on her lap.

"It's funny," she observed, "that I'm here on my first day instead of with my father. I feel at home here."

Ross was not surprised; not many people could resist his stepmother's quiet charm. His schoolfriends, the men he had sometimes brought to the cottage, even his girlfriends had all succumbed. He had now and then attempted to analyse the reasons for her effortless conquests, but had found himself unable to come to any satisfactory solution. Age seemed to have no connection with her power to inspire affection; Jass had proved as susceptible as the most senior citizen in the village.

She was addressing Gianna.

"Perhaps you should have rung your father to tell him where you were. He might be anxious."

"Anxious? No. He doesn't get anxious. When I stay out late, or if I miss trains or aeroplanes, he doesn't get anxious. He only gets anxious when I have men friends who like me, and I don't want to marry them. He thinks I should choose somebody and settle down. He would have liked me to marry Pierre, for example – but whoever marries him will have to go round the world watching him on concert platforms."

"Singer? Instrumentalist?" Ross enquired lazily.

"Violinist. I should have remembered to look and see if his passport was in order. He always forgets things – except his violin and his music. If he has those, he thinks he has got all that's necessary. Do you think he'll find his way to the house when he arrives? He doesn't speak good English, and I have got his car, so he hasn't any transport. Do any trains or buses come here?"

"Trains, no. But we have two buses a day," Laura told her. "And when he arrives, I daresay someone will direct him to the Coach and Four."

"The inn? But that isn't where he has to go," Gianna said in surprise. "He will of course stay at my aunt's house. He can't go to London to stay with his sisters because they are away."

"You mean he's going to stay with you?" Laura asked in surprise.

"Of course. He will stay until after Christmas and then he and I will go to London together. I asked another friend, Alexander, to come and stay too, but he couldn't come. His apartment is being repaired and he was invited by his grandmother to stay with her."

"Alexander?" Laura said on a note of enquiry.

"He's the Scotsman I met on the ferry. He works on

a newspaper in London, but I can't remember the name. Yes, I can. It's called *Newshound*. Do you read it?"

"Now and then," Laura replied. "It doesn't print daily news. It's more of a magazine than a newspaper."

"That's what he said. He has to travel a lot because he's their sports reporter. He has just come back from Italy – but he didn't go there about sport; it was about something else. He couldn't fly back to England because the weather was so bad, so he came by train to Paris and then to Calais and that's where we met. I'm sorry he can't come to stay, but he's coming to my party on Christmas Eve."

Ross raised an eyebrow.

"Does your aunt know about this party?" he enquired.

"Not yet, unless my father has told her already. It's only a small party, but when my mother was alive, we always had a party on Christmas Eve. My father and I couldn't have any when we were travelling about, but when he said we were going to spend Christmas here, he agreed that I should have a party, and I asked some friends who are living in London. It doesn't go on late because some of them want to go on to nightclubs and others want to go to Midnight Mass."

"You're a Catholic?" Laura asked.

"No. My mother won the battle for me to go to school in France, but my father won the battle about religion." She displaced the dog gently. "I must go. You'll both come to the party, won't you?"

"I wouldn't miss it for the world," Laura said with feeling.

Ross thanked Gianna for giving up her morning to him. Laura went with her to the gate. Her eyes widened at the sight of the car.

"Yours?" she asked.

Gianna laughed. Laura wished she could tape the sound and switch it on whenever she felt depressed.

"Not mine, no. It belongs to Pierre. His father gave it to him after he won a big prize in Geneva."

"Thank you for making the lunch."

"It was nothing. Does my aunt Beatrice have a cook?"

"No."

"Then perhaps I shall be able to do the cooking for her. You know" – she was in the car, the door still open – "it will be nice to be living in a house again, even if it's only for a little while. After Christmas I have to go to London to study, but I shall come back here for weekends. Since my graduation, my father and I have been travelling a lot. I thought he was enjoying it, but he suddenly said that it was too much for him, and we should go home to his house in England. It was the first time he ever told me about the house, and about my uncle and aunt. He said he had never mentioned them before because when he married my mother, he had a quarrel with his sister Beatrice, and never came back here. He wanted me to be sent to school in England, but my mother said no, it was to be France, and he promised her he wouldn't tell me about my English relations. So you can imagine my surprise when he said we would come to England and live with them. You know them well?"

"Yes."

"You like them?"

Laura hesitated, and then decided to be frank. This was an unusual girl – unusually direct, open, intelligent. She deserved the truth.

"Your aunt Beatrice," she answered, "isn't easy to like. I respect her and in many ways I feel sorry for her. Your uncle Walter is a scholar – one of those people whose whole mind is on their books, so he's not much of a companion. Your father . . . I don't have to tell you about your father. And you'll soon be able to judge the others for yourself. Thank you again for making that beautiful lunch and for being so kind to Ross. Please come and see us often while you're here."

"I would like to do that. Goodbye."

She drove away, and Laura returned to the living room. Ross was lying with his eyes closed. He opened them and addressed her.

"A violinist in residence, and a party on Christmas Eve. Should someone warn Beatrice?"

"Someone should have warned Gianna. What do you make of her?"

"She's no ministering angel. The poet who wrote those words had obviously never come across her. She took my accident with the utmost calm."

"She drove you to the hospital and stayed with you and brought you back here and made you a gourmet's lunch."

"Yes, all that. Didn't you hear me thanking her?"

"You were lucky she was around. I like her. I think she's attractive, and natural. And beautiful."

"Almost. What's going to happen, d'you think, when the invited guests knock on Beatrice's door?"

"It's not Beatrice's door. It's James' door. And perhaps after twenty-three years of shutting people out, Beatrice will make an effort to welcome her niece's friends."

"Perhaps. But my guess is that she'll take the padlock off the back gate and fix it on the front gate."

He gave a prolonged yawn. Moments later, he was asleep.

Laura went into the kitchen and began very quietly to tidy up the mess. Then she took a cloth and wiped the mud from the floor of the hall.

Ross woke two hours later. She was preparing tea.

"How's the leg?" she asked.

"I wish it was someone else's – but I don't think it hurts as much as it did."

"I'm sorry about the skiing."

"So am I. What did you do while I was asleep?"

"Cleared up the mess in the kitchen and the hall."

He thought this over.

"Perhaps," he suggested, "Beatrice will teach her to be tidy."

Laura poured hot water into the teapot.

"Somehow," she said, "I've got a feeling that nobody can teach Gianna anything. That's to say, anything she doesn't want to learn."

4

The next morning, Ross' car was brought round from the garage. Driving to the hospital to have his wound dressed, he thought he might drop in to see Gianna on the way home, not only to find out how she had settled down with her new relations, but also to discover, if possible, how Beatrice was reacting to the changes threatening her long and unchallenged rule. But the session at the hospital proved long and painful, and he drove back to the cottage with one overriding desire: to stay quietly on the sofa with only his stepmother for company.

He had learned with disappointment but without surprise that his friend David Forrest was unable to change the date of his holidays. There went two weeks of sun and snow and après-ski, he thought resignedly. He decided to stay in Downpass until visits to the hospital were no longer necessary; then he would return to London.

If Laura had hoped that James Hargreaves would come and see her, she would have been disappointed – but she neither expected nor particularly wanted to encounter him again. The past was the past, and she was content to forget it. She thought he would probably share this view.

She felt sorry for Ross, but not too sorry. His way through life had up to now been almost smooth. She did not consider him spoilt; his demands had never been unreasonable and he had never shown himself to be more self-centred than the average young man. The money he had inherited from his father had made him independent at an early age, but he was pursuing a profession he liked, and was making a success of it. Once it was established that the wound in his leg was to have no serious after-effects, she ceased to worry, and turned her mind to food.

Cooking was an art or a science she had never troubled to master. She was an average cook, but a limited one; the cookery book on whose instructions she had hitherto relied was entitled *Meals in a Trice*. When Ross was not with her, she subsisted on wheat biscuits, cheeses of various types and nationalities, fruit – and large draughts of milk, which she had liked since her childhood. But after watching Gianna Hargreaves perform a minor miracle in her kitchen, she had become markedly more ambitious. Never again, she told herself, would she make the mistake of thinking that eggs and butter were all anyone needed to produce an omelette. Here, in her kitchen, were storage jars containing ingredients she had used seldom and sparingly, always without suspicion of what she was missing in the way of miracles. There was not much point in preparing dishes for herself alone, but she would make them as practice, and astonish Ross when he came down on visits. She might even invite some of her local acquaintances to lunch instead of, as now, to mild tea parties at which she had offered no more than homemade cakes and scones.

Herbs. She must grow more herbs. Gianna had needed herbs and they had not been available. On the bookshelves in the living room were books on herb-growing which she had merely glanced through. Now she would study them carefully.

While giving her mind to this new interest, she went about her annual Christmas duties: putting the finishing touches to the angels' wings for the nativity play, telephoning members of the committee responsible for providing the gargantuan Christmas dinner for Senior Citizens – always an exhausting occasion, as most of the village inhabitants qualified for the feast. The numbers increased every year – a fact which always puzzled Laura, as she would have expected the most senior to die off and give place to their juniors.

She found that she had run out of the cardboard she needed to make haloes for the angels. It was not far to the shops; she wrapped herself up warmly against the bitter wind and walked briskly to the village and back. Turning

53

into the lane, she saw the car in which Gianna had brought Ross back from the hospital on the previous day. There was nobody in it. Gianna was standing on the doorstep of the cottage, huddled in a fur coat. When Laura reached her, she stood aside to allow the key to be inserted in the lock, and then spoke abruptly.

"I had to come and talk with you," she said.

Laura glanced at her. The quiet, calm manner was still there – but there was anger, and some other unidentifiable look in her eyes. It was almost a baffled look – after only one day of Beatrice? Surely not, Laura decided. This girl wasn't the crushable kind.

She led the way into the living room. Her example in wiping her feet carefully on the mat on entering the house was not followed by Gianna, who brought her mud in with her. She took off her coat and flung it on the chair in the hall.

"If you're busy," she said, "I can go away – or I can talk to you while you work."

"I'm not at all busy. Sit down," Laura said. Then she added in a gentle tone, "Is anything the matter?"

Gianna looked at Ross, and hesitated. He was on the sofa, his leg propped on it, reading a book.

"Can't get up," he apologised. "Nursing my leg."

"How is it?"

"It's enjoying watching my sufferings. If you want to have a private session with Laura, you can use my chalet."

"Thank you. There is nothing private in what I came to say."

Laura had piled logs on the fire. She sat down and pre-pared to listen.

"Problems?" she enquired.

"No. Not problems." Gianna, from the hearth-rug, looked up at her with a frown. "It's only that you . . . even you . . . You talked to me in this house yesterday but you didn't tell me one word, not one single word about you and my father. Why not?"

"So that's it," Laura said. "Did your father tell you when you saw him yesterday?"

"No. He said nothing. I know, all my life I've known that he is not a man who . . . who speaks out, who speaks frankly. Now that I have met my aunt, I can understand this. It wouldn't have been easy to talk frankly to her. So he said nothing. But couldn't you have told me? What was so secret about it?"

"Nothing," Laura answered. "At the time, it was anything but secret – the entire village knew all about it. But that was twenty-three years ago, Gianna – more years than you've lived. What was the use of dragging it all out of the past? I think your father should have told you before he brought you to Downpass. Perhaps he was waiting to see if I'd mention it. I wasn't being secretive. I was merely avoiding a delicate subject."

"Is there so much difference? When we came here, he knew that I would meet you. Why couldn't he have said at least a word or two?"

"How did you find out?"

"My aunt asked me whether my mother had known about my father's engagement to you. Just like that, without preparation. In the same way, without preparation, my father had said to me in Paris: 'You have English relations and we are going to England to live with them.' So you can imagine how I am feeling now. How many other things are there that he, or other people, haven't told me? What is going to be the next thing that is not secret but that nobody talks about?"

Laura spoke slowly.

"I haven't seen your father for twenty-three years," she said. "I don't know how much he has changed, but before he went away, I knew him very well. As you yourself said just now, he's a man who's incapable of uttering forthright statements, so – "

"But *that* I was used to. Why I feel so – so shocked now is because these facts that he has been keeping back were facts which were of great importance to me – things which I should have been told."

"They were facts which weren't easy to explain."

"What was so difficult to explain? He was going to marry

55

you. But he went away and married my mother instead. His sister Beatrice wrote and said she never wanted to see him again. Perhaps he behaved badly, perhaps he hurt you – but why did he say nothing? Why did my mother say nothing? She could have said that my father had a brother and sister in England but they quarrelled with him when he married her. Was that too much to tell me? So why didn't she? If there are secrets, real secrets, secrets which do not concern me, I don't want to know about them. But these things – having English relations, my father and you not marrying each other – these things I should have been told. But they said nothing, and now I feel all the time that there are other things I should know, but nobody will tell me. Secrets, secrets, secrets. How would you like to feel like that?" Her eyes went to Ross. "When you were older, did Laura tell you she had been engaged to my father?"

He had closed his book.

"By the time I was of an age to be interested in broken romances," he said, "this one had become ancient history, like the Trojan wars. I knew the facts in a vague kind of way, when I heard snatches of casual conversation, or passing references. But I regarded it as dead and gone. I never had much interest in Laura's pre-Mirren life, that's to say, the life she led before marrying my father."

"And you must remember," Laura added, "nobody thought that James Hargreaves would ever come back to Downpass."

"Your trouble," Ross told Gianna, "is that you're mixing up being secretive with merely avoiding subjects that are too delicate – too loaded – to be discussed. Why stir up what's over and done with? For example, there's no secret in the fact that I'm married. It – "

"Married!" Her eyes were wide with astonishment. "You mean you – "

"Don't interrupt. I've never mentioned the fact to you because the subject didn't come up in our conversations. Going out of my way to tell you would have seemed silly. So – "

"Married! But where is your wife?"

56

"I haven't the slightest idea, or the slightest desire to know."

"You're divorced?"

"No. Don't change the subject. We were talking about Laura's engagement to your father. When she knew he was coming back here, she might have given me a briefing on what had happened before he went away. But she didn't have to, because when I arrived the other night, I dropped into the Coach and Four, and there was only one subject being discussed: the return of the villain."

"My father?"

"Exactly. I heard enough to know what the general feeling was before someone recognised me and the subject was shelved. The next morning, I asked Laura for details."

"He asked me what had happened," said Laura. "The answer was nothing. Nothing had happened. I was engaged to your father, he went away, he married your mother – finish."

There was a pause.

"You loved him?" Gianna asked.

Laura smiled.

"Oh Gianna, that's a difficult question to answer. If I said no, would you believe me? I liked him very much."

"But not love?"

"No. In the sense you mean, not love."

"I can believe you, because after I grew up, I saw that my mother didn't love him either. And he didn't love her. In the beginning, perhaps it was different between them, but not when I was older and could see. I don't know how I knew, but it's the truth. They were friends. They didn't quarrel, they understood each other. But love? No. Perhaps it was because there was no passion in my father. Who can say? But if you didn't love him, you weren't hurt when he went away and married somebody else?"

"No. I wasn't hurt."

"But for everybody in this place to know about it – you didn't mind?"

"In cases of this kind, most of the comments are made behind one's back."

57

"Did my aunt come to see you, to talk about it?"

"No. They went away for a time. When they came back, your aunt came to see me, but very little was said about your father."

"But after that, you never went to visit her?"

"I was never invited."

"Now that he is here, do you want to see him?"

"I think the honest answer to that is that I don't care one way or the other. Though I'd like to see if he has changed."

"You will soon find out, because he will come to talk with you. He is already sorry that he came back."

"Do you mean that he and your aunt – "

"The trouble is not with him and my aunt. The trouble is between my aunt and me. I find her very strange. She insists to do . . . she insists on doing everything herself, even when she does it badly, like her cooking. After the terrible dinner she made last night, I said to myself, no more. I told her I would do the cooking. She got very angry. Then she complained that I was untidy, that I left things lying here and there. I asked why she didn't have people to come and work in the house, and she said she wouldn't pay women for doing work she could do better herself. My father said that a woman called Mrs Arnott, who worked in the house when she was a young girl, was willing to come, and he would pay her. She has a sister who will also come, and a niece. That makes three. When I told my aunt I had invited my friends to a party, she said they must not come to the house. I said this was nonsense – but then you know what she did? You won't believe. While I was out with my father in the village, arranging about the women to come and work, Pierre arrived. She sent him away and said he must go to the inn, the Coach and Four. So I went there and took him back and put him in one of the rooms for guests. There are three more to be used if I want my friends to stay. To say, as my aunt did, that there were to be no guests, no parties, no music, no dancing – this is absurd. I said to her that we must decide at once: is the house hers, or is it my father's? If it is hers, I must of course agree to what she wants, but if it is my father's, then I was his daughter and he had brought me to the house to live as my home, and so unless he had any objections to the things I did, I would go on in the way I have always done since I grew up. My father didn't have any objections, to the party on Christmas Eve or to anything else. He is used to the way I live, with friends and music and meeting together to talk. My aunt said if I was going to stay there and ruin everything she had done in the house for so many years, she would go away. My father should have spoken out then; he should have told her to go if she wished. But he didn't say anything. I said she must suit herself, but it was a big house and her rooms were where she could not hear much noise, and all my friends were very nice and would be pleased to see her if she wanted to meet them."

The clear, musical voice ceased. There was a long silence. When Laura spoke, it was in a somewhat awed tone.

"How did your aunt stand up to that?"

"She went up to her rooms to sulk. She is very silly, you know. She has not got good brains, like my uncle and my father. She has lived too long alone with Walter, who is interested only in Buddha. She is still living in the past – no television, no new ideas, no change of fashion in her clothes, no people to visit her. She goes to London and joins demonstrators, but not for long, because she complains they won't listen to her advice. All she wants is to get her own way in everything."

"Don't we all?" Ross asked.

Laura said nothing. She was feeling more sorry than ever for Beatrice, who had so recently stated her own side of the case and who, while stating it, had had no idea what was in store for her.

Ross, from the sofa, was looking at a group he thought could have been put on canvas: his stepmother in a low chair, Gianna leaning against it, the dog sharing the hearth-rug with her. Her hair was loose and made a smooth dark frame for her face. Her cheeks were flushed from the heat of the fire. There was no sound except that of crackling logs.

Laura spoke at last.

"I've forgotten all about lunch," she said.

"No hurry," Ross told her. "I want a drink first." He got up and limped to the cupboard. "Anybody joining me?"

Nobody joined him. Gianna said she would make the lunch.

"No." Laura spoke firmly. "I'm going to do it and you're going to watch me and tell me what I do wrong. I want to learn."

On one side of the archway, the two prepared a simple meal. On the other, Ross watched them.

"Who's cooking the lunch at your house?" he asked Gianna.

"I prepared everything before I came, and then Mrs Arnott arrived and I told her how she was to finish it. I wrote down everything. When I go to London, my aunt can cook again, but while I'm here, I am going to rule in the kitchen."

"Where did you learn cooking?" Laura asked.

"From my grandmother, simply by watching her when she cooked. We used to go to her house for my school holidays."

"Is she still alive?" Laura asked.

"No. I miss her sometimes. She used to tell me a lot about when my mother was young, how she was a very good pianist and wanted to study with good masters, but how there was never enough money to pay them. Then her godmother offered to pay, so my mother left France and went to study in Italy, but after a year she found she wasn't as good as she had hoped, and she went home to Nice again." Gianna, suddenly noticing Laura's knife poised over the lettuce, momentarily forgot her family history. "No, Laura, you don't do it that way. Watch me." Then she picked up the thread again. "My mother expected I would be musical, but I can't play any instrument. I just like to listen to music. You must come and hear Pierre when he gives his recital in London. It's at the end of January – you mustn't miss it. He gave a recital in Geneva, and one in Paris, and they were both very successful. In London, he's going to play the Cervin Variations, and the accompanist is going to be – you won't believe. Daniel Rekovitch."

60

"Who's Daniel Rekovitch?" Ross enquired.

She stopped work and stared at him to find out if he had spoken seriously.

"You don't know who Rekovitch is?" she asked in amazement.

"No. Fill me in."

"You've never even *heard* of Daniel Rekovitch?"

"Never."

"That is terrible. I suppose you are going to say next that you haven't heard of Cervin."

"You took the words out of my mouth. I'll look them both up."

"Don't bother," Laura said. "Rekovitch is a famous accompanist and Cervin is – was – a composer, as you'd know if you ever went to concerts."

"Where does Pierre do his practising?" Ross asked.

"In his room. For hours and hours."

"Can your aunt hear him?"

"Only faintly. She should enjoy listening."

"And does she?"

"No. She complained. This morning. She came into the hall when he was going upstairs and told him he had no right to use the house for practising. She said being a guest was one thing, but scraping away all day – those were her actual words – was something else. He asked if she knew who he was, and she replied that even if he were Yehudi Menuhin, it didn't give him the right to shatter the peace of her home."

"Where were you during the hostilities?" Ross asked.

"Coming out of my room. He leaned over the banister and told her that unless my father or I made any objections to his practising, he'd go on in spite of what she thought. She told him to go away and take his violin with him, and then I said no, he must stay as long as he needed to, and practise all he wanted to."

"That made it a three-cornered contest. What happened after that?" Ross wanted to know.

"Nothing, except that she frightened him by what she said about taking his violin away. He thinks she meant

61

that she would take it away, so now he takes it with him all the time. He even went out for a walk and took it with him."

"He'll be followed by all the village children, like the Pied Piper," Ross said.

"Not if Jass is around," Laura told him. "She'll see no harm comes to him or to his violin."

"She'll probably be heading the procession," Ross said.

"No, she won't. She called here twice to make enquiries about your leg; you were at the hospital – but I discovered that you've been displaced by Gianna as her first love."

"She's never set eyes on me," Gianna protested.

"Yes, she has," Ross said. "You were in the car with me when you drove me to the hospital. One look, and she switched, thank God. Now it's you who'll be followed round and pestered."

"Followed round, perhaps. Pestered, no," said Gianna. She sent a glance round the preparations for lunch. "Everything is ready," she announced.

During the meal, she said that she was going to drive up to London the next day to buy the things she needed for entertaining her friends.

"Laura, why don't you come with me?" she asked.

To Ross' surprise, his stepmother, who disliked and avoided London, gave an unhesitating acceptance.

"I'd love to. Any particular shops?"

"Yes. I'll show you my list. Then we'll have lunch at Crespins. You know Crespins?"

"She doesn't. I do," Ross said. "Have you got that much money?"

"Is it expensive?"

"If you don't know, that means someone took you. He must have been a millionaire. They make you pay in gold bars. Who paid?"

"A man I met when I was trying to find coins to put into the ticket thing at the Underground station."

"You'll never go hungry," Ross commented. "Just pick up a man before each meal, on a ferry or in the Underground, and reach for the menu."

"I do not 'pick up'." She rose. "I have to go. May I help you to clear up the plates?"

"No, you can't, thanks all the same," Laura said. She went to the door and opened it. "Come and see us whenever you want to."

Gianna would not allow her to go out to the car. She drove away, and Laura returned to the living room.

"Quick work," Ross remarked. "It took her just twenty-four hours to get the drawbridge down." He frowned. "Do you say down, or up?"

"In this case, you say up." She paused. "No. Down."

"Will Beatrice go, or will Beatrice stay?"

"Perhaps she'll stay and fight. But she probably realises that things will never be the same again."

"They might. It doesn't sound as though James is going to settle. When Gianna goes to London, he might go too. All Beatrice has to do is wait."

"You mean that if she hangs on, she'll find herself in charge again?"

"Yes. But while she's hanging on, there'll be battles – and James will be right in the middle of them."

Laura was on her way to the kitchen.

"Serves him right," she said over her shoulder.

5

It was not Laura who went up to London with Gianna. The telephone began to ring before half past eight the next morning and continued to ring at five-minute intervals; distressed female voices communicated the news that the proposed nativity play had suffered some severe setbacks: two of the kings from the East had developed measles and the Archangel Gabriel had fallen off his toboggan and now had two black eyes. The cast was being hastily reset, and as a result, bitter feuds had sprung up, jealous mothers were withdrawing their offspring, and panic had set in. Laura realised that she was the only one with the necessary authority to restore peace and reconcile the combatants.

"Why you?" Ross demanded when he came across the garden to breakfast. "You're not the one who decided to have a nativity play in the first place – let them sort it out on their own."

"If I don't go and pull things together, there won't be a nativity play at all."

"So what? Who'll miss it? Only a handful of mothers who want to show off their children. You were looking forward to getting out of this village for once."

"I can go some other time. I'll ring Gianna – she'll understand."

"It won't be much fun for her, going up alone." He pushed down the bar of the toaster. "I've a good mind to take her up myself."

Laura looked at him in surprise.

"Do you feel up to it? You had a bad day yesterday."

"It must have been a kind of crisis. When I woke this

64

morning, I knew my leg was on the mend. Will you ring Gianna and ask if she'll object to an escort with a leg and a half."

"What about the hospital?"

"I'll pick her up at her house and drive to the hospital and she can wait for me – I won't be long – and then we'll go straight up to town."

"Would you like me to pay for your lunch at that restaurant . . . I've forgotten its name."

"Crespins. No. Thanks for the offer, but money's all right at the moment. Incidentally, how well off is James? His daughter wears expensive clothes."

"All the Hargreaves – I mean these three here – have a lot of money. It came from old Jasper and I don't suppose they've made much of a hole in it. They're not spenders, any of them. Walter only buys books, and Beatrice is a hoarder. James went from tea to silk importing and owns both companies."

Even without this information regarding James Hargreaves' financial position, shopping with Gianna would have showed Ross that her allowance was more than ample. It also showed him that the entertaining she had in mind was by no means on the pot-luck plane. The ingredients for the Christmas Eve supper took up most of the space in the luggage compartment of his car, and she bought champagne by the case.

"Here, steady on," he protested at last. "These friends of yours aren't expecting a banquet. Or are they?"

"Party food costs a lot. And it's Christmas. Besides, it isn't only for parties that I'm shopping. Do you know that my aunt has nothing, simply nothing in her kitchen? No stores, nothing that can be used to make a good meal." She consulted her list. "I think I've got everything."

"If you haven't, you'll have to go without the rest of it. I'm hungry, and I ordered the table for one thirty. It's now ten to two."

"Then let's go."

At their table at Crespins, she glanced briefly at the metre-square menu, laid it aside, and told him exactly what

65

she wanted to eat. Then she sat back contentedly watching him choose the wine.

"You've been here before, haven't you?" she asked when they were alone.

"Once and once only."

"With – ?"

"With a beautiful girl."

"Lunch or dinner?"

"Lunch. It was her birthday."

"Were you in love with her?"

"No. And she was obviously not in love with me, or she wouldn't have let me squander all that money."

"What is squander?"

"Spend unwisely – I think. Why didn't you ask me into your house when I called for you this morning? I wanted to meet Pierre."

"How could you meet him? He was practising. He begins after breakfast and then goes for a short walk and then practises again until lunchtime and again afterwards. And before you meet Pierre, you're going to meet Alexander."

"Alexander?"

"Alexander Rannoch. He's the man I met on the ferry and fell in love with."

He stared at her. She appeared to be perfectly serious.

"Fell in love? I thought you told me you spent your time on the ferry eating croissants and honey."

"With him. You can eat and fall in love too. Before I left the house this morning, I telephoned to him and said we were going to have lunch here. He couldn't join us for lunch, but he's coming for coffee and we're driving him back to Downpass for tea and dinner."

"Are we really? How about a word or two to me before making your arrangements?"

"I knew you wouldn't mind."

"You couldn't have known. You merely hoped I wouldn't mind. Why couldn't he have gone down to Downpass on his own?"

"I wanted you to drive, so that I could sit in the back with him."

"There's such a thing as a rear-view mirror. If he starts anything, I'll stop the car and kick him out with my good leg. Damn it, you only met the fellow yesterday."

"Not yesterday. Two days before yesterday. He has telephoned seven times."

"Isn't it a bit too soon to go overboard?"

"Too soon? I met him, I had breakfast with him, I crossed the Channel with him. And just as Dover was coming into sight, I knew I was in love."

"Do you always succumb so precipitately?"

"Do I what?"

"Have you ever been in love before?"

She looked at him in amazement.

"Don't be silly – of course I have. All the time."

"*All* the time?"

"Most of the time – but not like this. It's fun to pretend you're in love, but this is different. This is serious."

"How can you judge? Just because a man filled you up with croissants and honey – "

"It's strange they don't have croissants in England. They make them, but they make them wrong."

"Never mind about croissants. Do you claim you can fall in love with a total stranger between Calais and Dover?"

"I just told you – I did. Why can't you accept the fact?"

"Because it doesn't tie up with my first impressions of you."

"What were those?"

"That you had a clear head, and seemed to use it."

"I use it when I meet a man who attracts me. You can learn a lot about someone in a short time, in some circumstances, that is. He saw that Pierre had got into trouble with his passport, and that I would need help getting the car on to the ferry, so he came and offered to do it. He spoke very good French and he did everything efficiently and without fuss, and then we were sitting at a table in the middle of the English Channel, eating – "

"Yes, yes, yes. Croissants and honey. Did he fall in love too?"

"Of course. I wanted him to come and stay for Christmas, but he had to stay with his grandmother because his apartment is being repaired, and he thought it would be unkind to leave her alone. But he's coming home with me today."

"I hope he'll make a favourable impression on your aunt."

"You don't like her, do you?"

"No. And she's never really taken me to her heart. She wrote me off as frivolous."

"Is that bad, to be frivolous?"

"Very bad in the eyes of the aunt Beatrices of this world. It means trifling and lack-of-purposefulness and so on. Have you ever noticed that there's something about a happy person that rouses the gravest suspicions in people?"

"No."

"You should be more observant. The way to get on in the world is to be like that chap in Shakespeare who gave the impression of being wise simply by saying nothing. Put on a serious air, and people think you're up-and-coming, bound to do well in the world. Look as though you're enjoying life, and you're written off as a lightweight."

"That's how you sound most of the time. Look at the way you spoke about your wife."

"I didn't know we'd discussed her."

"You only began. I'd like to hear more."

"Why?"

"Because it would fill in a gap in your history."

"You're interested in my history?"

"I'm interested in knowing why you never got divorced. It sounds to me silly to get married and then spend years not knowing where your wife is. If you're still married and you meet someone and fall in love and want to marry again, there you are with a wife already. Didn't she ever want a divorce?"

"No. She needed to be free enough to have all the fun she wanted – still wants – and at the same time able to use the fact of being married to cut short any affair that became a bore or a nuisance or an embarrassment. You can see her point."

"No, I can't. In her place, I would like to be free."

Their food was brought and served. He was interested but not surprised to find that she had some knowledge of wines, as well as of food. They ate in silence for a time, and then she put a question.

"How did it begin?"

"How did what begin?"

"Getting married and not divorced."

"Are you prying into my secrets?"

"You said it wasn't a secret. You said it just hadn't come into the conversation and that's why you hadn't mentioned it. I'm mentioning it now."

"Aren't you afraid of opening old wounds?"

"You didn't sound wounded. Were you?"

He considered.

"Not wounded. I was – let me think of the right word – I was scarred."

"But no wound, no scar," Gianna pointed out. "Why don't you tell me about it?"

"Do you want facts, or facts mixed with emotions?"

"Just facts. You met her – where?"

"At London airport. I'd been asked to go and meet her. She'd come over from New York – she spends a lot of time in the States – to be bridesmaid at her best friend's wedding."

"Best man friend or best girl friend?"

"Girl. They were cousins and they'd been brought up together. They'd always done everything together and they'd planned to marry together."

"But they weren't being married together?"

"No."

"Why not?"

"Because they'd tried to get the same man – and the bridesmaid had lost."

"But she still agreed to be bridesmaid?"

"Yes. I thought at the time that it showed great generosity of spirit – to lose but to accept defeat gracefully. To lose and yet to – "

"Never mind. Go on."

69

"She was very pretty. Small. What they used to call petite."

"And still do. So then what?"

"I drove her to the bride's house in London. We got on so well on the way up that she said she'd dine with me. She explained that the bride's method of winning the battle for the bridegroom had been, to say the least of it, unethical. I felt very sorry for her."

"So you took her to dinner."

"Yes. Not croissants and honey. A very expensive meal, almost as expensive as this one. Next night, we dined and danced, and the night after that, the bride's parents gave a reception at which champagne didn't so much flow as cascade. The occasion was marred by the bride's boast to the bridesmaid – in my presence – that she had won the bet she'd made about being married before the bridesmaid. The bridesmaid didn't like that remark; in fact, it made her come into the open and tell me she considered she'd been made a fool of. She added that she was planning a neat revenge. By this time, I'd like to mention, she'd embarked on her tenth, or perhaps it was her eleventh, glass of champagne. And I was keeping up fairly well."

"What of this revenge?"

"To get married first."

"I suppose to the first man who happened to be available – which was you. How could you be married in so little time?"

"Something called a special licence. When we attended the wedding, she announced that we were man and wife. As revenges go, it was a great success."

"It was a mean trick."

"Exactly. It more than equalled the previous mean trick."

"How old were you?"

"Old enough to know better. I was just twenty–one. I was floating on clouds of expensive dinners and swimming on seas of champagne. My one clear thought – not very clear – was that I had done a good deed for a deserving and incidentally very atractive girl. I felt like a knight errant."

70

"A what?"

"Don't you know what a knight errant is? Was?"

"I know knight. I don't know errant."

"It means wandering. They used to go round looking for maidens in distress, and rescuing them. At least, that was their story. After this experience I'm telling you about, I wouldn't have chosen knight erranting as a profession."

"How long did you go on feeling like this knight errant?"

"How long?" He frowned in an effort to recall the past. "Two, perhaps three days. Then I sobered up. I'd like to say that this lamentable episode, this disgraceful escapade, this tasteless adventure had three immediate results."

"One?"

"It showed me that beneath my suave and sophisticated exterior, I was nothing but a bumpkin."

"A – ?"

"A country clod. A hayseed. A . . . well, a bumpkin."

"Two?"

"It proved that I was a weak fool who could be used."

"Three?"

"It taught me to limit my intake of drink. A useful lesson which I've never forgotten."

"You lived together?"

"We went on what people called our honeymoon. Three weeks in a hotel in Cornwall."

"And after that?"

"We parted. And believe it or not, we parted friends. Neither of us liked what we'd done. The sooner we lost sight of one another, the sooner we could forget the whole thing. So we talked things over and she promised that if ever I wanted a divorce, I could have one, but if I didn't mind, she'd rather go along as what she called separates. I agreed, and that was the end."

"Didn't you want to know where she was all this time?"

"No. She got into the headlines once or twice – nothing very serious: speeding, rowdy parties with film stars, that kind of thing."

"Do you feel as free as she does?"

"I've never felt fettered, if that's what you mean. If I'd

71

wanted to marry, I think – in fact, I'm sure – she would have kept her promise to let me go. Has that filled the gap in my history?"

"Yes. Thank you. But I don't think I'll listen to your advice about falling in love with strangers on ferries."

"I suppose you won't. All the same, you should."

"When he comes here and you meet him, you'll understand."

"Understand what?"

"Why I'm so sure about loving him."

"What about all those other men you were in love with all the time?"

She waved a careless hand.

"Overboard," she said.

They moved from the dining room to Crespins' famous winter garden for coffee. They were about to settle at their table when Gianna spoke.

"Here's Alexander," she said.

Ross turned. A man was coming towards them – and at sight of him, the winter garden faded, the surrounding tables dissolved into the mists of the past, and Ross found himself back where so many of his happiest hours had been spent: on a rugby field. This was no ferry-traveller coming in to sit down and sip coffee from blue and gold cups. This man was a front-line forward, stocky, solid as a goalpost. Memories of swift and successful lineouts flashed into Ross' mind; brilliant passes, dropped kicks, a race down the field, ball held in a desperate clutch, tacklers shaken off and that last glorious moment, full-length on the muddy earth, the try scored. Even the newcomer's conventional suit could not dispel the illusion.

He came out of his dream to find his hand in a painful grip.

"Nice of you to let me come and join you," a cheerful voice told him.

Almost square face. Fair hair, blue eyes – unusual in a Scotsman, Ross thought. And the look he had just been telling Gianna was one to be avoided: one of untroubled calm, of happy confidence in the workings of fate.

"Glad you could come," Ross told him. "I understand I'm driving you both down to Downpass."

"Yes. Nice of you. I've got a car, but – like you – one of its supports has come to grief. It's more a rattle-trap than a car, but it goes now and then." He walked round the table and kissed Gianna lingeringly on the lips. "I missed you. Nice to see you again, love."

"As the stepson of one of her family's oldest friends," Ross said, "I've been warning Gianna against too-impulsive decisions in the emotional field."

"I'm the one you ought to warn." Alexander drew up a chair near to Gianna's and sat. "I took one look at her, and – this I swear – something seemed to hit me. It had never happened to me before. I had the feeling – have you ever had it? – that I'd seen her before, somewhere, anywhere. She wasn't a girl I had to get to know. I *knew*. She said she felt the same. There are some signs you have to follow, and I followed this one. There, I said to myself, is *the* girl. It made me forget that I was on my way home after mucking up an assignment."

"You look as though you play a lot of rugby," Ross remarked.

Alexander's face lit up.

"My God, do I! Did you when you were younger?"

Ross took this blow as well as he could.

"Yes. I still play seven-a-side occasionally," he said.

"Strenuous stuff, seven-a-side. I play for the Mayfleet Club. Ever heard of it? I thought not. We're not exactly Five Nations material. The Mayfleet's one of eighteen clubs in or around Berkshire devoted exclusively to rugby. Most of us are average, some of us are good, and all of us are dead keen. We give up all our leisure to practise, and we've got fixtures for all eighteen clubs to play each other, the winner to get the Mayfleet Shield, donated by my father just before he died. Mayfleet's never managed to win it, but we were runners-up last season and we're hoping to win it this year. We've knocked out one of the best clubs – the Bingley – already."

He pushed aside his cup of coffee, put his elbows on

the table and continued with what Ross guessed to be his favourite – and might prove his sole – topic of conversation.

"Funny how this thing has mushroomed in just over four years – or perhaps it was only natural that the idea would catch on. There are chaps like me in every town, every village all over the country – young, fit and prepared to give up their weekends to playing rugby. But getting games – regular games – was practically impossible. The point – "

"Your coffee's getting cold," Gianna told him.

"So it is." He picked up the cup and drained it. "The point," he proceeded, "was that there was all that individual talent, but there was no grouping, no coordination. So suddenly I had an idea, and I got half a dozen fellows to listen to it, and they" – he leaned sideways to allow a waiter to refill his cup – "they thought I was on to something good. So we went ahead. We put notices in every pub within a radius of fifty miles, asking anyone interested in forming local clubs to get in touch with us. The response was fantastic. We weeded out the chaps who were doubtful about giving up a lot of their time. Not that they weren't keen, but you know how it is? Some wives begin to get restless, girlfriends get resentful, that sort of thing. We divided the rest into groups on a kind of geographical basis, and saw to it that everyone was in easy reach of a club. We appointed a general secretary, and each club appointed its own officials. It worked. The not-so-keen dropped out, the keen stayed on and new blood kept coming in from the ranks of school-leavers. At the other end of the scale, there were the getting-on-for-thirties who'd let themselves get out of condition and wanted to get fit again." He sipped his coffee and looked at his audience of two. "Have I given you the picture?"

"Yes," said Gianna. "But – "

"We've only seven more games to play before the final. Three are no problem. The other four'll be tough, and we'll need to be in peak form. That's why this job the boss gave me, this trip he sent me on, came at the worst possible time. I should have been working up to a hundred per cent fitness instead of loping round in airports and conducting abortive

74

interviews. 'Why send me?' I asked him. I reminded him
that I was a sports writer, not a music reporter, and not a
bloody detective, either. 'What you need,' I told him – of
course interpolating a respectful 'sir' between every six
words – 'what you need, sir, is someone who knows something, sir, about music.' And also, I added, the kind of chap
who's good at nosing round digging up past history. Not
only did he not agree, he didn't even listen. So I had to go,
and he gave me no idea whatsoever of what I had to do
when I got there. I came back with exactly nothing. Wait till
he reads my report. I couldn't stretch it to more than a page
and a half. He won't sack me, because I happen to be a good
reporter in my own field. The truth – I only discovered
when I got back – is that he wanted me out of the way for a
few days. He . . . Sorry; am I monopolising the conversation?"

"Yes. But why did he want you out of the way?" Gianna
asked.

"In order to land me with an assistant in my absence. A
girl. His daughter, God help him. He thought she was well
out of the way, living in their baronial castle in a damp
corner of Scotland, but no. She got tired of the set-up. Her
mother writes poetry and keeps a pet piper and celebrates
Burns' Night – that kind of thing. So Daphne – that's the
daughter's name, though it should be Daffodil, because
she's the blondest blonde I ever laid eyes on – came south,
and then she crossed the Atlantic and tripped round the
States for a couple of months, and then walked in on her
father and announced that she was ready to be a newspaper
chief's assistant. This in spite of the fact that she can't type,
has never heard of shorthand and hasn't caught up with any
of the latest systems or machines or computers that today's
secretaries have added to their repertoires. She's living in a
high-toned hostel somewhere in Kensington, full of titled
octogenarians. The boss – her father – found her three jobs
and she was in and out of them in three weeks. But by then,
he'd remembered something: that years ago, when my
parents were alive, we'd lived next-door to the baronial
castle. We'd been neighbours, if that's the word when you're

75

six miles apart and there's nothing but heather in between. He promptly appointed her my assistant, and she started, quote, work, unquote, just after I left on this mission. God knows what she's been doing with my files while I've been away. I was afraid she'd been put into my room, but, thank God, she's got one of her own next-door which she calls her office."

"What was your mission?" Ross asked.

"Chasing up details of a defunct composer. He died some years ago – it was one of those cases where nobody heard anything about him when he was alive and nobody heard his music because nobody ever played it. He wrote four symphonies and one of them got on to the programme of a Prom concert last season. So the boss thought he might become newsworthy and decided to write him up. But he found we hadn't any facts to write, so he sent me to Switzerland to dig some up. This chap had been living in Lausanne for the past twenty years or so, but it turned out he wasn't Swiss; he was German. I found the boarding house he'd been living in, but all I learned about him was that he took no interest in food or clothes or his fellow-guests, but liked women. He'd had several mistresses who'd all disappeared without trace long before I got to the scene. I'm surprised I could stretch it to a page and a half."

"Couldn't you have written about his music?" Gianna asked.

"No, love. Sport, yes, Music, no."

"But you like music, don't you?"

"It depends. There's music and music. There's the music you hear and go away whistling, or the music that takes you back to the school chapel so must be Bach – and there's the music you have to take on trust, like some of the modern painting. I belong to group one."

"If he wrote four symphonies," Ross said, "wouldn't somebody have the copyright? If you could find out who –"

"I did. He sold the copyright of all four to a music publisher in London. I rang them as soon as I got back. The only fellow in the firm who'd ever heard of this composer was in hospital after falling off his bicycle. So I remembered I had an assistant, and told her to go on from there. Did I shake my head when you mentioned cognac with my coffee?"

"Yes. Changed your mind?"

"A drop, just a drop would lull my fears of throwing the boss' daughter out and then being thrown out myself to join the unemployed millions. Though it might not come to that. London's never been my idea of the good life on earth, so I took a chance a couple of weeks ago and applied for the job of running this vast new sports complex they've just built near Edinburgh."

"But you told me you came to London to be a journalist," Gianna reminded him.

"I did, and I am, love. But anyone – almost anyone – can be a journalist whereas only a fellow like myself, steeped in sport, can get a massive sports complex on to its feet. As well as which, I won't have the boss' daughter foisted on me as assistant."

"Why don't you ask her to my Christmas Eve party?" Gianna asked.

He stared at her in horror.

"Ask . . . you don't mean ask Daphne Maxwellton to . . . What on earth for?"

"You said she lived in a hostel with a lot of old people."

"So she does. But she can go and spend Christmas with her father in his Park Lane pad, can't she? I daresay that might be even drearier than spending it in the hostel – but come to think of it, I'm not going to have such a bright Christmas myself." He turned to Ross. "I've been living on the top storey of a house in Bayswater. The owner lives on the ground floor and refused to do any repairs until the snow began melting from the roof on to my furniture. I had to get out until the place was made weatherproof, but I hope to get back in about three weeks. In the meantime I accepted, in a mood halfway between sentiment and stinginess, my grandmother's offer to move in with her. She lives in that vast converted mansion in Belgrave Square – Belgrave Towers, they call it. Very, very classy. Lounge, bar and dining room on the ground floor, and sixteen extremely pricey suites on storeys two and three. But if I'd known the actual size of her spare bedroom, I'd have gone to a hotel. It's roughly ten by ten, with a bed made for a pygmy. My legs hang out all night. And only one bathroom, which my grandmother never seems to be out of. When I'm in real trouble, I have to go down to the ground floor and use the facilities there. Nice word, facilities. How did I get on to facilities?"

"We were talking about your assistant, Daphne Maxwellton," Gianna said. "If you'll tell me the name of the hostel she's living in, I'll ring her up and ask her to the party."

"Must you?"

"Yes. If she's going to work with you and be with you so much, I must see her and decide whether you are in any danger."

"I don't like blondes. I like beautiful brunettes like you."

"What's the hostel?"

"It's called the Empress Eugenie Club. You can see where they've painted out the 'for Gentlewomen' on the sign. God knows why a free-wheeler like D. for Daphne Maxwellton installed herself in a place like that. I can't give you her phone number."

"I'll look it up."

"How's she going to get down to your house?"

"I'll get one of the others to give her a lift."

Ross drove home thoughtfully. On the seat behind him, the two sat hand in hand, saying little. He took them to Hargreaves House, helped to unload the shopping and refused an invitation to go in and have tea.

"Pity," said Alexander. "You could have met Pierre. He's the highest violinist I ever came across – well over six feet. The audience must get cricks in their necks looking up at him."

"Some of them look down on him," Gianna pointed out.

"Not the stall holders. Thanks for the coffee and the lift,"

78

he said to Ross. "I hope Gianna'll take me round to meet your stepmother."

Ross drove to the cottage. When he entered, tea was laid on a round table in front of the living room fire. Laura put water on to boil.

"Enjoy yourself?" she asked.

"Yes. I met this fellow Gianna claims to be in love with – the man on the ferry. They both look as though they're deep in."

"Did you like him?"

"Yes. Young for his age, which is twenty-four. Talks too much, but you don't mind listening because it's all so full of . . . well, zest."

"What does he look like?"

"He's built like an oak tree. Fair hair, blue eyes, square face, but good-looking. He reminds me . . . Do you remember at one of my school sports days asking me who the boy with the biceps was? This man is the boy with the biceps grown up. Now he's the man with the muscle. What sort of day did you have?"

Laura did not answer. She was in the kitchen and he thought that perhaps she had not heard. But carrying in the kettle, she answered the question.

"I had a visitor."

He turned to look at her, but he did not speak. She filled their cups and handed him his.

"He came," she continued, "not long after you went out."

"Long enough to make sure that Gianna and I were out of the way."

"Perhaps. I saw him coming up the path, and I opened the door and said, 'Hello, James, it's nice to see you again.' He came in without saying anything – he never used to say anything until he'd got into the living room and taken a stand by his favourite chair – your favourite chair – and waited for me to sit down. Then he'd seat himself and look at me and say, 'Well, Laura?' He did exactly the same today, and I had a feeling we were back where we were all those years ago." She paused. "He's worn well. I told him so. But he looked tired – spent, I think is the word. He said he didn't see much change in me."

"And then?"

"Then there was a long silence. He's good at silences. He sat staring into the fire, and I waited."

She had waited patiently. Then he began to speak, and his tone had a kind of desperation.

"It was a mistake to come back, Laura. I made a grave mistake in imagining that Beatrice would have changed, would have mellowed. I didn't expect a welcome. I was prepared for recrimination. I wasn't afraid of meeting her again, as I was afraid – half-afraid – of meeting you. I came back because . . ."

Another long silence. Then the gentle, hesitant voice went on.

"I came back because I was driven back. I needed a refuge, and my house seemed the only refuge left to me."

"Refuge from what, James?"

"Not refuge. Refuge is the wrong word. I wanted rest. I wanted a place where I could be quiet. I'd been crazy to have allowed myself to believe I could keep up with the kind of life the young lead nowadays. I should have found a small hotel somewhere, and settled into it, and let Gianna go on travelling alone, or with a younger companion. But she wanted me to go with her, and I allowed myself to be persuaded. I kept up as long as I could, and then I found myself longing to be back in Downpass."

"You didn't want to travel?"

"No. I'd never liked moving around. None of us three – Beatrice, Walter or myself – did much travelling when we were young. But I wanted Gianna to see more of the world than she'd seen up to now. She hadn't known much of England when she was at the university. She knew France, but she didn't know any other Continental countries, and I thought seeing them would, as it were, complete her education. So she travelled, and I travelled with her."

Through his halting sentences, Laura pieced the story together. An ageing man with a beloved daughter of whom he had seen little during her school and university days, and

80

who was flattered by her wish that they should go travelling together. They had embarked on what, to Gianna, had been a delightful journey through many lands. But to her father it had developed into an increasingly exhausting series of stops and starts, of trains, planes, days of sightseeing and evenings when he, ready to drop, craved rest but she, tireless, was ready to set out on the evening's amusements.

"Didn't she see it was too much for you, James?"

"In the end, yes. But it was my fault she didn't see earlier. I should have given in – but giving in meant losing her company, admitting I was too old to keep up with her, and watching her go away with younger companions."

Another silence. She put logs on the fire and offered him coffee. He shook his head.

"Thank you, no. You see, Laura, part of the trouble was that – thank God – she's fond of me. She wanted me to enjoy all the lunches and dinners, she wanted me to enjoy meeting new people. But all I wanted was rest. And so I decided to come back here."

"And only then did you tell her that she had relations in England."

"Yes. Only then. While my wife was alive, the question had been settled once and for all: Gianna was not to be told. Beatrice's reaction to my marriage, and the little I had told her about life with Beatrice, hadn't disposed her to send Gianna here. But I realise that it was wrong to have kept her in ignorance for so long."

"And wrong, surely, to have told her nothing about our engagement?"

"Yes. Yes, Laura, quite wrong. But I have never been a man with any moral courage – you must have realised that long ago. Perhaps Walter and I had all our spirit bullied out of us – I don't know. All I know is that as soon as I came here, I realised that I was still unable to stand up to Beatrice, still unable to take a line of my own, still unable to insist on what I know or knew to be right."

"Isn't Gianna doing the insisting for you?"

"Yes. She doesn't lack courage, moral or any other kind." He sighed. "Things aren't easy in the house. Beatrice and

81

the violinist, Pierre, have become open enemies. There are daily women to do the work, but Beatrice is doing her best to make things impossible for them. The only hope of peace I can see is that Gianna will decide to live in London."

"Would you go and live there too?"

"No. It would be a young circle, and I have had enough young company for the present. I've discovered that nothing ages one more quickly than the effort to remain young. I would stay here and live as peacefully as Beatrice will allow me to. Fortunately, she goes up to London several times a week, so there will be intervals of freedom for me."

"How seriously are you taking Gianna's statement that she's in love?"

He hesitated.

"All I can tell you," he said at last, "is that she has known a great many men, and a number of them have wanted to marry her, but to my knowledge, she has never shown much interest in any one of them. This is certainly the first time I have heard her say that she is in love."

"Ross is with her today. Perhaps she'll talk to him and give him some idea of what she plans to do."

"This young man is a journalist. If she does end by marrying him, they'll live in this country and perhaps I can pay them occasional visits. It's strange: she only met him a few days ago, but she didn't give me the impression that she was acting impulsively. We can only wait and see how it develops. Beatrice will be happy if Gianna goes away. But it won't prevent her from making things in the house very difficult in the meantime."

"Beatrice can't do much harm, can she?"

"Harm? No. But she can make my life a kind of hell. Not Gianna's. I think she's afraid of Gianna. She's never before been up against anyone who takes it for granted that every sane person will see the sense of what she's doing, and agree with it. Unfortunately, she jars on Beatrice in many ways. She's untidy, she's unpunctual, and she's impervious to Beatrice's sneers or snubs. At times – and this may sound curious – I even find myself actually feeling a little sorry for Beatrice."

"Well, don't feel sorry. See to it that she doesn't spoil Gianna's life as she spoiled yours and Walter's. I'm glad to hear you've opened the house to Gianna's friends."

"I think Gianna did the opening."

"Then stand by her and see that the doors stay open. When the parties begin, if the atmosphere becomes too charged, or if you find the noise and confusion too much, shut yourself in your room, settle down with a book and have some of Gianna's lovely food sent up to you on a tray. There are daily women to do the work. Relax. Be happy because Gianna's happy. Let Beatrice rage as much as she wants to – she's got to let off steam. You've got a lovely daughter; look after her."

"Lovely? Yes, she is, isn't she."

"You told me in a letter that her mother was beautiful. Does Gianna look like her?"

"She has the same features – but her expression is very different. Her mother was not . . ." A long pause. "Her mother, I was going to say, was not a happy woman, but I mean that she hadn't Gianna's vitality, Gianna's capacity for laughter. I tried to make her happy, but I never succeeded."

"Was she sad all the time?"

"No, oh no. I don't want to give you a wrong impression. It was just that always, even in her happier moods, there was a trace of sadness. And she and Gianna were always very close to one another."

That was all he had said of his marriage. And most of what had passed between them she repeated to Ross.

"Didn't he want to know anything about you?" he asked.

"Yes. I told him about your father, and how you and I came here when he died. But – "

"But what?"

"It's odd, but I had a feeling that he was going to tell me more about his marriage, and then stopped himself. It made me feel as though he was keeping something back. I remembered what Beatrice had said about his being evasive. He told me a lot about what led up to the marriage, and it all sounded frank enough: he'd known her as a child, he'd visited her family when he went to his office in Nice, he had known her father for years – her father worked in the office. He missed her when she went away to study music. She got back just after he arrived – engaged to me. You'd think that was just the beginning of the story, but that's where he ended it."

"I suppose what he left out, if he left out anything, was how he switched from you to her. And you could hardly expect him to tell you about that. He must have seen her with what they call new eyes when she went back to Nice. Something must have hit him – the kind of thing Alexander Rannoch said he felt when his eyes fell on Gianna. Did he mention Alexander, by the way?"

"He said it was the first time he's ever known her to be serious about a man."

"She's certainly in love. So is he. You couldn't doubt it, looking at them both. They sat at the back of the car on the way home holding hands like teenagers. They made me feel sixty-two instead of thirty-two. Incidentally, she said her mother went back to Nice because she hadn't made the grade as a pianist. Perhaps that accounts for what James called the trace of sadness."

"Perhaps. It's strange, isn't it, that when we go to this party on Christmas Eve, it'll be the first time you've ever entered Hargreaves House. And the first time I've set foot in it since James went away."

"I'm looking forward to finding out whether the inside is as ugly as the outside. Who was old Jasper's architect?"

"He didn't have one. He just told the builder what he wanted."

"Exactly what I surmised. What made him build such an oversize mansion?"

"Money, I suppose. And the desire to show the world that he had it. He was in advance of his time, in many ways: the house has always had very efficient central heating, for example."

"If he'd been in advance of his time, it would have been solar heating."

"Perhaps. But there's lots of light – lovely long windows. The ceilings are too high and the bedrooms are too large, but there are two nice drawing rooms, one large, one smaller, opening into each other, and there's a spacious library. When my father and I went to visit them, which was usually on Sunday evenings, the only rooms in use were the library – for Walter – and one drawing room. Most of the bedrooms had dust sheets over the furniture."

"Sounds bleak."

"It was. Big square entrance hall, marble floor. Lots of bathrooms – not quite one to every bedroom, but almost. More tea?"

"No, thanks."

"What did you have for lunch?"

"Don't ask what I had. Ask what I paid."

"You shouldn't have refused my offer."

"Is it still open?"

She smiled.

"Sorry. Opportunity only knocks once."

6

On the evening of the party, Laura and Ross decided to walk to Hargreaves House. The moon was almost full, the roads clear of snow. The patches remaining on hedges and grass verges had frozen into grotesque shapes, and in the moonlight looked like strange, wild figures peering out at them as they passed.

They had been late in setting out; Ross had experienced some trouble in arranging his bandages and Laura, as always on formal occasions, had discovered that since she last wore her go-to-meeting dresses, fashion had decreed they should be shorter or longer, or looser or tighter. And her hair, so easy to arrange as a rule, had suddenly developed a maddening tendency to hang in wisps.

They left the cottage at last, their footsteps sounding metallic on the rutted surface of the roads. When they spoke, vapour floated from their lips into the night. But their conversation ceased abruptly when they turned into the road on which Hargreaves House stood. They could not yet see the house, but above it was a brightness that made Laura think of fire. They reached the imposing gateway, and through the wrought-iron design saw a sight that made Laura gasp.

"Ross, look! Just look!"

He was looking. The large gate lamp shone down on them and, at the end of the drive, almost every window was glowing with light.

"That's what I call a welcome," he said. "Did they light up the place like this when you and your father came on visits in the past?"

"Never. They used to put on the gate light and the porch light, and you could see lights in one or two of the downstairs rooms. But this? No."

The front door was opened by Mrs Arnott, well known to Laura but tonight unfamiliar in a black dress with a frilly apron. The hall also looked unfamiliar, being bright with anoraks and scarves that hung from hooks or lay heaped together on benches.

Behind Mrs Arnott lurked the small figure of Jass.

"I'm keeping an eye on her," Mrs Arnott said. "She wanted to come and see the ladies' dresses."

"Don't say my name," Jass pleaded. "Mrs Risdon's got big ears and she'll hear you. Twice she's come down to see what's going on in the kitchen, and I had to hide under the table. My Mum said I could stay as long as I want to."

"I'm sending her home with my niece, soon as we've served the supper," Mrs Arnott said. "But she's behaving herself, I'll say that for her."

Gianna came into the hall, slim and lovely in a long green dress. She took Laura's hand.

"Come in and meet everybody," she invited. "Jass, if you're good, Mrs Arnott will let you help her to carry in the ices at supper."

Jass, squirming and simpering, was understood to say that she would be goodness itself. Ross was interested to note that Gianna accepted the signs of homage calmly, and with no sign of the irritation or impatience he himself had frequently shown.

The distance from the hall to the large drawing room was only a few steps, but for Laura it represented a journey into the past. Her mind swung back to the days when Beatrice Risdon had made a habit of inviting the vicar and his daughter to supper after evening service on Sundays. It had always been a plain meal, and it never varied: cold meat, potato salad, large crushed-looking lettuce leaves, dry biscuits with even drier cheese. And afterwards they had always sat in this drawing room, the three men – James, Walter and the vicar – in one corner, discussing the politics of the day; Beatrice and Laura in another, each with her embroidery. At five minutes to eleven Beatrice had folded her work and the visitors knew that this was a sign for them to depart. James showed them out and the gate light was extinguished as soon as they had closed the gate behind them.

She wondered how much James recollected of those evenings. Looked at from this scene of revelry, they seemed to have a certain quiet charm. Dull and predictable though she had found those Sunday meetings, they had possessed a peace, a serenity which she did not often encounter in the gatherings of today. She and Beatrice had not found much to talk about, but from the corner of the room in which the men were seated had come the sound of exchanges and sometimes arguments – the interesting talk of intelligent men.

This evening it was difficult to distinguish any one conversation. Instead of the murmur of voices, there was dance music from a record player. Some of the guests – they numbered about two dozen – were drinking, others were dancing. James, wearing a dinner jacket and an anxious expression, was moving about the room refilling glasses or carrying empty ones into the kitchen. There was no sign of Beatrice or of Walter.

Gianna lowered the volume of the music and performed casual introductions. There was Pierre, as elongated as Alexander had described him. Alexander was there, and Pierre's two sisters, Simone and Denise, who were teachers in a London school of languages and whose flat Gianna and Pierre were to share while Gianna looked for one of her own. It was not difficult to identify Daphne Maxwellton – tall, pole-thin, in a clinging gold dress. She was dancing with a long-haired man who wore black silk trousers and a white silk blouse; in response to Gianna's introduction, she waved a languid hand in Laura's direction. The other guests were no more than a sea of faces, and Laura was glad when James led her into the smaller drawing room and settled her on a sofa.

"It's quieter in here," he said. "Not like old times, is it?"

"No. Not quite. Isn't Beatrice coming down?"

"No. Walter looked in – and vanished."

"Are any of the guests staying overnight?"

"Only one – the girl in the gold dress, the one they call

Daphne. She's rather intimidating. I suppose you're going to the Midnight Service, as usual?"

"Yes."

It was an occasion Laura never missed. It was conducted by candlelight and she loved the peace and the flickering shadows in the ancient little church. It was her father who had held the first candlelit service, and every Christmas Eve since that time had seen the church filled to capacity.

"Are you enjoying yourself?" she asked James.

"Yes and no. I'm glad Gianna has got friends round her, but – as when we went travelling together – I can't get used to the odd garments they wear, and I still find myself getting embarrassed when they make casual references to subjects which were certainly not current when I was young. And then, I worry because Beatrice is shut away upstairs, when she could have been down here with us. I often puzzle over whether we could have – should have – done something like this when we were young. I mean my family, the Hargreaves. But if we ever had a party, it didn't take place in this house."

"My father used to say – d'you remember? – that you had to choose between keeping peace in the home and doing your entertaining elsewhere, or making the home the centre of hospitality."

"In his day, there was a choice. The disappearance of servants left most people to choose the first alternative." He gazed at the animated scene in the adjacent room. "I didn't realise most of them would be French."

"Neither did I; I would have brushed up on my verbs if I'd known I'd need them. Why did you find the Maxwellton girl intimidating?"

"She called me James, for one thing. And every time I took her a drink, she polished it off and handed the glass back to be refilled. When I attempted, as a polite host, to join in a conversation she was having with a young man, she patted my cheek and said 'Home, James' in a commanding voice."

Laura laughed.

"No wonder you want Beatrice down here," she said. "She would have – "

Laura suddenly stopped in mid-sentence. Her eyes had fallen on a small framed snapshot on a table beside them. She reached out a hand to pick it up, and saw a look of acute embarrassment on James' face. She spoke in a casual tone.

"Gianna's mother?"

"Yes. That is, er, yes. I didn't know she'd put it . . . "

She sat looking at it – a lovely young girl on the steps of a villa set among pine trees.

"She was beautiful, James."

"Yes. Yes, she was. You can see her better in larger photographs, but this was the one Gianna always liked best."

"It's very clear. Most of the snaps I've got have faded."

"This hasn't, I'm glad to say." He took the frame from her and replaced it on the table. "She was a beautiful child, and she grew into a beautiful woman."

"I think Gianna looks like her. How are you getting on with Alexander?"

"I like him. He seems to be a steady sort of fellow. There doesn't seem to be much money at present, and he won't get his inheritance – I mean the capital – until he's thirty."

"In my opinion, not early enough," Laura said.

"I'm inclined to agree with you. His father was the head of a shipping firm. Alexander was to have joined it, but preferred to go into journalism. They lived up north until his mother died – his father was a Scot but his mother was English. She was educated in Switzerland. I don't think Alexander goes up to Scotland very often; all his interests seem to be down here in the south."

"What do you call 'all his interests'? Ross seemed to think he had only two: Gianna and rugby."

"That's true." He rose. "I'm so sorry – I haven't even thought of bringing you a drink."

But as he was returning with one in his hand, he was intercepted by Daphne Maxwellton.

"Whoa there, James," she said. "I'll take that to Mrs Mirren. I want to talk to her. You can go and play games in the other room."

She approached the sofa, her own drink in one hand, Laura's in the other.

90

"I'm coming to sit with you. All right?"

"Please do."

It was interesting to see that the dress, tight though it was, could stretch sufficiently to allow its wearer to sit down. Daphne achieved this manoeuvre without spilling any of her drink, and directed a long, keen scrutiny at Laura, who felt entitled to make as frank a survey in return. Long face, high cheek-bones, blue, up-slanting eyes – and that extraordinary silvery hair. Manner: confident to arrogance; casual. Speech: slightly affected, laconic, voice rather high and drawling, but musical. She was a type Laura had seen on the covers of fashion magazines, but had never met. The caption, she thought, would need only one word: sophistication.

"You're Ross' stepmother, aren't you?"

"Yes."

"I think he's sweet. Rather elusive, but then, that's not surprising. He got badly scorched once, didn't he?"

"You'll have to translate that."

"Well, he got married. Did you know her?"

"No."

"I was too young to know much about it – I was only about twelve when it happened. But do you know, the *oddest* thing, I ran into her last month when I was in New York. I was telling Ross about it just now. He was *riveted*. He hadn't had any direct news of her for years and years. She's rather fascinating, but I think she's beginning to let her figure go." Her eyes swept over Laura's curves. "Isn't it a tragedy that so many women do? I shall never be anything but slim."

"Lemon juice for breakfast, lettuce for lunch, a lean cutlet for dinner?"

"Goodness, no. No cutlets, fat or lean. The one thing, the one useful thing my mother ever taught me was how to avoid putting on weight. Do you worry much about yours?"

"Should I?"

"Well, it's obvious that you don't, but it's such a pity. I'll tell you how you can be as slim as I am." She paused to light a cigarette. "What you do is, you choose a dress – a

91

staggering, eye-catching sheath like the model I'm wearing, and you take every cent you have in the bank *out* of the bank, and you buy the dress but, but, *but*, you must make sure that it's too small for you. They'll try to persuade you to take a larger size, but you must be ab-solutely firm, and refuse. You buy one you can just squeeze into, and you take it home and swear you'll make yourself fit into it."

"But I – "

"There is only *one* way of being able to drive your women friends mad with jealousy and get your money's worth; you get your weight down until you fit into the dress. How do you do it? By thinking of it every time you see food. You reach out a hand – and draw it back when you remember that your object is to be the best-dressed woman in London. In no time at all, you fit the dress – and your figure is perfect. You must try it. You really must."

Laura saw Ross approaching on what she thought was probably a rescue operation. If he intended to remove Daphne, she forestalled him.

"Draw up a chair," she invited. "Daphne's giving me fashion hints."

"Not that she needs them," Daphne said. "Those curves suit her."

"That's what I think too," Ross said. "If I have to choose between curves and angles, I'll go for curves. I can't offer you another cigarette, I'm afraid. I'm a non."

"I was also telling Laura – I may call you Laura, mayn't I? – about your wife. I told Ross" – she turned to Laura – "that I was at a party in New York, and this woman came up and said wasn't I Daphne Maxwellton, and I said yes, and she said she'd met my mother once. I asked her name and she said she was Mrs Mirren and if ever I ran across her husband, Ross Mirren, I was to give him her love. She's running a gift shop – lovely things, wildly expensive. She didn't finance the venture – it was Gould Schneider who put up the money. They're sharing a penthouse and having a lot of fun. I can't imagine why she doesn't divorce Ross and marry Gould – he's rolling. Rolls of fat, rolls of money – he sounds awful but he's really quite nice." She focused a keen

92

gaze on Ross. "In your place," she advised, "I'd go over there and grab her. She's ready to settle – you can see that. After all, she's not all that young; she must be all of nearly thirty. I quite liked her. In fact, I liked her so much that although I'd like to keep you for myself, I'm willing to let her have you."

"I don't want you," Ross informed her. "You'll starve yourself until you die of that disease I can't pronounce."

"No, I won't. In the summer, I can forget about clothes and eat all I want until the autumn. Do look at Alexander – he's in the sulks. He didn't want me to stay here tonight."

"Why not?" Laura asked.

"Because it meant that Gianna would have to stay here too, and he had other plans for her – I didn't ask him what they were. Do you know, he lives on the top storey of an awful leaky house in one of the back streets of Bayswater. He's got enough money to live decently, if not graciously, but he won't. He won't even buy himself a decent car. It's the Scots streak in him," explained Miss Maxwellton. "Where do you live?" she asked Ross.

"The Barbican."

"One room, even if it is forty by forty, with only a tiny bedroom and bathroom and a smaller kitchen. When I heard what he was paying," Laura said, "I felt ill."

"What's Alexander going to do," Ross asked Daphne, "if you forget about clothes all summer?"

"What on earth has it got to do with . . . Oh, you mean the *job*! He'll just have to find another assistant, that's all. One who knows something about sport, which I don't."

"Didn't he pass on to you the job of – "

"Oh, that composer. Sometimes my father has brainstorms. This was one of them."

A door on their right opened, and Mrs Arnott was seen signalling: supper was ready to be served. Daphne put out a hand and Ross drew her to her feet; she went to join Pierre, and James came to escort Laura. Ross, about to follow them, caught sight of the framed snapshot and picked it up.

"Gianna's mother," he said. "Right?"

"Yes," answered James.

93

"There's a strong likeness, isn't there?"

"Yes."

"What's the building?"

"The building? Oh, you mean the villa. It was the house her music teacher lived in in Italy. She was very sorry to give up her studies."

The guests were filing into the dining room. Laura saw that two tables had been laid beside the long oak one she remembered. The food, she thought, could not have been surpassed by a first-class restaurant. The meal was simple, but perfectly cooked. It was laid on the sideboard, and the guests helped themselves and carried their plates to the places at which name cards had been put. Laura was seated with James on one side of her and Pierre on the other.

"A pity Beatrice and Walter are missing this wonderful food," she said to James.

"Trays were sent up to them. They came down empty."

"Does Beatrice show any signs of getting used to the new order?"

"Not the slightest. I think she's merely waiting for Gianna to go away."

"When do Gianna's classes begin?"

"Early in January; I'm not sure of the date. I think she and Alexander are talking of her getting a flat in which they can live after they're married."

"Isn't it too soon to talk of marriage?"

He smiled.

"My opinion won't be asked. Young people do as they please nowadays. I'm sorry about that affair of Ross'. A pity, wasn't it?"

"More than a pity. I wish they'd get divorced and finish with it all."

"You never met her?"

"No. The whole thing happened too fast."

"Does he spend much time with you?"

"Not in the summer. I scarcely see him from May to October. During the rest of the year, he comes down about once a month."

"He's a fine young man."

94

"He's good company. And – apart from the marriage – he's got a lot of sense."

He lowered his voice.

"I thought the young lady sitting opposite was taking rather an interest in him."

Laura made no reply, though her own opinion was that Daphne Maxwellton's open advances to Ross were made with a view to diverting attention from her interest in Alexander.

"It's time I talked to Pierre," she said. "Do I speak French or English?"

"He won't speak French to you – or to any English person. I can't decide whether he does it to improve his English, or because he thinks his English needs no improving. I think you'll find talking to him rather a strain."

She turned to Pierre, who had just ended an animated conversation with Simone, seated on his other side, and was preparing to give his attention to Laura.

"I'm told you're giving a recital in London soon," she began.

"Please?"

She repeated the sentence more slowly.

"Ah. Yes, yes. This is true."

He seemed uninterested in the topic; she tried another.

"Do you find it cold over here?"

"Cold? Yes, I find it so. I don't like to be cold. You like the cold?"

"Not too much of it."

"Russia is more cold."

"Yes, so I believe."

"And Sweden. Especially Sweden. You have visited there?"

"No."

"Stockholm is beautiful. Also Copenhagen. And I think most of all, Norway."

Laura, feeling that this was developing into a travelogue, went back to music.

"I hope to go to your recital. I'm looking forward to it."

95

"There are no more tickets. They are all sold. Only my sisters have kept some. You must speak to them. Only the expensive tickets are left; perhaps you will not want those. You play the violin?"

"No. I'm afraid I don't play any instrument."

"You have never made a study?"

"No."

"It is a pity. Who is the girl sitting on the other side of the table, eating nothing and drinking so much?"

"She's Alexander Rannoch's assistant."

"For what?"

"Well, a kind of secretary, I think."

He studied the gold dress, the expensive make-up, the glossy cap of hair and the gold-lacquered fingernails.

"She *works*?" he asked disbelievingly.

"Yes. At any rate, she's got a job."

"That is not the same thing."

"I suppose not."

She was relieved to see James rising to announce that coffee would be served in the drawing room. There was a general movement to disperse, and Laura took the opportunity of slipping upstairs to see Beatrice.

She knocked on the door of her sitting room, and Beatrice opened it.

"Oh, it's you. Come in. I was wondering if you'd take the trouble to look in on us."

Walter struggled out of an uncomfortable-looking arm-chair. Like all the furniture in the house, it was heavy and ugly, its look further marred by the covers Beatrice had chosen when she came back to live in the house.

"I wish you'd both come downstairs," Laura said. "It's not at all a noisy party, and they're all very nice."

"I'm glad you're enjoying it." Beatrice gave a con temptuous sniff. "It isn't our kind of amusement. I went down to the kitchen – what the food has cost James, I dread to add up. That daughter of his will ruin him. And oceans of champagne. She couldn't have learned extravagance from her mother – the family had nothing when she married James."

96

"I'm sure he enjoys watching her spend his money."

"That's nonsense; no good businessman would enjoy watching waste. I'm filled with disgust when I see how he spoils her. She seems to have robbed him of any caution he might have shown in the past. For example, how much has he done to find out something about this man she's talking of marrying? Nothing. Judging by the dreadful little car he brought here, he can't have much money – but I hear he has a grandmother who lives in Belgrave Towers. If that's true, there must be money somewhere in the family. They don't give those suites away."

"You'll like Alexander when you get to know him better."

"I doubt it. He calls himself a Scot, but he was educated in England and he talks like an Englishman, which in my view means that he's neither one thing nor the other. As for that Frenchman, I've come to the conclusion that he's off his head. Do you know that he carries his violin about with him wherever he goes? I wouldn't be surprised to hear he'd put it under the table while he had supper. He takes it into meals, he takes it with him when he goes out for walks and I daresay he takes it to bed with him."

Laura leaned back in her chair, listening and relaxing. It was barbed, it was spiteful, but it was a change from the scene downstairs. When she rose to join the guests some moments later, she felt rested and ready to enjoy herself again.

Gianna, she found, was waiting for her. She led her to Alexander.

"We want to ask you a favour," she said.

Ross was passing, and Alexander grasped his arm.

"Wait a minute," he said. "You're in this too. The thing is" – he turned to Laura – "I told my grandmother about Gianna, and she said she'd very much like to meet her."

"Naturally," said Laura.

"I want to meet her too," Gianna said, "but I don't want to go by myself."

"Won't Alexander be with you?" Laura asked.

"No. She said it would be nice if he wasn't there and she

97

and I could get to know each other. But I thought . . . " She paused. "I wondered if you would mind going with me. Don't say no straight away, please. Normally, I'd ask my aunt Beatrice to go, but that wouldn't be . . . well, I wouldn't want her with me. But you're a friend and if we said we were going up to do some shopping and would drop in and have tea . . . don't you think that would be a good way of doing it?"

It was Ross who answered.

"Yes, it would," he said. "I'm speaking for Laura, because I can see she's wondering how she can accept and not give away the excessive curiosity she's feeling. All you have to do is tell Alexander to fix a date with his grandmother. What did you want with me?"

"Another favour," explained Alexander. "I've got a match at our club ground on Saturday. I'll be in Wales on Friday, but I can drive straight to the game and get there in time if I don't have to pick up Gianna. I'd like her to be there. Would you take her?"

"Yes. How much does she know about rugby?"

"Nothing. At least, nearly nothing," Gianna said.

"If you took her," Alexander said, "you could explain the finer points of the game. Will you be here or in London?"

"Here. What time's the match?"

"Three. It's quite an important one for us, because if we knock out this lot – they're coming up from Reading – we won't have much trouble getting through to the final. Will you do it?"

"I've just said I will."

"Good. If you get too cold, you can make yourselves comfortable in the clubhouse."

"Laura, how do you feel about rugby matches?" Gianna asked.

"If that's an invitation to join you, the answer's no. I did enough freezing on fields when I used to go and watch Ross playing. I'd like to warn you that if you let your attention wander and miss what Alexander calls one of the finer points of the game, you'll never be forgiven."

98

"I won't let my attention wander. I shan't be seeing much of him between now and the day of the match. I'm just beginning to realise how much time I'll have to spend in the future just waiting for Alexander to come home from his travels."

"Has your father," Laura asked her, "said anything to you about these so-to-speak functions which take place in the village at this time of the year?"

"Yes. Do you go to them?"

"No. At least, only to one or two. The idea is to find an outsider if possible. It gives a kind of stimulus to the proceedings. Ross always gets roped in. He isn't exactly a stranger, but he's very good at giving the impression that he's come down from London especially for the occasion."

Gianna turned to him.

"I'd like to go with you, if you'll take me," she said.

"I'll take you – but you don't know what you're letting yourself in for. I've cut out the gymnastic display. I saw no point in limping up to the platform and lecturing on the perfect physique. That leaves the handicraft display and the band parade."

"When?"

"Both on the same day – day after tomorrow. The band parade's at eleven in the morning and the handicrafts are on view from three o'clock onwards."

"Will you come and fetch me?"

"If you're sure you want to go."

"Yes, I'm sure. I want to get to know some of the people here."

"Then you can begin with the Junior Band. Ages six to nine. But don't bring Pierre – I don't think it's quite his idea of real music."

7

Christmas Day was celebrated quietly at the cottage. Ross spent most of the day sitting in a comfortable chair, reading. There was no fear of being disturbed by callers, for it was the village custom to confine the exchange of greetings to the church porch after the morning service. Gianna and Pierre called in for a few moments on their way to London to spend the day with Pierre's sisters, and brought flowers for Laura. They brought Daphne with them; they were to drop her at her father's house, where she intended, she told them, to see that his Christmas spirit, such as it was, would be written on a cheque.

The mince pies were brought out and eaten at lunch, which Laura and Ross ate in the kitchen. Dinner was a more ceremonious meal on a holly-decorated table in front of the living room fire. The Christmas pudding had been made by Laura; Ross had brought wine down from London.

"How many bottles of champagne do you think we got through last night at the party?" she asked.

"I wasn't counting. Daphne Maxwellton disposed of several of them."

"Without turning a hair. Your father once told me that your grandmother had a head like that."

"I wish I'd inherited it."

"You've had a very dull day. Do you wish you'd spent it with some of your friends in London?"

"No. One of the reasons I come down here is to recharge my batteries. There's something about you, or about this cottage, that breathes peace. Where else would I get that? And it hasn't been a dull day; it's been just what I needed. Do you want to listen to some music, or do you want an early bed?"

"Early bed."

"Good. So do I. I need to rest before facing that Junior Band."

"It won't be any worse than it was last time you heard it."

But on the following morning, Ross found this statement to be incorrect. The sounds created by the twenty members of the Junior Band caused Gianna to turn pale.

It was an orderly assembly. The band members and their parents met punctually in the school hall, together with some other spectators Ross presumed to be deaf. The band lined up, instruments in hand. The band's organiser and conductor, an elderly lady named Mrs Colton-West, stood, baton in hand, in an ill-fitting tweed suit and a matching hat not unlike the battered one worn by Beatrice Risdon.

It had been hoped, when the band was inaugurated, that Beatrice would provide at least some of the instruments, but she had pursued her usual policy of giving advice and leaving others to make the necessary financial contributions. The parents had held a collection, but this had not realised the amount hoped for; thus there were no gleaming trumpets, no clarinets, no trombones. There were a number of drums, three bugles borrowed from the Boy Scouts, several tambourines, four recorders and two triangles. Mrs Colton-West had been advised to settle for a percussion band, but she had allowed ambition to override discretion, and now waited to give the signal for the music to begin.

The first command was 'Quick march' – this was a peripatetic band. The juniors, drawn up in five lines of four, marched. Their steps did not synchronise, but the stamping was full of spirit. At a given signal, halfway round their circuit of the hall, they began to play. They blew and thumped and banged, but listeners were unable to decide whether they were playing 'The British Grenadiers' or 'Men of Harlech'. All guesses proved to be wrong, for when the noise stopped, Mrs Colton-West announced that it had been her own adaptation of 'Good King Wenceslas' into marching rhythm.

The second item was a duet for recorders. One of the

soloists was Jass, who did well enough until her eyes fell on Gianna, after which she lost her place and obviously failed to find it again.

More marching followed and some of the spectators slipped unobtrusively away. Instruments were laid aside as the juniors performed a complicated chain movement; then the finale was given by the band forming a semi-circle and playing a barely recognisable version of the National Anthem. This over, they gave three cheers for their conductor, broke into disorderly groups and joined their parents. Mrs Colton-West, beaming and triumphant, stationed herself at the exit to shake the hands of the departing audience. Ross and Gianna were the last to leave and she accompanied them to their car.

"A worthwhile task, I feel," she told them. "I have to put in a lot of hard work, and of course I'm not claiming that the results are all one hoped for, but it does, I think, give the younger children an introduction to music. I wish I could have afforded to buy instruments for them, but that was impossible. However, I've started a fund and I put into it any small contributions I receive from time to time. It . . . Oh, *thank* you, Mr Mirren. That is so kind – and far, far too generous. How very nice of you to take such an interest; it really does encourage one to go on."

Gianna promised that her father would send a cheque.

"He's not musical," she said, "but he'll be interested to hear how you've trained all those children."

"I'm so grateful, Miss Hargreaves. I didn't realise who you were when you arrived. I asked somebody and they told me. You've no idea how much difference it makes to the children to know you've troubled to be present. Thank you, thank you very much for coming."

They drove away, leaving her waving her baton. Ross felt the usual mixture of embarrassment, compassion and shame that gripped him after attending such village functions.

"Why don't people help her more?" Gianna asked.

"To produce that cacophony?"

"That what?"

"That appalling row."

"She's trying to get a lot of little savages interested in music, and nobody's helping her. Why not?"

"Nobody's interested."

"The parents must be."

"Not to the extent of providing instruments. Can you imagine what would happen if those twenty children were given instruments and then told to practise them at home?"

"They could use a room at the school to practise in, couldn't they?"

"No. They tried that, but there had to be a supervisor to see that they stuck to practising and didn't wreck the place. Nobody volunteered for the job. One reason was that nobody's too keen on Mrs Colton-West. She's a newcomer. She moved into one of the larger villas, brought an immense amount of luggage and immediately started off on the wrong foot by inviting the neighbours to table-tapping sessions. That didn't get moving, so she switched to yoga, and that folded too. There's something about this community that resists organising – as your aunt Beatrice discovered. Mrs Colton-West hasn't given up yet, but she might soon. Her name doesn't help – people think it sounds like a station. Are you still prepared to go to the handicraft display?"

"Yes."

"Laura's offered to give us lunch."

"Please thank her – but I'll go home, and I'll be ready at about three."

Fortunately, the handicraft display, also held in the school, was not an assault on the ears, as the morning session had been. Desks were ranged round the room, and on or round them were arranged the results of the work done during the year by the more artistic – or the more energetic – members of the village. Ross and Gianna were greeted by the chairman of the work committee. He offered to show them round, but they told him they would rather browse and see everything unaccompanied.

"There's not as much to see as there was last year," he said. He lowered his voice. "My opinion is that people are

103

losing interest in this sort of thing. It's this television. They all sit down to watch it of an evening, and they keep on watching it until it's time to go to bed. If they haven't got colour sets in their own homes, they go round to the pub and sit there until closing time."

"So there's not much time left to do handiwork," Gianna said.

"No time to do any, and no *wish* to do any. That's the truth, Miss Hargreaves. What you'll see now, as you go round, is what's been done on afternoons when they didn't mind missing a programme."

This sounded discouraging, but when Ross and Gianna slowly walked past each display, they found no lack of articles and no lack of variety. There was woodwork, some of it with carved decorations; there were woven baskets, book-ends, paintings in watercolour or oil, children's toys both woolly and mechanical, photographic displays, models of ships, pottery in strange shapes, embroidery and innumerable knitted garments. Some of the exhibits were as fragile as the exhibitors seated by them; others were of almost professional standard. The better articles all had 'Sold' notices beside them.

As Ross expected, Gianna bought so many things that several journeys to the car were needed before they could leave. As he had also expected, most of her purchases were from the badly executed sections. He confined himself to choosing articles which Laura could give away. When at last they left the building, laden with purchases, they had the satisfaction of knowing that business was moving more briskly than when they had arrived.

"And that's the lot." Ross stacked the last purchases into the car. "I suppose you know that the two baskets you bought are shedding their straw?"

"Yes, I know."

"And the shawl you bought for Laura, who doesn't wear shawls, is losing its fringe."

"Yes, yes, yes. And the paintings I bought are terrible, but who else would have bought them? Just think of all those old people sitting there until the evening and nobody buying anything except the good things. Just think how happy they must be when they've sold something and got a little money."

"I'm thinking."

"They're not rich, are they? To earn a little more money for themselves, don't you think that's a good idea?"

"I don't know. Let's say I've got a dark side to my nature. When I'm asked to buy an article that's falling apart, I can't decide whether the transaction is a business arrangement or a charity."

"Then don't try to decide. Just buy the things and make the people who've made them happy. That's all."

"It isn't quite all. Why did I feel embarrassed when I handed over the money for this calendar and two of the pages fell out of it?"

"That wasn't embarrassment. That was pity for the poor old lady who'd made it."

"So it's a charity?"

"All right, if you like, then it's a charity and you shouldn't argue about how you feel about it. Do you know that my aunt Beatrice goes there and buys hardly anything? My father told me."

"He misled you. She goes there when they're beginning to clear away the things at the end of the exhibition, and she waits until the prices are halved."

"So there's your answer. It's a charity – for my aunt's benefit." She got into the car. "Anyway, thank you for bringing me."

"Don't forget I'm taking you to Alexander's match tomorrow. Why don't you have lunch with me first?"

She gave an unhesitating answer.

"Thank you. I'd love to."

"Incidentally, won't Pierre be leaving soon?"

"He isn't going yet. He's staying a few days longer because he says this is a good house for him to practise in. My aunt doesn't speak to him and my father and my uncle don't disturb him – and he likes my cooking. When we go to stay with Simone and Denise, he won't be so comfortable."

"What about the arrangements for his recital?"

"Rekovitch is looking after everything in London. Pierre needn't go up yet; they will only have to make the final arrangements together."

"I see. Mind you wrap up warmly for the match – it'll probably be freezing. Are you quite sure you want to watch it?"

"Quite sure. Alexander told us – don't you remember? – that if it got too cold to stay outside, we could shelter in the clubhouse."

But on the day of the match, even sheltering in a clubhouse seemed to Ross to be an occupation for the hardy. During the morning, sleet laid a white carpet on the lawn, and the wind seemed to be whistling a warning that this was no weather for watching games. But on the point of ringing Gianna to counsel staying at home, he remembered that a few years ago, his sole concern about weather conditions had been to ascertain whether the field was waterlogged. He was sure that Alexander was equally impervious to the elements; the match would take place, and Gianna would no doubt insist on being there to watch it.

Before getting ready to leave, he prepared two rounds of ham sandwiches. Then he filled a flask with hot coffee, and as an afterthought, decided to take a rug. That would ensure that Gianna had food and drink – and warmth.

Driving out of Downpass with her beside him, he left her to decide where and how they would lunch. He found that she, like himself, did not want to go to a restaurant.

"Somewhere like a pub," she suggested. "A nice warm fire, hot soup and sandwiches. Do you know where we can go for that?"

"Yes. There's an old coaching inn near Ascot that I discovered on a misty night a few years ago when I was driving back to town after a dance. I wasn't too sure that I was on the right road, but just as I'd made up my mind to, as it were, retrace my wheels, I saw through the murk the faint lights of – "

"Through the what?"

"Murk. M–u–r–k."

"What's murk?"

"Well, it's . . . it's murk. I saw through the murk the faint lights of an ancient hostelry, and – "

"I suppose you use words like that to show me my English isn't as good as it should be."

"There's nothing unusual about the word 'hostelry', except perhaps that you read it more often than you say it."

"So you saw the lights, and went in?"

"I did. There was a large lounge with oak beams, a roaring fire and – "

" – hot soup?"

"No. A double whisky to warm me. It was served by a beauteous maiden who told me her name was Elaine. Her red hair was natural. She had to work for another hour but was free after that and wouldn't mind a lift home as she'd quarrelled with her gentleman friend and it would serve him right if he found she'd gone off with someone else."

"Why are people always using you to get their revenge on someone else?"

"I've often asked myself that question. I can't make it out."

"Did you take her home?"

"Of course. A natural redhead."

"And beauteous. Where did she live?"

"In a sort of villa a few miles from the coaching inn. With her mother, she said."

"Was her mother at home when you got there?"

"No. Elaine said she must have slipped out to see someone."

"In the murk?"

"Elaine said she must have lost her way in the mist."

"Did you wait for her all night?"

"I might have done if the gentleman friend hadn't arrived. He thought he was going to be aggressive, but I was in fairly good trim and at least a head taller than he was."

"So you sent him away?"

"Actually, I sent myself away. You've heard that three is a crowd?"

"Yes. What other adventures have you had?"

"You wouldn't call that an adventure, would you?"

107

"No. I'd call it a lost opportunity."

He gave her a glance in which there was curiosity as well as amusement, but he did not speak. Only when the car was parked and they had entered the inn and by good luck captured the armchairs of a couple who were leaving, did he resume the conversation.

"Isn't it time you told me some of your adventures?" he asked.

"First you order the hot soup."

He ordered drinks, hot soup and sandwiches. The lounge was full, but nobody present seemed in convivial mood; most, like Ross and Gianna, looked relaxed and grateful for this comfortable refuge.

"I like this place," she said. "I'll ask Alexander to bring me here."

The words gave him a slight shock; he had completely forgotten Alexander.

"You're still in love with him?" he asked.

She frowned.

"Why do you think this isn't a serious thing?" she asked. "What does time matter? Two days, three days, three weeks, three months – if you're in love, why should you look at a calendar and say: 'Not long enough'."

"I wouldn't say so after three months."

"You wouldn't say it at all if you knew me better."

"All you've told me about yourself is that you were in love all the time."

"But in a different sort of way. I have never – will you listen and believe? – I have never felt for another man what I felt when I was standing beside Pierre's car at Calais and a voice said, *'Puis-je vous aider?'* and I looked round and – I suppose you'll laugh – I felt in some strange way that this was not our first meeting. I can't explain that, but it's true. I felt there was no need for us to begin to know each other; we knew straight away. We talked about the arrangements for the car, for going on the ferry, and then stood on deck watching France go out of sight, and then we went down to have breakfast – all quite naturally, as if it was meant to be like that. Is that love?"

He made room on the small table between them for the drinks.

"I think we could say it was mutual attraction," he said.

"I want you to understand that it was – is – love. So please don't say any more about it being too soon to know our minds, too soon to get married. I think perhaps you don't like him very much – do you?"

He sipped his drink.

"I like him very much," he answered. "I think he's a nice fellow, and in spite of that *Puis-je vous aider* to a girl he didn't know, good husband material. You ought to be very happy once you get used to the idea of sharing him with a rugby ball every winter."

"I'll enjoy watching him play. I wouldn't like a husband who didn't play some sort of game to keep himself fit."

"You'll have a lot of mud to wash off his shirts and shorts. You can't just throw them into the washing machine. Laura tried that with mine. It wasn't a success and the machine never got over it. Of course, you might have an army of Mrs Arnotts working for you."

"Not a whole army, but certainly somebody to help. Especially if we live in London and I continue to go to my classes."

"What made you want to study computers?"

"Because computers and – oh, electronics, space missiles – I couldn't begin to understand what any of them were about, though I enjoyed maths and physics at school. All I wanted was to find out just a little, so they didn't seem such total mysteries. These classes won't teach me much, but I'll get some idea of what it's all about. I began learning this at the university, and now I want to go on."

Soup was brought, and she finished hers and asked for more. He sat watching her. A wonderful girl, he thought. Good to look at, good to listen to, natural, relaxed, able to laugh. Lucky, lucky Alexander.

"It's a pity," he said when they had drunk their coffee, "that we have to leave this place. Every time I look out of the window at the weather, I feel we're crazy to stand on a frozen field watching a bunch of maniacs – with the exception of Alexander, of course – rolling in sub-zero mud."

"I thought you used to be as enthusiastic about rugby as Alexander."

"Once upon a time, yes. But since meeting him, I've begun to feel the weight of my years."

"Thirty-two. At that age, my father married my mother."

"How old was she?"

"Eighteen."

"He'd known her for a long time, hadn't he?"

"Ever since she was a child. Her father – I suppose you know this – worked in the office in Nice. When his wife died, my mother was only seven, so her grandmother came to look after her. My mother told me that everyone spoiled her – especially her uncle Philippe. He never married, and my mother said he looked on her as a daughter. Nobody refused her anything – she was everyone's pet, and got her own way always, which she said was very bad for her. When she **was** seventeen and wanted to take up music because she was such a good pianist, she couldn't accept the fact that her father hadn't enough money to pay for her to go and study in Italy. There was only one person who could have paid – her uncle Philippe. He had an important post in the Government and had saved some money. But he said that if he paid for the lessons, it would be like sending her away, and he didn't want her to go. So she wrote to her godmother, and it was her godmother in the end who paid for her studies. Everybody tried to – "

" – persuade your mother to drop the whole idea?"

"Yes, though she went just the same. But after only a year, she came back to Nice because she found that her talent wasn't as great as she had thought, certainly not enough to justify paying such high fees. That was when my father had just arrived in Nice on one of his visits to the office, and he said he saw her not as a child but as a woman. They married, and Philippe bought them a house in Biarritz. I was born there. We lived in the house until my mother died."

"How old were you?"

"Sixteen. Philippe died when I was fourteen, and I remember how upset my mother was. She told me she could never repay what he did for her. My father – James – wasn't so upset, because he had never got on well with Philippe, I don't know why. Philippe used to come and visit us, and you could see my father didn't like him. I was sorry when we left Biarritz. Have you ever been there?"

"Yes. Wonderful surfing."

"I know. When you said you felt the weight of your years, it reminded me of my father saying that he wished he had been younger when he married, because my mother always seemed to him so young, so much younger. If you had known about him and Laura and their engagement, would you have been angry that he didn't marry her?"

"No. Being selfish, I would have been glad to keep her to myself."

"It's strange, isn't it, how things turn out?"

"Sometimes. The strange thing to me, if you don't mind my saying so, is the thought of your father as a father. He doesn't seem to me to be cut out for fatherhood."

"I always knew that he wasn't like other fathers. I liked that, though the teachers at school didn't think he had enough authority – he never made me do anything I didn't want to do, because he said he thought I had just as much sense as he had and he trusted me to work out things for myself. He was more of a companion than a father. I used to think sometimes that perhaps he ought to be more firm, more . . . more decisive, but since coming to England and meeting my aunt Beatrice, I've understood a little more why he was . . . as he is. I think that she drove him and Walter inside themselves, took away their initiative, made them, if you want to say so, weak. I suppose my mother knew that he was weak, but I'm not sure. Certainly we both, she and I, always felt safe with him, secure. I don't think I'll feel very secure when I marry Alexander, but then, I'm not like my father or my mother. I'm stronger, I think, and more independent."

"It's going to be an odd marriage," Ross commented. "He'll share you with his rugby ball, and you'll leave his

111

dinner in the oven and go off to concerts. Or computer classes."

She laughed.

"Perhaps. It's a pity, isn't it, that he isn't musical? But music seems to have no effect at all on him?"

"Isn't he going to Pierre's recital?"

"Yes, but only because I asked him to go with me. I can't believe he'll listen to Pierre playing and feel nothing."

"He might feel something very strongly – and audibly."

She shrugged, and reached for her coat.

"Time to go," she said. "If I can endure to watch Alexander playing on a day like this, he should be able to –"

" – endure in his turn."

"Are you going to the recital?"

"Yes, but only because Laura asked me to go with her. Have you got that sketch Alexander made of how we get to the rugby ground?"

"Yes. I'll direct you."

Whether the sketch had been imperfectly done, or whether she was a poor navigator, he did not know, but they had to change direction several times before they saw the signpost they were looking for.

"There it is: Mayfleet, two miles," she said. "You turn down this road."

Turning down it, he found that it was not a road but a narrow, winding lane pockmarked with deep holes. More than once, the car seemed about to overturn, and it became increasingly difficult to avoid bumps, shaped like icebergs, that threatened to tear a hole in the bottom of the chassis.

"This accounts for the state Alexander's car is in," he said. "Can you see anything that looks like a clubhouse?"

"No."

They had arrived at a desolate, windswept plain. No houses could be seen. There was a shack on their left, a deserted hut on their right. The lane was becoming all but impossible – and then the sound of voices was carried to them on the wind and they rounded a curve to see in the distance a field on which were assembled about twenty men in red or white shirts and white shorts. The home team bore

112

large letters on their shirts: M.C. The visitors, in red shirts, had no distinguishing letters. On the far side of the field was a wooden shed surmounted by a flagpole from which fluttered a pennant bearing the name: Mayfleet Rugby Club. Round the shed stood an assortment of cars, bicycles, motorbikes and one rather old minibus. There was no sign of Alexander, but from afar they could hear a signal played on a car horn, and soon his car, looking more shabby than ever under its coating of mud, jolted its way over the adjoining field and stopped beside the other vehicles. Alexander got out and came to join Ross and Gianna.

"Sorry I'm a bit late," he called as he approached. "Glad you got here all right – I was wondering if I'd put enough detail into that sketch map."

Close though he was, it was difficult to hear him above the violent gusts of wind. He was wearing an overcoat over a suit; he looked cheerful, eager and totally unaffected by the weather. He took Gianna in an embrace, told her that he would introduce the team to her after the game, and then gave a rapid glance round the players waiting on the field between the ramshackle goalposts.

"Three of our lot missing, Ted," he yelled to a white shirt. "Any idea what's keeping them?"

"I know what's keeping Hartley," Ted shouted back. "His wife won't let him out till he's finished the washing-up. I dunno about the others. They . . . Oh, wait a minute – here they come."

A motorcycle came bumping across the adjoining field. The rider drew up beside Alexander, removed his helmet and goggles, wiped his streaming nose and spoke.

"My brother couldn't make it – sorry," he said. "He's down with the flu. Gotta high temp, hundred and two."

Those who heard this bulletin showed no signs of sympathy; they looked as though having the flu on the day of an important game was merely a way of letting the side down.

"Well, we'll just have to do without him, that's all. I'll go and change," Alexander said. "If I were you two," he told Ross and Gianna, "I'd go round to the other side. You'll have your backs to the wind. Pity we're a couple of men short, but we'll try to put up a good show for you."

He was about to go up the steps of the clubhouse when he saw the flask Ross was carrying.

"That's not hot coffee, by any chance?" he asked.

"Yes. I brought some coffee and sandwiches for – "

"Good fellow," Alexander said gratefully. He raised his voice to shout. "Here, Bob, come and get a sandwich inside you. Ted, want a dose of hot coffee?"

An eager group gathered round. Short of snatching the flask and the rapidly disappearing packet of sandwiches, Ross had no option but to stand and watch. A few minutes later, the empty flask was returned to him, together with the crumpled sandwich paper.

"Those," he told Gianna as they walked on, "were for you."

"Thank you. But they looked as though they really needed them, didn't they?"

He thought she looked as though she needed them more. They had turned up the collars of their coats and plunged their hands deep into their pockets. He saw that her expression was the one she had worn while waiting for him at the hospital: interest in her surroundings, patience, expectation as to what was coming next.

"You're going to find it too cold to stay out here for long," he said.

"Perhaps. Let's watch the start, anyway."

Alexander and two late arrivals from the opposing team emerged together from the clubhouse. The referee blew his whistle, the linesmen unrolled their flags. Alexander's side won the toss and the next moment the ball was in play. In a short time, Ross saw that in spite of the general dilapidation and austerity of the surroundings, the standard of play was high.

"They're good," he said to Gianna.

"You sound surprised. Did you think they wouldn't be?"

"I didn't think they'd be as good as this. They looked a scratch lot."

"They do a lot of training, like Alexander. And they try

114

to improve the ground and the clubhouse. Do you know they built it themselves?"

"No."

"They bought the ground and had water laid on from that farm over there. They decided not to have electricity because they're never here after dark."

"Cold showers?"

"Yes."

A tough lot, Ross thought, not without envy. His own rugby matches had been played on well-kept grounds; the clubhouse had had rows of changing rooms and hot showers, and there had been a well-stocked bar.

"I wouldn't say this to Alexander" – her words came to him on the bitter wind – "but watching the other kind of football seems less confusing."

"That's because you don't know the rules. Rugby is – "

He stopped. Alexander, clasping the ball as though it was a beloved mistress, had disappeared under a dozen heavy bodies. The whistle blew, the bodies heaved themselves up and revealed Alexander uninjured. Gianna drew a deep breath of relief.

"Do they get hurt sometimes?" she asked.

"Now and then. It's all in the game."

"Why are they shouting?"

"Alexander nearly scored a try."

"A – ?"

"He nearly got the ball over the line. He – Oh, well done, well done," he yelled. "Keep it going, keep it going. Keep . . . oh, the damn fool's lost it."

"Alexander did?"

"No, not Alexander. The – "

He felt it was useless to continue. She was not watching the game; she was watching Alexander. For all she cared, he thought, the rest of the team could have walked off the field. And as she had none of the mounting enthusiasm that was beginning to warm him, she would soon freeze where she stood. He draped the rug over her shoulders.

"I'm ready to go into the shelter if you are," he said.

She nodded, and walked beside him to the shed and up

115

the slippery wooden steps to the interior. Then they stood and looked about them.

A wooden partition divided the space lengthwise. Through an open door in the centre they could see rows of pegs hung with coats and scarves. There were two benches, and beyond them, three primitive showers fixed above slatted boards that allowed water to drain out. In the front half of the partition was a small, square wooden table covered with handwritten notices of future fixtures. On the wall hung a large notice-board and some photographs of teams. Two windows with several panes of glass missing over-looked the playing field.

"Alexander said the windows got broken in the summer," Gianna explained. "The shed was rented to some cricketers, and the balls – "

" – did the damage. I'd stand in front of this window if I were you – it lets in less wind. Want a bench to sit on?"

She shook her head. They stood looking out of the windows. A few hardy spectators had appeared, some standing round the field, others seated in their cars. A tractor from the farm had stopped some distance away and the driver was watching the game. In spite of his concern for Gianna, Ross found himself more and more interested in the players, occasionally shouting encouragement or advice through the window.

At half-time, the players did not leave the field. They formed into two groups, and a woman from one of the cars walked over to them holding a plate on which were seg-ments of orange. She handed this round to the teams; then the interval was over and play was resumed.

"Sometimes," Gianna said, "there's a lot of mist, and they can't see to finish the game."

He looked at her in wonder. She must be feeling bitterly cold. She had had to readjust her ideas on clubhouses. She had received very little attention from Alexander, and was now faced with several more weekends of watching games in these harsh conditions – but still she gave no sign of disappointment. He thought he could detect an undercurrent of uneasiness, but could not be sure. In fact, all he knew for

116

certain was that his regard for Alexander was not now as high as it had been. Certainly today he appeared either insensitive or selfish.

The game, which at half-time had been even, resulted in a win by a small margin for Alexander's team. There was back-slapping and handshaking, and a general move towards the shed. Ross and Gianna went outside and met Alexander, mud-covered, on his way in to a shower.

"Well, what did you think?" he asked Ross.

"It was a good game. Congratulations."

"We're not bad, are we?"

"You're damn good. Do you want me to take Gianna to your car?"

"Yes, thanks. I won't be long, love," he promised Gianna.

The tractor, they found, was not there solely to provide the driver with a grandstand view. He was waiting outside the shed with a large sack, and into this the home team, appearing now and then naked in the doorway, dropped their muddy and sodden shirts and shorts. When he had collected thirteen outfits, he heaved the sack over his shoulder and went towards the tractor.

"Where are you taking those?" Gianna asked as he passed.

"To the farm. Mr Rannoch's got a contract – so much a shirt, so much a pair of shorts, after the game. Home team only. Cor! Fancy wanting to play in this weather," he remarked finally as he went on his way.

"You told me I'd have to do that for Alexander," Gianna said to Ross. "But you see, I won't." She stopped before the small, mud-covered car. "I wish we had a hosepipe – we could get this mud off."

"By 'we', I assume you're referring to yourself and Alexander."

"I meant you and me."

"If he wants his car washed, all he has to do is drive it through – "

"Yes, I know. One of those mechanical washers."

"What was he doing in Wales?"

"Interviewing a sports personality – I don't know which one. He's been given a list of top sporting men and women of the year and he's got to go round and interview them."

"Where's he taking you now?"

"First to the newspaper office to write a short report, and then to dinner. Thank you for bringing me. Here he comes."

Alexander, clean and once again dressed in suit and overcoat, put Gianna into the car and climbed into the driving seat.

"Thanks again, Ross. See you around. Bye."

He pressed the self-starter. The engine shuddered, gave a weak cough, and died.

"Don't tell me she's going to stage one of her dead-stop demonstrations," Alexander said irritably. "Come on, come on, you she-devil."

Nothing availed. The engine refused to start. Some of the home team got out of their cars or off their motorbikes and came to offer assistance.

"We'll shove you down that slope," a linesman said. "Ready?"

The car, pushed by a group that included Ross, rolled down the slope, spluttered, and stopped. There was a brief inspection by two mechanics, who then voiced their verdict: the car would have to be harnessed to the tractor, towed to the farm and left there for the night. In response to shouts and signals, the driver returned with the tractor.

"Not again?" he asked in disgust. "This makes three times I've had to tow you. In your place, I'd sell this bag of nuts and get myself a proper car."

"She came like a bird all the way from Wales," Alexander protested.

"Don't worry," Ross said. "I'll take you anywhere you want to go."

Alexander got out of the car.

"It's not as easy as that," he said. "I need this car tomorrow. I've got to drive down to Kent to interview someone."

"Hire a car," Ross suggested.

"The one and only time I put a hired car on my expense account, I was also told to make it the last." He turned to one of the mechanics. "How long d'you reckon it's going to take to get this one going?"

The man looked doubtful.

"You've got distributor trouble," he said. "A matter of four, five hours. I don't suppose you'll find a garage that'd do it on a Saturday evening."

"If you paid me on the nail," the tractor driver offered, "I'd tow you to a chap I know who can fix anything on four wheels. But you'd have to pay him on the nail too. How about it?"

"Looks as though I've got no choice," Alexander said. He opened the door on Gianna's side, and spoke ruefully. "Sorry, love. You'll have to go back with Ross."

She got out of the car and stood beside him, her hand in his.

"When do I see you?" she asked.

"Soon as I get back from this interview tomorrow. I'll go straight down to Downpass."

"In time for lunch?"

"No. I've got an idea." He turned to Ross. "Could we have tea at Laura's cottage?"

"Of course."

"Then that's it." He kissed Gianna and got into his car, which had been harnessed to the tractor. "Bye, love. Tea-time tomorrow."

The car was towed away. Gianna walked beside Ross to his car.

"Home?" he asked.

"Please."

He boosted the car's heating and they drove for the most part in silence, but he guessed that both their minds were on Alexander. He felt sorry for her, but was not sure he had any reason to be. She had chosen a man who happened to enjoy playing a rough game in rough conditions; she could scarcely expect him to give up the habits of years in order that they might spend their weekends in more comfortable

119

surroundings. The boot, he argued to himself, might well have been on the other foot; he had known women, actresses for example, for whom he had waited many a long hour during rehearsals or performances. People had to adjust, to compromise – though in this case he was almost certain that it was not Alexander who would do the adjusting.

She spoke after a time.

"This isn't the way home."

"Yes, it is. Not to your home – to my home. I'd like to show you where I live. But that's not the prime reason for taking you there. I want some hot tea and half a dozen slices of thick buttered toast. How about you?"

"It sounds a wonderful idea."

"Have you thawed out?"

"More or less."

"I enjoyed the game. I don't suppose you did."

"I enjoyed watching Alexander – except when they all jumped on top of him. Why are we stopping?"

"There's a shop here that's open late on Saturdays. I want a couple of loaves of bread."

"And butter?"

"And butter, yes. I've got some of Laura's homemade jam."

When Ross opened the door of his flat and ushered her inside, she gave a sigh of contentment.

"Lovely and warm," she said.

He was drawing back curtains, looking out into the growing darkness.

"Come and look at the lights. These rooms aren't high enough to give much of a view, but there's always this panorama of lights every evening to cheer me up. Sit down while I get tea ready. There's a bathroom through my bedroom." He opened the bedroom door. "Plenty of hot water. You'll find me in the kitchen."

She had paused on her way through the bedroom and was looking at a photograph on his dressing table.

"Laura," she said, "And – your father?"

120

"Yes. Taken on their wedding day."

"That boy is you?"

"Yes. Aged nine."

"Did you like her from the beginning?"

"Yes."

"Where did you first meet her?"

"My father brought her to one of my school half-terms. She had decided that it would be better to tell me at once that she was going to marry him, rather than leave me to work it out for myself. All he told me was that he was bringing down a friend. I kept a table free for tea, and they arrived and he asked how I was. Then he simply said: 'Ross, this is Miss Tenby. I'm doing my best to persuade her to become your stepmother. Laura, this is Ross.' Then after that little speech there was a long pause. I waited for her to say something and wondered why she didn't, and then I realised the reason she wasn't saying anything was because she was struggling against her shyness. It gave me a shock."

"Why a shock?"

"Because it had never occurred to me that a grown-up could be tongue-tied by shyness. I pulled myself together, and the first words I said to her were: 'I'd like to call you Laura.' We just went on from there."

She had picked up the photograph.

"She looks so pretty."

"She was. She is. Go and get yourself brushed up."

She lingered to look at the group photographs on the walls.

"That one" – she put a finger on a figure at the end of a row – "is you?"

"Yes. The year I got my rugby colours. The following year, I was elected captain. I thought that was as high as a man could rise in life."

"And this one?"

"Back view of me rowing at Henley. I wasn't much good. I'm better in the water than on it."

"There's no photograph of your wife?"

"No. Nobody with a camera was present at the wedding,

and we never made – correction, never wanted – a record of our honeymoon, such as it was."

"It was strange that Daphne Maxwellton met her in New York."

"I suppose it was, America being the size it is. Would you like strawberry jam, or a rather successful mixture of raspberry and gooseberry?"

"All three, please."

When she joined him in the kitchen, he was lifting a loaded tray and carrying it to the living room.

"If you'll pour out the tea, I can begin on the toast," he said.

They were so hungry that a fresh supply of toast had to be made. There was little conversation until it was finished and the jars of jam scraped clean. They poured out the last of the tea and then leaned back in their chairs, relaxed and contented.

"I enjoyed that," she said.

"Me too. I'll get Laura to give you some of her jam."

"My mother used to make jam, when we lived in Biarritz. After that, my father and I were moving about most of the time, so it wasn't possible to have a store cupboard like my mother's."

"Do you think of yourself as French, or English?"

"French."

"Do you think in French?"

"I used to, but at the university, towards the end, I began thinking in English. Before that, I wrote my essays in French in my head and put them on paper in English."

"Were you at school in Biarritz, or did you go away to school?"

"I was a weekly boarder at a school called Roche-en-Haut, between Biarritz and Guethary. There were some English girls, but not many. Only French was spoken, and we had lessons in English and German and Spanish."

"Games?"

She laughed.

"Not what the English think of as games, no. We played tennis on hard courts that were covered with weeds; as soon as we pulled the weeds up, they grew again. And if you hit a ball too hard, it bounced through the holes in the side net and rolled down the hill into the sea. We had bicycles, but we weren't allowed to ride them on public holidays, because of the heavy traffic. We were all in love with the visiting masters. My father used to come in the car to fetch me every weekend, and if we gave a lift to one of the masters, the other girls were green with envy. Why is envy green?"

"The matter's being studied at the highest level. I suppose your habit of being always in love began with the visiting masters?"

"Perhaps."

"What made you decide to come to an English university?"

"It was my father who decided for me. My mother was dead, and it was she who had insisted on a French education. Now he thought I should learn something about England – and so I came."

"Didn't it strike you as odd that you didn't meet any of his relations in this country?"

"Sometimes I wondered about it. But I thought they would all be old. At first I thought that I might have been able to spend some of the vacations with them, but I was always invited to stay with friends at Christmas and Easter, and in the summer, I went back to France. I used to go camping. Do you like camping?"

"With congenial companions, yes."

"Do you go skiing every year?"

"Yes, except when I get an iron hook in my leg."

"Does it still give you pain?"

"No. A certain amount of discomfort, that's all. You like skiing?"

"If I said I was a champion, you would think I was exaggerating?"

"I'd reserve judgment until I'd seen you on the slopes. Is Alexander keen?"

"No. He says he likes climbing up mountains, not skiing down them. How long have you lived in this apartment?"

"Between three and four years."

"I like it. I like this big room, and the little kitchen. Is there a restaurant in the building?"

"No. Just kitchens. If you want a full-scale lunch or dinner, you have to give a few hours' notice; otherwise you can ring down for anything you want, and it comes up on the service hatch."

"Do you invite many visitors?"

"My experience is that you don't have to invite them; they invite themselves. People are always dropping in."

"Girls?"

"Sometimes."

"My aunt Beatrice said you liked women."

"What man doesn't?"

"Pierre for one. He's not interested in anything except his music. He lives for it. Rekovitch says this recital will make him very well-known in England. After this, he goes to the States."

Ross got up to close the curtains, and then carried the tray to the kitchen. She helped him to put the cups into the dishwasher, and he did his best to view the scene objectively: man and woman clearing up after a friendly tea party. But he was aware that he longed for a replay. The thought of more Saturday matches assumed a new and attractive aspect, until he remembered that this interlude had been possible only because Alexander's car had broken down. Next week, she would have to be surrendered to him, while he himself drove home in solitude.

"Music?" he asked when they left the kitchen.

"Yes."

"All my records were chosen by Laura. Come and look. Sibelius, Mahler – several Vaughan Williams. Holst. If I put on 'The Planets', it would take us to the point of discussing where you'd like to go for dinner."

She looked at him with raised eyebrows.

"Lunch. Tea. Dinner?"

"You've got to eat, haven't you?"

"You didn't expect to have me on your hands for so long. Why did Alexander have to stay with the car? Why couldn't he have left it and taken me out to dinner?"

124

"When he was towed away, he wasn't even sure he could get the car fixed. He'd rather be looking at you than at a distributor."

"Wouldn't you like to go to Laura's cottage and have me cook dinner for the three of us?"

"Some other evening – and with Alexander to make a fourth. I know a nice roadhouse on the way to Downpass. In the meantime, we could listen to music and you could explain the finer points of Holst to me."

She hesitated.

"Shall we toss for it?" he suggested.

"No. You decide."

He decided by selecting a record and putting it on.

8

The next day, Gianna walked over from Hargreaves House soon after lunch, accompanied by James and Pierre. James apologised for coming uninvited.

"I wanted to phone," he told Laura, "but Gianna said you wouldn't mind our dropping in informally."

"Of course I don't mind – it's nice to see you both." She took Pierre's violin from him and placed it on a chair in the hall.

"I hope nobody will touch it," he said anxiously.

"Nobody'll lay a finger on it. Come and sit down and get warm. I'm glad to see you're giving yourself a rest from practising."

He chose the largest chair, sat down and said that he would soon be going to London.

"It is very cold there," he added.

"I believe it is," Laura agreed. "I can never make up my mind whether January or February is the coldest month of the year."

"January," said James.

"But in Australia, hot," pointed out Pierre. "In New Zealand also hot, I think."

"Yes, that's true. Gianna, sit down – it's too early to make tea. Alexander's cake is ready for him."

"He's late," Gianna said. "He should be here by now."

"You wouldn't want him to speed in that car of his, would you?" her father asked.

"No. I have decided that he must ask his grandmother to buy him a new one."

"I'm not looking forward to visiting her," Laura said. "Are you sure it wouldn't be better if you went by your-self?"

"Quite sure," Gianna said firmly. "But I'm also dreading the occasion. She sounds . . . I don't know . . . inquisitive. She has already asked Alexander all about me, why I'm in England, what classes I'm going to, where I'm going to live in London."

"Naturally she'll ask questions," Laura said. "Your father ought to have presented Alexander with a long questionnaire, instead of merely accepting your prejudiced opinion of him. All he knows about his future son-in-law is that he plays good rugby and has no ear for music."

The telephone rang when they had waited an hour for Alexander's arrival. Laura handed over the receiver to Gianna and returned to the living room, but it was clear from Gianna's dismayed comments that he was not coming. She rejoined the others and spoke without emphasis, but Ross felt certain there was anger hidden beneath her disappointment.

"That was Alexander. He was ringing from a house where he'd walked when his car stopped and wouldn't start again. He says it's not far from Guildford, but all the garages he tried refused to let him have a taxi because it's Sunday and Downpass is too far. He says to tell Laura how sorry he is, and we're to have tea without him."

James and Pierre looked relieved; now they could eat at last. Laura and Gianna brought two trays into the living room: there were hot scones and the large walnut cake that had been made specially for Alexander. Gianna sat on the hearth-rug as usual. She spoke very little. Ross would have given a great deal to know what she was thinking.

When he and Laura were alone, he asked if she had any clue.

"She was angry," Laura said.

"I suppose she can't blame him if his car breaks down."

"If it hadn't been the car, it would have been something else. She was very angry – and I'm glad."

"Why?"

"Because I was beginning to fear she'd make too many excuses for him. She's not going to have an easy time. He's a man who's probably basically unselfish and considerate, but he's had things his own way for too long. From the sound of it, that grandmother of his doesn't do much for him."

"What should grandmothers do?"

"This grandmother should buy him a new car. She must be rich; nobody could live in the Belgrave Towers set-up if they weren't very well-off. I think it's wicked of his father to have made him wait until he's thirty before getting his inheritance."

"He gets the interest on the capital, and it's a pretty large capital if what I've heard about his late father's assets is correct. The interest ought to be enough to buy him several new cars. Perhaps Daphne Maxwellton was right when she said he had a canny streak."

"When I see his grandmother, I'll see what I can get out of her."

"Cars?"

"No. Facts about the family."

But on Wednesday Laura was to find that no effort was required to get any family details out of Mrs Rannoch; they were all supplied unasked.

She was driven up to town by Gianna. They went in Pierre's car. James had announced his intention of buying one, but was going about it in his usual indecisive way, studying sheaves of advertisements, visiting numerous showrooms, doing intricate sums to compare prices and performance and petrol consumption, deciding on a model and then changing his mind. And so, while he dithered, Gianna continued to use Pierre's.

They had told Alexander they would do some shopping and call on his aunt for tea, but this had been said to make the visit look informal. They did no shopping, and drove straight to Belgrave Towers.

The mansion, once a ducal residence, was now divided into suites. These were numbered, but each in addition was named after one of the eminent personages who had graced the receptions once held in the magnificent state apartments. Laura and Gianna, hesitating after entering a palatial hall, were approached by a haughty woman who, after a survey that registered with electronic speed their appearance and probable status, enquired coldly whether they were looking for anyone. Since Laura was momentarily distracted, gazing wide-eyed through enormous glass doors at the scene in the adjoining lounge, it was Gianna who answered.

"Suite number two, please."

"Ah. You mean Wellington. You are visiting Mrs Rannoch?"

"Yes."

"May I know your names?"

Informed of these, the questioner walked to a table, picked up a telephone and spoke into it. Then she went towards the glass doors.

"Follow me, if you please."

The doors opened mechanically as they approached. A footman attired in red and gold livery left the tea table at which he was serving, and met them at the entrance.

"Take these ladies up to Wellington," ordered the elegant woman. "Mrs Mirren and Miss Hargreaves to see Mrs Rannoch."

He bowed and led Laura and Gianna to a distant lift. They walked past table after table at which were seated beautifully groomed men and women whose average age, Laura calculated, must be at least eighty. On the tables were set gleaming silver trays and delicate china cups. The conversation was animated, if a trifle shrill, and the laughter was extremely well-bred.

The lift was a vast glass cage. As it took them smoothly upward, they could see the lounge as though from the dress circle of a theatre. Laura longed to ask their guide to press a stop button and allow her to take in details of this scene from what she had imagined to be a dead past. But in truth, it wasn't dead at all, she told herself in wonder. There it all was, down there, spread out rich and colourful, and inhabited by the last survivors – surely the last? – of the age of privilege.

Moments later, the lift came to a halt. The man in red and gold led them along a wide, richly carpeted corridor and knocked discreetly on a door to which was affixed a small brass '2'. A voice answered, he opened the door, murmured the visitors' names, and withdrew. From a high-backed chair rose a slim, slightly stooping figure in a long, trailing gown.

"Please come in," said a soft voice. "How nice of you to come and see me. Mrs Mirren . . . "

A delicate hand, beringed, was graciously held out.

"How do you do?"

"And . . . Gianna." Not a hand, but a soft, scented cheek. "My dear, you're even lovelier than Alexander said you were. Come and sit beside me on the sofa. Mrs Mirren, I think you will be comfortable over there. Now, my dear Gianna, let me look at you."

While she looked at Gianna, Laura looked at the room. Large. Rich rugs, antique furniture, every piece of a frailty that matched the exquisitely preserved woman seated beside Gianna. She wondered how Alexander managed to thread his way through the small space left between articles of furniture. There were mantraps everywhere: those low tables, those two beautifully worked footstools, the three little Chinese figures. She recalled his brief description of his grandmother: 'She's a perky old lady,' he had said, and that was all. Perky she certainly was not. She had retained much of what must once have been considerable beauty; her manner was soft and in a younger woman could have been called beguiling. But under it, Laura already sensed a certain hardness.

"One imagines that this is a spacious room," she was saying, "but when one's things are in it, one sees they didn't make it large enough. Heaven knows they had enough space to use."

"Have you lived here long?" Laura asked.

"From the beginning. I was one of the first, if not *the* first, to come here. They tried, you know, to find other uses for the house – it was so beautiful – but everything failed. When they decided to convert it, they knew there would be an outcry about carving up the interior of so historic a building, so they kept the plans a great secret. Only a few people knew what was going to be done. Dear old Lord Padsey was the person who gave me a hint, and I acted at once – I chose this suite from the plans. My son, who was alive then, was sorry I left Scotland, but I reminded him that although he was a Scot, I was English. You live in the country, Mrs Mirren?"

"Yes. Not very picturesque country, but not too far from London. And as it doesn't lead anywhere, we're not disturbed by much traffic going through the village."

"But there's a motorway close by, isn't there? Don't you find that something of a trial?"

"Not after a time. One gets used to the noise. In fact, it becomes rather soothing – a kind of continuous hum."

"And you, Gianna" – Mrs Rannoch obviously considered she had done her duty by Laura – "you're not going to bury yourself down there, I hope? Alexander mentioned some classes . . ."

"I'm going to study at a college in Kensington."

"Something to do with computers, he said. That sounds very ambitious."

"It's very interesting."

"You've only spent three years in England?"

"So far, yes."

"One can scarcely realise you're not completely English – your accent is so good. It's just a little matter of intonation, but I daresay you'll lose that when you've spent more time in this country. You fell in love at first sight, I understand?"

"We both did."

"I'm wondering whether you have discovered that you've fallen in love with not one man, but two. There are two Alexanders – you realise that?"

"I'm beginning to."

"There are, you know. Please believe me. I know him so well. He is the *dearest* person, and he is speaking no more than the truth when he assures me you are the first and only girl he has ever fallen in love with. But he has other loves."

"I know." Gianna spoke calmly. "Rugby. I'll get him back in the summer."

131

"Ah, but will you? Only if you're a mountain climber. Not Himalayan – Alpine. When he puts away his rugby boots, he will put on his climbing boots. I have scores of snapshots showing him – as he puts it – scaling the heights. I'm afraid you'll have to get used to waiting for him in mountain chalets – picturesque, but rather lonely, I fear. Anyway, enough of my chatter for a moment. Shall we have tea? Would you most kindly telephone and ask them to send up tea for three people in Wellington?"

Gianna went to the telephone, dutifully gave this rather odd-sounding order and resumed her seat.

"What you must be anxious to learn, my dear, is something about Alexander's family. I feel any girl about to marry should know, as it were, something about the family she's marrying *into*. But there is one thing I must say first: that I did my utmost to persuade my son – Alexander's father – not to make it a condition in his Will that Alexander would have to wait until the age of thirty before coming into his full inheritance. The interest seemed adequate enough when the Will was drawn up, but since then, we've had years of inflation, and poor Alexander has had to make economies which are hard on a young man living in London. My son was naturally disappointed at Alexander's refusal to join the family firm, but that wasn't the reason for making that provision. The truth, my dear Gianna, is that he was afraid Alexander might have inherited his mother's tendency to extravagance."

There was a pause. Mrs Rannoch sighed, and seemed to be recalling an unhappy past.

"The role of mother-in-law," she resumed, "is not an easy one. I know few women who have been successful in the part. My own position, I think, was peculiarly difficult. You have no son, Mrs Mirren, so you will never be faced with what I went through."

"Didn't you like her?" Gianna asked in her most direct manner.

"Oh my dear" – Mrs Rannoch spoke in a shocked tone – "I'm not saying that I *disliked* her. In many ways, I admired her. But I was sorry for my son when he fell in love with her, because she had a kind of mania for travelling; she was forever going abroad, and she didn't always keep her promises to return quickly. It made him very miserable." Mrs Rannoch paused, as if pained by what she was revealing. "She was very gifted, and there was nothing amateur about her accomplishments; she was a splendid horsewoman, she won prizes for skiing, and played excellent golf and tennis. But above all, she was a brilliant violinist; in fact, she wrote to my son informing him that she was thinking of taking up music as a profession. That was only one of the ways in which she tormented him. She didn't keep long to any one hobby. She had no mother. Her father had a great deal of money, but there wasn't much of it left after she had rented a chalet in Switzerland, an apartment in Milan, and a studio in Paris. This reckless expenditure continued after she married my son."

She broke off at the sound of a knock on the door. Tea was wheeled in on a trolley and placed before her. The door closed and she busied herself pouring out. The service was silver, the cups Crown Derby. Laura wondered if guests were expected to be so overcome by this display that they would fail to notice the sparseness of the food. On one plate were a few slices of paper-thin brown bread and butter; on another were arranged half a dozen wafer-like biscuits, and that was all.

During tea, Mrs Rannoch spoke only of general subjects. But when the trolley had been removed, she leaned back and again took up the topic of her daughter-in-law.

"We were talking of Stroma," she said.

"Was that her name – Stroma?" Laura asked.

"Yes. It's rather unusual."

"It's the name of an island off the coast of Scotland, isn't it?"

"Yes. My son fell in love with her when he came down from Oxford, and for years she kept him . . . I don't like the word 'dangling', but it can be applied here. She wouldn't marry him but she wouldn't let him go. Wherever she went – and she was seldom long in one place – she kept in touch with him. I did my best to make him look at other women.

I introduced him to the most charming girls, but he couldn't be made to forget Stroma."

She took up a cigarette box, opened it, found that nobody smoked and closed it again.

"The trouble," she continued, "was that she had had a rather disciplined upbringing. She had been educated at a very strict convent in Switzerland, and so when she left, it made her determined to enjoy her new-found freedom to the full."

"Did she ever settle down?" Laura asked.

"In a sense, yes. She stopped wandering from one country to another. She came back from Italy and told my son she was ready to marry him. He bought her a beautiful house in Scotland and they were married almost immediately because he was afraid she might become restless again. Alexander was born the same year. She never had any other children; perhaps that was why she filled the house with hosts of her friends and entertained on a scale which I can only call sumptuous."

"That's not the way Alexander lives," Gianna said. "Have you ever seen his flat?"

"No."

"We stopped once to look at the outside but couldn't go in because it was being repaired. What I saw, though, didn't look very comfortable. And to add to his troubles, he doesn't seem to be able to afford a new car."

Mrs Rannoch looked distressed.

"Those are the economies I mentioned earlier," she said. "If I could give him any financial assistance, of course I would. He will get something when I die, but who, in this appallingly expensive age, can really manage to leave anything at the end?"

"When did Alexander's mother die?" Laura asked.

"Stroma? When Alexander was four. She was very young. I think she really wore herself out. My son died a few years ago – when Stroma died, he sold the house and moved to Edinburgh." She leaned over the arm of the sofa and from a small table near-by took a silver-framed photograph. "This was one of the wedding groups. It isn't a very good likeness of my son, but you can see how good-looking Stroma was. It's such a pity Alexander didn't inherit those looks."

"Or yours," Gianna said in a matter-of-fact tone that robbed the words of any suggestion of flattery.

Mrs Rannoch laughed softly.

"That's a very nice thing to say; thank you. What Alexander *has* inherited is his father's love of sport – though my son didn't devote as much time to it as Alexander does."

She passed the photograph to Laura, who looked with interest at the tall, graceful figure of Alexander's mother. A lovely face. A faint smile on the lips – not one of those radiant bridal smiles, she thought; there was something enigmatic and distant about it.

When she and Gianna got up to take their leave, Mrs Rannoch moved towards the telephone to summon red and gold, but Gianna stopped her.

"Could we walk down?" she asked. "It's such a lovely staircase."

"I'm so glad you noticed it. So many people don't," Mrs Rannoch said. "Yes, do walk down if you prefer to. But" – she offered her cheek for a kiss – "you must come and see me again soon. And you too," she added graciously to Laura. "Alexander told me you had been very kind to him. And I should very much like to meet your stepson someday."

She did not go with them to the door; she stood instead in the middle of the room, her hand raised in a queenly gesture of farewell. They closed the door behind them and walked along the corridor to the stairs; on their way down, they paused and leaned on the velvet-covered balustrade to gaze down at the scene in the lounge. Most of the tea tables had been removed; chairs and sofas had been brought in and were occupied by elegant figures whose wigs and toupees, seen from this high view, were only too evident.

"They're not real," Gianna explained after a time. "We're in Madame Tussauds and they're all made of wax."

"Why did I imagine that this way of life had gone for ever?"

135

"It has. I've just told you – these are wax. Or stuffed, I'm not sure which. I find it strange that only not so many years ago, they lived like this in their own houses. Mansions. Castles. 'Let them eat cake,' Marie Antoinette said – and here they are, two hundred years later, eating it."

"What I find strange," Laura said, "is that they had such a long innings."

"Innings? Oh, I see. Are those jewels they're wearing real, or do you think they had to sell the real ones before coming to live here?"

"Real. I wonder what they feel about giving up their own homes."

"The homes were no use once the servants disappeared. But there'll always be individuals with lots of money who'll be able to live like this – if they want to."

"When you're as old as these people are, what else is there to do but enjoy luxurious living, if you can still afford it. At least they're buying independence. They're not imposing any burden on their families."

"But if they're all like Alexander's grandmother, they're not doing much to help the families either. They ought to be using their money for better things than" – she waved a hand – "than this sort of thing."

"Buying their grandsons cars?" Laura proffered somewhat sarcastically.

"Why not?"

"Could I – I'm asking myself – live like this if I had the means? The answer's no. I was brought up in a relatively humble vicarage. We had two Crown Derby pieces, but they were kept in a glass-fronted cabinet. They still are. But if I'd been born the daughter of a duke, growing up with priceless treasures all round me, perhaps I would have been determined to finish off as I began." Then she turned to Gianna, suddenly changing the subject. "I'm hungry. Are you?"

"Yes. Couldn't we stop somewhere on the way home and have something to eat? That tea she gave us was just for mice."

They did not talk of Alexander's grandmother again

136

until they were in the car. And it was Gianna who spoke first.

"She was a spiteful cat, wasn't she?" she asked Laura.

"Your future grandmother-in-law? Well yes, I think she was."

"She needn't have told us all those things against his mother."

"My feeling," said Laura, "is that Stroma got the best of it in the end."

"I hope so. Do you think she was as bad as Mrs Rannoch said?"

"How do I know? She seems to have made up for whatever she missed at her convent."

"I don't believe what she said about her son being afraid that Alexander would be extravagant, like his mother. That other spiteful cat, Daphne Maxwellton, tells people that he's mean with his money. He isn't mean at all. Most of his money goes to help his rugby club. I went there; I saw it, and I saw the other men too. They weren't rich, any of them. They were just workmen and I don't suppose their wives would let them spend money on the club even if they had any to spend. Alexander pays for the field, he paid for what they needed to make the shed – I mean the clubhouse – better. He's also going to spend money putting up a small stand for spectators. Why did he go and live with his grandmother while his roof was being repaired? Not because he wanted to. Not because he liked her. He went there to save money for his club."

Laura wondered how much of James' money would in future go towards improving the club facilities. She felt relieved at the thought that all Alexander would need when climbing Alpine mountains would be a pair of boots.

"Ross told me he's taking you to the match on Saturday," she said.

"Yes. I said I could go alone, but he won't let me. Alexander will be interviewing someone in the morning and he'll go straight to the match afterwards. Did you notice that his grandmother didn't say one word about what a good journalist he is? She must read *Newshound* – there was a copy on one of her tables. She could have praised some of his articles – but she didn't."

They decided to drive straight home instead of stopping to eat on the way. Ross' car was at the gate; they found him walking over from the chalet.

"Been sorting my things," he told Laura. "I'll be leaving soon."

"Everybody'll be leaving," Laura said with resignation. "You, Gianna, Pierre. It'll be like the old days – myself, James, Walter and Beatrice. And even Beatrice is spending more and more time up in London."

"My father's worried about her," Gianna said. "She's become interested in youth clubs, and she's going round visiting some of them – and making trouble. She tells them all that they're doing too little, and doing it all wrong. But that's better than getting herself mixed up in violent demonstrations and risking going to prison."

"Alexander ought to write a column about people like her, entitled 'English Eccentrics'," Ross said. "What was his grandmother like?"

They walked up to the house. Once inside, Ross poured drinks and the two women made sandwiches.

"Gianna's opinion of Grandmamma," Laura told Ross, "is that she's a spiteful cat."

"On what do you base that view?" Ross asked Gianna.

She told him, in detail and at times with ferocity.

"The old lady seems to have upset you," Ross commented when she had come to an end. She – "

He stopped. The front doorbell had given a faint ring.

"That sounds like Jass," Laura said. "She's afraid of pressing too hard."

She opened the front door to be greeted by Jass' piping voice.

"It's a telegram for Mr Mirren. I was in the post office and they were going to telephone it to him, but I said I'd bring it over."

"Come in and give it to him," Laura invited.

Jass came into the living room, held out the telegram to Ross and then stood on one leg gazing adoringly at Gianna.

138

"Thanks for coming round with it," Ross said.

"Oh, that's all right, Mr Mirren. I was just there, so I brought it. Why don't you open it?"

Ross opened the telegram, glanced at it, rolled the paper carelessly into a ball and tossed it into the fire.

"Was it good news?" Jass asked.

"Yes. Very good news. Do you want me to run you home?"

"I'll take her," Gianna offered. "I've got to go home and it's on my way."

Ross saw them to the car and returned to join Laura.

"A reply from my wife to the letter I wrote her," he said.

"You wrote to her?"

"Yes. I asked if she'd divorce me."

"She must have agreed. You said it was good news."

"Yes, she's agreed."

"That means . . . that means you'll be free."

"That's right. I'll be free," he said.

9

There was no rugby match on either of the two following Saturdays. On the first of these, the ground was unplayable and on the second, so many of the team had succumbed to the current epidemic of influenza that only four were available to join Alexander. He used the first match-free weekend to go over to Spain and interview a retired boxing champion in Alicante; the second weekend was spent helping Gianna to find a flat. She was by now attending her computer classes, but much as she liked Simone and Denise, found life in their apartment somewhat too disorganised for comfort. Pierre's accompanist, Rekovitch, had already moved him to quieter quarters.

On the following Saturday there was to be a match near a village called Shepland, which was about thirty miles from Downpass. Ross assumed that Gianna would be taken there by Alexander, but on Friday afternoon received a call from him at his office.

"Ross?"

"Yes."

"Do you happen to be free tomorrow afternoon?"

"I was going down to see Laura, but I can put it off if it's anything important."

"It's this match out at the sports ground near Shepland. I was going to take Gianna, but three of our team are without transport and they've asked me for a lift. Could you take her?"

"Wouldn't it be better if you took her and let me take the others?"

"I thought of that, but it would mean giving you three different sets of directions. I know where these fellows live, but you'd have difficulty in finding them."

"Did you ask Gianna what she wanted to do?"

"Yes. She'd like you to take her if you're free."

"All right. Where do I pick her up?"

"At Simone's. You won't need a sketch map from me – you can find Shepland without any trouble. It's a couple of miles from Stanton. There's only one place you can go wrong, and that's at the Stanton crossroads. Keep straight on, past the cinema on the corner, and you'll find yourself at Shepland. The playing field is on the near side of the village. Got it?"

"Yes."

"I'll see you there. After the match, I'll bring Gianna back and you can deliver the three fellows back to their places of abode. Thanks."

Ross looked for Shepland on the map he kept in his car, failed to find it but located Stanton. On the following morning, however, he felt that he need not have troubled himself, for the day began with a freak storm that drove horizontal sheets of rain against his windows, and raging winds that made the bare boughs of the trees dance in frenzy. The storm went on unabated until half past ten, when it ceased with a suddenness that made the ensuing silence seem eerie. Putting down his morning paper, he studied the black clouds that threatened more rain, and decided there could be no hope of a match in conditions like these.

But shortly afterwards, emerging from his shower, he saw to his surprise that the sun had come out – a sun so warm that a faint vapour could be seen rising from the streets. He felt optimistic enough to put in a call to Gianna, but before he reached the telephone, it rang. He picked up the receiver and heard Gianna's voice.

"Ross? Alexander telephoned just now; he said he is sure the ground will be all right for the match. But there is a little difficulty my end. My father came up yesterday to go to a theatre with me, and I promised to drive him back to Downpass because he is having lunch with Walter and the vicar. Pierre is going too."

141

"Pierre? I thought Rekovitch had got him hidden away somewhere."

"My father said a day in the country would do him good. Can you go to Downpass before we go to the match?"

"Yes, easily. Would you agree to a sandwich lunch at the Coach and Four?"

"That sounds a very good idea."

"I'll be round as soon as I've dressed."

He picked up Gianna and James and was directed to the quiet, secluded mews flat in which Pierre was installed. He came up to the car muffled in woollen scarves, his oilskin-protected violin case held firmly under his arm. Ross left the two men at Hargreaves House and took Gianna on to the Coach and Four. They got there shortly after opening time, and were the first to enter the warm, beer-smelling bar. They ordered mulled wine and sandwiches and took a table in a window overlooking the narrow, featureless street. Other customers came in and were served by Mrs Farley, Jass' stepmother, a smiling, apple-cheeked young woman who, Ross felt, would look more at home working in a milk bar. Across the road, the garage was visible, with one or two self-serving drivers at the petrol pumps. Neither in the bar nor in the street did anyone show any sign of haste or purpose; given a different climate, Ross thought, it could have been a somnolent Mexican scene.

"When you were a student in England," he asked Gianna, "did you visit any historic pubs?"

"Sometimes. A man I knew was doing a thesis on old coaching inns, and we went round together inspecting them. How old is this inn?"

"Your great-grandfather, old Jasper Hargreaves, fixed the date round 1780 though he thought the sign was earlier than that. He bought the building – it was in bad shape and he had to rebuild it, but he wouldn't touch the sign. When he sold the place to Jass' grandfather, he made it a condition that the sign stayed as it was."

"My father says Jasper discovered Downpass."

"He didn't discover it. He developed it. The only – "

He stopped, his eyes on the street. There were indications

142

that something was astir. The garage owner, the drivers, a group of men crossing over to enter the inn had all stopped to look down the road at the cause of a disturbance which Gianna and Ross could hear but could not see. Then, to their amazement, they saw passing the window the tall, bony figure of Pierre. Under his arm was his covered violin case. He was walking with his gaze fixed straight ahead, oblivious to, or heedless of, the group of children following him. They were almost on his heels, jeering, shouting, imitating the movements of a violinist, interlarding insults with one or two French words they happened to have picked up.

Gianna stood up and made her way quickly to the door. The customers in the bar crowded to the windows to see what was going on. Ross reached Gianna and caught her by the arm.

"Steady," he warned. "Those kids are rampant. You'll get hurt."

There was undoubtedly a suggestion of mob violence about the children. They numbered about fifteen, most of them boys, all between the ages of eight and ten. The volume of sound increased as they began yelling.

Gianna was struggling to get her arm free. She was white with fury.

"Let me go. Ross, let me go. They're tormenting him — can't you see? Let me go. Why don't these people *do* something?"

As she spoke, there emerged from the side of the inn a small, flying figure. It was Jass, without coat or cap, in a woollen dress and a pair of scruffy slippers. She moved so fast across the road that she seemed to catapult herself into the middle of the yelling children. Before any grown-up could interfere, she had knocked down Tom Lunt, butted his two brothers in the stomach, torn out a handful of his sister's hair, driven a fist on to Rodney Miller's nose, bitten Charlie Cooper's ear and was halfway to strangling Emily Richards when Ross lifted her bodily from the fray.

"Lemme go," she panted. "Lemme go. Lemme get at 'em."

143

But there could be no further combat. Mr Lunt had emerged from the bar and was herding his wounded off-spring homeward, encouraging them with a series of cuffs on their ears. Mrs Miller had appeared from nowhere and was staunching the blood pouring from her son's nose. Mr Cooper and Mr Richards, hastily finishing their beer, put down their tankards and went out to deal with their young. The rest of the children were doing their best to escape, but the onlookers, incensed by this baiting of a harmless-looking foreigner, were holding on to the delinquents until their absentee parents arrived to deal with them.

Throughout, Pierre stood watching the scene, motionless, expressionless. Gianna was beside him offering words of comfort. The road, which a short time before had been almost empty, now looked more like a crowded city thoroughfare. Only when peace had been restored did Pierre move to the door of the inn, where Jass was being held prisoner by her parents. He addressed her father.

"You have a very brave infant, Monsieur."

"Don't you believe it," Jass' mother replied. "She just likes to get into a fight, that's all. She learned it from me. I was the terror of Camden Town in my day."

Jass' father addressed her sternly.

"You go upstairs with your Mum and get cleaned up." He turned to Ross. "Bring the gentleman in, Mr Mirren. We owe him a drink or two."

There followed a demonstration of Anglo-French amity. The entente cordiale wasn't in it, Ross observed to Gianna. Pierre was given a seat and surrounded by those citizens of Downpass who had witnessed the scene and who were now anxious to make amends. He was offered beer. *Non, merci.* Whisky? *Non, merci.* Then – ?

Ross suggested mulled wine, and Pierre's countenance brightened.

"On the house," said the landlord.

Also on the house were cold beef sandwiches, slices of veal and ham pie and chicken rissoles. Halfway through the feast, James and Walter entered, having searched everywhere for their guest. He had refused a lift to the vicarage,

144

saying that he preferred to walk. When he failed to arrive for lunch, search-parties had been sent out, but nobody had thought of looking in the pub. He was led away, but not until he had accepted and drained another glass of mulled wine. He departed between James and Walter. His gait was dignified, his speech of thanks clear, but there was a slightly glazed look in his eyes, and his hold on the violin was not as firm as usual. With his departure, the bar emptied. Ross and Gianna walked to his car and set out for the rugby game.

"Why did I think that Downpass was a place where nothing ever happened?" she asked him.

"That show was put on especially for you. I wouldn't be surprised to learn that Jass organised it so she could stage a rescue and impress you."

"Will the children try to get their revenge on her?"

"Not if they're wise."

There was silence for a time and when she spoke again, it was of Alexander. Something of the pleasure he had been feeling left him as he realised that once they got to the match, her interest would be transferred to the game, or to one figure in it.

As they neared Stanton, the sun vanished. A few moments later, rain was falling, running so swiftly down the windscreen that Ross had difficulty in seeing the road ahead.

"This'll probably put paid to the game," he said. Then he spoke optimistically. "It may stop soon."

They were almost at the Stanton crossroads. Alexander's instructions had been to go straight ahead, but as they reached the intersection, Ross saw that the road was closed for repair. A barrier had been erected across it, and behind could be seen the small tent used by the workmen, who would be off duty today. A yellow diversion arrow indicated the route to be followed.

He stopped the car, took out the map, opened it and handed it to Gianna.

"This is where we are." He put his finger on the spot. "We have to go through here and turn right at this point – there'll be a sign of some sort."

But there was no sign of any sort in evidence, and if there had been, they would have found it difficult to discern through the mist that had been rising since they left the crossroads. Gianna studied the map.

"We have to go straight on," she said. "Then we turn to the left."

She sounded so confident that he decided to let her guide him. He followed her directions, peering through the windscreen and the still-pouring rain, doing his best to avoid the water-filled ruts that seemed to get deeper as they turned into narrow and still narrower lanes. At last he stopped the car.

"It's no use going on through this downpour," he said. "The ground will be inches under water."

"Yes, it will," she agreed. "But Alexander must be there – we can join him. You turn to the right here."

Reluctantly, he went on. But turning to the right, he was confronted by a herd of cows coming slowly through a gate. Behind them were extensive farm buildings; in the distance was a farmhouse. He stopped and switched off the engine.

"Let me see that map," he said.

She gave it to him and pointed out the route by which they had come. He saw that they had been driving in a circle.

"How the hell did you manage to miss that turning?" he asked rather too brusquely.

He immediately regretted the roughness in his tone, but he was trying to suppress feelings which were a mixture of frustration and jealousy. She was not interested in weather conditions or appalling road surfaces or the state to which they were reducing his car; all she wanted was to get to Alexander. For that, she needed a driver – and that was how she regarded him. She and Alexander, he thought bitterly, merely used him, and when his usefulness was ended, they forgot him. He was nothing, he told himself gloomily, but an extra leg. Now he was marooned in a farmyard and surrounded by cows, without a single dwelling – except the farmhouse – in sight. Across sodden fields he could make

146

out through the mist vague shapes that might or might not be the village of Shepland.

"We'd better go home," he said. "If we get to the ground at all, which seems doubtful, there'll be nobody there."

"Alexander will wait for me," she said with a confidence that only served to increase his irritation.

"No, he won't. If he's got any sense, he'll realise there can't be a match, and he'll go home. And what's more, if he'd looked at the weather report, he wouldn't have left home. Neither would we."

The cows, after standing in front of the car eyeing it doubt-fully, had divided into two tributaries and were pushing their way past, two or three of the more curious stopping to gaze into the interior. Ross turned to Gianna.

"It's up to you," he said. "Go on and drown, or go back to tea."

"I'd like to go on," she said.

There was a note of obstinacy in her tone which put the final touch to his anger. Without saying anything further, he started the car, turned with difficulty and felt his way back along the lane.

"You haven't given me back the map," she pointed out.

"No. We'll get on better if I do the navigating."

"If you're implying that I made you go the wrong way –"

"We didn't get to the ground, did we?"

"And so you are angry." She sounded even angrier. "I did my best, but it is not a good map, and that village isn't even marked on it, and there was a roadblock and after that, mist, and so we went wrong. I'm sorry. I'm sorry Alexander asked you to bring me here."

"He didn't ask me to bring you here. He asked me to drive you to the sports ground. Perhaps you ought to lay off computers and study map-reading."

For a moment, he thought she was about to open the door and get out. The look of the lane, however, deterred her. She sat in silence while he put the map aside, deciding instead to trust his sense of direction to lead them to the ground, which he was certain they would find deserted. He would not be able to ask anybody the way, for there was not a soul in sight.

After negotiating a few more cart-tracks, he reached the point at which they had left the road – and here a pleasant surprise awaited him. They were on a rise, and the mist which had been so thick had dispersed and was now merely a haze that gave the scene a kind of Impressionist beauty. Before them was a narrow, undulating road ending in a line of low hills. On their left, far off but now clearly seen, was a small village. On their right were the farm buildings which had blocked their passage earlier, and beyond them was the beautiful, mellow old farmhouse. The intervening fields, now under water, formed a lush, green valley whose charm not even these weather conditions could dim. The only incongruous detail in the picture was a lopsided shed topped by a small flag which the wind was tearing to tatters.

"Well, we've made it," he said. "That must be the club-house."

He steered between fields along a narrow, stony lane which ended in a sea of mud a hundred yards from the shed. They could now read the sign painted on the side of the shed: Shepland and District Rugby Club. The door was closed, and a padlock hung from it.

They sat and looked on in silence. When the silence became unbearable Ross began to speak in the tone of a commentator.

" 'The match was played in conditions that gave the players no chance to show their real merit. Several of the younger players were excellent in the scrums, but the lineouts were –' "

"Now you can do what you wanted to do," she broke in frostily. "You can go home. There's nobody here. I'm sorry for all the trouble I've caused you."

His ill-humour, never of long duration, had vanished.

"It was worth coming, just to see this wonderful view," he said. "Who would have believed, from the unpromising approaches, that this Happy Valley existed here?"

He had already resolved to return in the spring to view the lovely scene under sunnier conditions. He could not understand why the site had not been built on; it adjoined the village, which was picturesque but had a look of wanting to expand. Two or three cottages like Laura's . . .

He turned his attention to Gianna. She was looking angry and disappointed, but he could think of nothing consoling to say. She had insisted on coming; she now saw for herself that their journey had been a waste of time and petrol, and she was ready to go back. Whether Alexander had been here or not it was impossible to say.

He put the car into gear. Seconds later he became aware that the back wheels were spinning, throwing up spurts of mud that blocked the rear window.

He sat considering the situation. It seemed hopeless, with no help in sight. There was no visible approach to the village and the farm buildings looked deserted. He could see lights in the farmhouse; someone was obviously at home, but too far away to be of any assistance. There was nothing to do but get out of the car and shore up the back wheels. He could use the stones which were lying in abundance on the lane along which they had come, but to get them and put them under the wheels would entail several journeys in pouring rain across an area round the car which was ever-deepening mud. He had a serviceable mackintosh, but no head covering. He was wearing stout shoes, but what he needed, he told himself, was a pair of fisherman's boots.

"Why don't we go?" Gianna asked.

"We're stuck. We won't be able to get moving until I've shoved some stones under the back wheels."

He reached into the back of the car for his mackintosh and struggled into it. Then he opened the car door and stepped out. Before he had reached the stones, rainwater was pouring down his face and trickling inside the collar of his mackintosh. The wind whistled about his ears. The mud was so deep that he feared his shoes would be sucked off.

He went back to the car with the first armful of stones and banked them as firmly as he could round one of the back wheels. Straightening and turning to go back for another load, he found Gianna beside him.

149

"Don't be a fool," he shouted over the wind. "Get back into the car."

But she gave no sign of having heard. She went on her way to the lane, picked up some stones and carried an armful back for him to put round the wheels. She had put on a headscarf, but it was already soaked and her hair hung in strands on the shoulders of her suede jacket. Her boots, calf high, had looked both strong and smart, but they were now covered in mud and it soon became evident that they had not been made to keep out water.

They worked steadily, passing and repassing one another – and then something about her, the combination of bedraggled appearance and dogged persistence, made him smile. The smile became a laugh. Having begun, he was unable to stop, and leaned against the car, helpless with mirth.

She paused to look at him in surprise – and then she, too, was laughing until tears mingled with the raindrops on her cheeks. He went up to her and with a sharp stone attempted to scrape away some of the mud that was clinging to her boots and impeding her progress. She shook her head, still laughing, and leaned against him, clinging to his soaking mackintosh.

As they stood together, there was a lull in the storm. The rain became a drizzle, the wind dropped and they saw, to their amazement, a car approaching over the stony lane. It was a large station wagon, which drew up on the edge of the muddy area. Seconds later, a man wearing a large sou'-wester, thigh boots and a black leather mackintosh, jumped out: everything save his broad red face was wrapped up against the elements. He stood surveying Ross and Gianna for some moments, and then put his head back and gave a bellow of laughter. Finally able to conquer his mirth, he addressed them in a broad Welsh accent.

"Well, you've got yourselves into a rare mess," he told them. "My name's Evans. I own that farm over there, at least my wife does. We saw you from our windows and I guessed the car was stuck. It's always happening with those rugby chaps – they never learn. I've told them many a time

150

to get some concrete put round that shed, but they haven't done it yet. I've brought along a couple of lads and some planks to get you out of trouble."

"It's very good of you – " Ross began.

"Never mind about speeches," Mr Evans broke in genially. "Just you get your young lady and yourself into my car and I'll take you to the farm so that you can get cleaned up a bit. Never mind about bringing some mud with you – we're used to that. These lads'll get your car out and follow us later."

Ross put Gianna into the station wagon, but elected to stay and help the two youths. When Mr Evans drove away, Gianna was trying to squeeze the water from her sodden headscarf out of the window.

Ross and the two helpers arrived at the farmhouse just as dusk was falling. They stepped out of the car into what seemed to Ross to be a sea of dogs – some barking, some snarling, old and young, pure-bred or mongrels. Sheltering in doorways were families of cats. A friendly pony came to the edge of a field to see what was going on, and two small donkeys gazed impassively over a hedge.

The front door of the building appeared to be disused; its paint was peeling, and three weed-covered steps led to an equally neglected garden. The two rooms facing the front looked large and bare, and were unlit.

It was the wide double doors at the back that Mr Evans – seen without his oilskins to have ox-like shoulders and a protuberant paunch – opened to admit Ross. He led him to a vast, stone-floored, bitterly cold room in which there were concrete slabs round the walls, large stone sinks, a number of taps, some with short lengths of hosepipe attached to them, and a ceiling from which dangled large, lethal-looking hooks. Against one of the walls stood a dishwasher, two large refrigerators and a deep-freeze.

"Used to be a dairy," Mr Evans explained, "but that was in the old days, when there were a dozen men and women employed on the place. There were fine hams hanging up here once, and rows of great bowls of cream, and butter churns – but that's all finished and done with. Now we only

151

feed four – me and my wife and the two lads you've seen. They're cleaning up right now but they'll be over for tea. They come from Shepland and they go home every night, but they have all their meals here." He opened a tap over a sink. "Plenty of hot water. Towels on that hook. Get a bit of dirt off and then go through that door over there into the kitchen. Take your time; there's no hurry."

"It's really very good of you – "

"Nonsense, boy. It's not often we see a girl as pretty as that one of yours."

Left alone, Ross hung up his mackintosh and cleaned himself up as well as he could. The water was piping hot, the towels satisfyingly absorbent. Before going into the kitchen, he removed his shoes, and on stockinged feet walked to the door and knocked. Mr Evans admitted him, and from the threshold Ross looked at a scene he was to remember whenever, in the future, anyone spoke the word comfort.

A bright fire burned in a huge grate that was a combination of open fireplace, three cooking-rings and two blue enamel ovens. The room was as large as the one he had just left, but it was warm, with deep, shabbily upholstered chairs placed haphazardly round the fire. Wooden kitchen chairs were ranged round an oval table. On this was a blue checked cloth which could scarcely be seen for the number of plates resting on it. Mrs Evans, short, stout, with a manner that was a mixture of the practical and the fussy, was making room for more, cutting thick slices of home-made bread and keeping watch on the food sizzling loudly on the stove.

"Now there you are," she called to Ross. "Come in, come in and sit yourself down. Tea's all but ready."

She had a flat Midlands accent. She was wearing a floral overall; her cheeks were as red as her husband's and her hair was scraped carelessly into a bun on top of her head.

Of Gianna there seemed for the first few moments no sign. Then Ross saw her two bare feet protruding from the end of one of the decrepit chairs that was pushed close to the fire. He walked over and looked down at her over its back.

152

"She looks a treat, doesn't she?" Mrs Evans said. "That's my dressing gown she's wearing. Soaking wet, she was."

"And cold," added Gianna in a drowsy voice. Her eyes were closed. She opened them to remark that she had rung Alexander to say they would be home late; then she appeared to settle down to sleep.

"You'll both be hungry," Mrs Evans remarked. She pushed several plates into new positions and set others between them. Ross began a half-hearted protest.

"Look, Mrs Evans, you shouldn't be giving us tea. We –"

"High tea," she corrected. "We don't have supper. Come six o'clock, we sit down to a good, healthy, hearty meal and that's all for the day. When the lads have eaten and helped to clear away, they go home."

"They look like brothers, but they're cousins," Mr Evans explained. He pushed two chairs nearer to the fire, dropped into one with a force that explained its battered look, and waved Ross to the other. Before seating himself, Ross again looked across at Gianna.

"She's asleep, and I don't wonder. We won't wake her yet," Mr Evans said.

"Not till I've got the teapot filled," said his wife.

"It's the warm room that makes you drop off," Mr Evans went on. "If we didn't have visitors, I'd be nodding off myself."

"He falls asleep, visitors or no visitors," said his wife.

"Old age, that's what it is," said Mr Evans. "I'm well on the way to sixty, so I'm not as active as I was."

"That's true enough," said Mrs Evans. She was moving thick rashers of bacon round a frying pan. "When he was younger, he never stopped. Now he likes to take it easy. Not like my Dad; he never took a rest in his life till he went to his last one. Near eighty, he was."

"And strong as a horse," said Mr Evans. "But you've got to remember that in his day, there were farm labourers to be had, as many as you could pay for. Then they began to leave the land, and they're still going. Try and get men to come and do the manual work they did when I was a boy and you'd be wasting your time."

153

"There were Land Girls during the war," Mrs Evans said. "I was one of 'em. But they disappeared too. If you get a man today, all he wants to do is wear out the seat of his pants sitting in a tractor. He won't even bend down to pick up a potato."

"Things had got that way when we got married," Mr Evans said. "But I liked this place, so I took it on."

"He had to take me on too," said his wife. "My dad said he couldn't go on for ever, and advised me to look for a man to run the farm. I looked, but I didn't see one I fancied. Then I went to a cattle sale up in Yorkshire and there was this Evans bidding for the calf I was after. He got the calf and he got me too."

"That's right," said Mr Evans. "She agreed to let me be the boss, and so I left my little mountain patch in Wales and here I am still, and always will be. It's not a place where there's much going on; most people would say it was too quiet, but we like it. We live simply; no frills, as you can see, but we keep warm and we eat well, as do the two lads who work for us."

Mrs Evans went into the washroom and rang a large bell. Gianna stirred, stretched, and Ross got up and held out a hand to pull her to her feet.

"You sit here" – Mrs Evans indicated a place at the table – "and your young man next to you. You're not married – I saw you weren't wearing a ring, but I daresay you're paired up, the way it's done nowadays."

"As a matter fact," Ross began, "we – "

"Here come the lads. This one," said Mr Evans, "is Barney and the other one over there with the red thatch has been called Skipper for so long, I've forgotten what he was christened. You know where to sit, lads."

They gathered round the table, hungry and expectant. Mrs Evans carried a frying pan from the stove and from it expertly shovelled eggs – two apiece – and slices of bacon on to the plates. She filled the cups with tea so strong that it looked the colour of the mud the car had been stuck in. Into it, before Ross or Gianna could stop her, she had put large heapings of sugar. Before them stood a spread of

154

thick brown bread, yellow butter, jugs of cream, a bowl of honey, fresh cheeses, homemade buns and a large round cake decorated with lemon peel. Ross did justice to it all, and Gianna's eyes grew rounder as she watched him.

"Everything home-grown or home-baked," Mrs Evans said proudly. "No cardboard or plastic food in this house."

It was not a hurried meal. Mr Evans and the two boys had second helpings of eggs and bacon, and went on to eat their share of everything on the table. When at last the chairs were pushed back, Mr Evans made up the fire while the others carried the plates out and stacked them in the dishwasher. Then the two boys cluttered noisily away on a motorbike, Barney on the saddle and his cousin riding pillion. Mrs Evans removed her overall, hung it on a hook behind the door and gave a sigh.

"Done for the day," she said. "After we've had our tea, we take it easy, him with his evening paper and me with my knitting. This evening, though, we can have a nice chat instead."

"We should be on our way," Ross said.

"Nonsense, man. Not on top of your tea," said Mr Evans. "You've got to let it settle. Take a chair."

They sat round the fire and talked – of the weather, the farm routine, the Government, and of the Evans' two grown-up sons who had gone to Australia and were farming successfully there, but who could not persuade their parents to go out and join them.

"We're too old," said Mr Evans, "but old or not, we've never wanted to leave this farm. We hoped our sons would build their own homes on that land we own between the farm and the village. There was room enough for two houses, and plenty over, but they preferred to go to Australia. Since they went, a lot of people have been after us to sell the land, but my wife and I didn't like the idea of a row of villas spoiling our view, though our sons can do what they like with the land when we're gone. Mind you, I don't blame them for going – neither does their mother. They're doing well, and they say it's a good life."

"Are they married?" Gianna asked.

155

"Yes. Both of them. They took their girls with them. They say they're happy and they certainly sound it, but if they want to see us, they'll have to make the journey."

"I certainly won't go there," Mrs Evans said with decision. "I can't see why people enjoy gallivanting. I know people over in the village, Shepland it's called, where whole families pack up every summer and go to Lord knows what outlandish places. Turkey, if you please, and Yugowhatever, and they fly both ways and come back with a lot of trashy souvenirs and boring films they make you sit and look at. I stay at home and save myself a lot of trouble."

"And expense," added her husband.

"Yes, money too. They tell me I miss a lot, but when it comes down to it, all they've seen, for all their journeying, is a few bars and beaches."

"It's the sun they go for, Mother."

"So they say. They certainly go as pale as plaice and come back red as lobsters. They leave their animals for the neighbours to look after. I don't know who'd look after our lot, if we ever decided to go on a trip."

Silence fell. It was very quiet outside. The wind had dropped, the rain had ceased. When Ross and Gianna made their farewells and left their new friends, they drove away into a darkness unrelieved by moon or stars or streetlights.

When they had driven a short distance, Ross stopped the car and switched off the lights.

"Blackness, and silence, and distant spots of light far away in the village windows," he said. "Would you think I was exaggerating if I told you I'd fallen in love with this place?"

"No. I think it's beautiful."

"Even in this kind of weather and at this time of year. It'll be a wonderful sight in summer. Odd, the way we congregate in towns and cities."

"You could build yourself a house in the country."

"That's exactly what's been in my mind ever since Mr Evans said he owned the land between the farmhouse and the village. I'd pay him anything he asked – in reason – if

156

he'd sell it to me. He'd have my guarantee that I'd only put up one house on it."

"There'd be a lot of land left over."

"Swimming pool, tennis courts, sauna, squash court, stabling."

"Even after that, there'd be quite a bit left. What would you do with it?"

"I'd . . . well, I suppose you could call it realising a long-cherished dream." He paused. "I think the Evans sons probably went away because the farm wasn't producing enough to keep three families."

"You said you were going to realise a dream."

"I meant it. It's not a new idea. I've had it in my mind for a long time."

"What is it?"

"I'd like to create a kind of animal retreat. I said it wasn't a new idea and it isn't particularly original either. I saw my first retreat when I was still at school; I went in for one of the Duke of Edinburgh Awards and had to tramp for days in open country over the Pennines. A test of toughness. Most of the ground I had to cover was uninhabited, but I came to a group of wooden buildings which a man – an elderly man, retired – had put up on about ten acres of land where sick or neglected or ill-used or worn-out animals could stay and be cared for. I talked to him while I ate my sandwich lunch. He told me he was doing it with the help of a friend who was a vet. On the ten acres there were animals roaming freely – those of them still able to, that is. There were horses, donkeys, ponies; there were smaller animals and wounded birds recovering from being shot and left to die. Watching it all, I told myself it was something I'd like to do. I was about sixteen. I knew I was going to be an architect in my father's firm, but I made up my mind that if ever I saw my way to setting up a place like that one, I'd do it."

"So you'll go ahead – if Mr Evans will sell the land to you?"

"Yes. It's only taken me sixteen years. You can't accuse me of being impulsive, can you?"

157

"No."

"Do you think it's a worthwhile idea?"

"Yes. I don't think you have an impulsive nature."

"Didn't my marriage come under that heading?"

"No. I would call that the result of a combination of circumstances; a pretty girl, the excitement of being asked to help her . . . I don't think you rushed into anything. You were pushed into it. This dream . . . I like it very much. I think you should do it if you can. And if you ever do, I'll go round stealing all the poor cats who never get out of the apartments they're cooped up in, and dogs who can never go for walks except on the end of a lead, and birds in too-small cages, and poor little animals given to uncaring children to play with. There won't be enough room for your tennis courts and your sauna; you'll need it for the animals. But you must be careful to marry someone who likes animals, who believes in dreams and who doesn't want to live in a city."

"I'll be very careful."

"Will you go and see Mr Evans again?"

"Yes. And when I do, will you come with me?"

"I'd like to. I liked them very much. But when I meet two people as happy as they are together, I wonder what will happen if one of them dies."

"Not if, when. It has to happen, and the survivor goes on and makes the best of it. The Evanses must miss their sons more than they admitted, but their way of life reminded me of Laura's; people have always said she leads a dull life, but it isn't dull at all. Did you ever want brothers?"

"Yes. Did you mind being the only child?"

"No, not really. I once asked Laura why she and my father didn't have any children. Her answer was that she liked things the way they were; having a second family, she thought, might be a complication. She also said she looked on me as a real son and often forgot I wasn't. But when my father died, I was sorry she hadn't any children of her own. She and I moved back to the cottage and it became my home."

"What about uncles and aunts and cousins?"

"Both my parents were only children, so the cousins were all distant."

The questions and answers were all casual, coming between intervals of contented silence. The darkness enclosed them; neither of them felt inclined to move. The minds of both were on the Evans and on the events of the afternoon.

"What did you say to Alexander when you rang?" he asked.

"Just that we'd be back late. I said we'd had car trouble."

"Where was he?"

"In his office. He told me he'd be there if the match had to be cancelled. There are going to be some changes made to the building, and he has to move out of his room, so he was getting his papers together."

"Are you dining with him?"

"No."

It was a simple negative, but something in her tone made him wish there was still light enough to see her expression.

"Why not?" he asked.

"Because when he knew there couldn't be a game, he asked the three men with him to go out to dinner. He asked me to go along too, but I didn't want to. What I want, and what I never get – what I'm beginnning to think I will *never* get – is to see him when we can be alone, when we can talk, when we can make plans for the future."

"My father used to say that the future always had a way of working itself out. He sometimes quoted the saying about mice and men – you know it?"

"No."

" 'The best laid schemes o' mice an' men
      Gang aft a-gley.'
Robert Burns, Scottish poet. He seemed to think a lot about mice – he called one a wee, sleekit, cow'ring, tim'rous beastie. Get Alexander to put on an authentic Scots accent and you'll get the full flavour. I would have liked Burns better if I hadn't had an ancient great-aunt who went on singing long after she should have stopped, and liked to give renderings of Scottish poems set to music. The poets must

159

have writhed in their graves. What English poets did you study in school?"

"Wordsworth, mostly. And Keats."

"He's my favourite. Who else?"

"Shelley. I once wrote an essay about his death. It was very sad – and very bad. It had to be written in English and I was only twelve and made lots of mistakes. I could never make my teachers understand that having an English father didn't help me much with my English essays."

There was another silence, broken eventually by Ross' tentative suggestion of a meal at his apartment. But neither of them seemed willing to end this quiet interlude and start the journey home.

"Shall I tell you something?" she asked after a time.

"If you're sure it's nothing Laura wouldn't like me to hear," Ross replied, with mock seriousness.

"Anybody can hear it, for all I care. Quite simply, I don't mind if I never see a rugby match again in all my life."

He thought this over.

"No match, no Alexander," he reminded her.

"Yes, I know that now. But am I really to spend my time watching him do everything he wants to do, even if it isn't what I want him to do? Is this how things must be, that a man meets a girl and say he loves her, but makes no change, no allowances in his life and just goes on as if nothing special has happened? Is it?"

"Give him time. He hasn't realised yet that any change is necessary."

"What *will* make him realise? Shall I have to be one of those girls who complain about being left alone? Am I to make scenes and threaten him and say he mustn't play games any more? I can't do that. It just isn't in my nature."

"Just give him time," Ross counselled again, but though outwardly calm and dispassionate, he nevertheless felt some small stirrings of unease.

"Ever since I arrived back in England, things started to go wrong. The ferry, that wasn't England. England was seeing that ugly house and meeting my aunt Beatrice and learning that my father had never told me things I should have been

160

told, and being in love with a man who says he loves me but does nothing to prove it. Isn't marriage, successful marriage, meant to involve a kind of . . . a compromise between two people who each give up a little? What has Alexander given up? Nothing. Not a single game, not a single meeting with his friends. You say I must give him time, give him time, give him time. But time for what?"

"Time to adjust. Time to outgrow some of the things –"

"How can he outgrow what is ingrained?"

"Where did I get the idea that Frenchmen don't change much when they marry? Isn't their idea to maintain a wife and home and children, and having done that much to ensure the future, allow themselves some extra-marital amusements?"

"They don't have to be French to do that. The point of what I'm saying is that Alexander should have asked me if I was happy about all the things he has gone on doing even though we are supposed to be engaged. At first, I was patient. But now, I'm asking myself questions, and I don't like the answers. I ask myself if he is selfish. I ask myself if he is incapable of seeing below the surface of things. I ask . . . Why am I telling you all this?"

"To get it out of your system."

"You like him very much, don't you?"

"Yes."

"And you believe that soon, by a sort of miracle, he'll take his mind away from his rugby clubs and make plans for our wedding?"

"No, it may not be what I believe. It's what I hope."

"What did your father do when he met Laura? Did he go on living as he had been living before he met her?"

"Well, not entirely. She didn't like London, so he sold the house he owned in Chelsea and bought one a little further out of town – in St John's Wood – because it had an enormous garden and she could imagine herself in the country."

"You see? He did that for her. For Alexander, I would live anywhere he wanted. I would go out to work, which I would enjoy, but if he asked me to stay at home, then I'd do that instead. If he didn't want children at first, I'd wait, although I want to have them very much. All these things, he and I should be talking about – but he doesn't talk about the future, unless it's about the next rugby fixture. Did I fall in love with the man he is, or did I fall in love with somebody who looked like him outside, but who remained a complete stranger? And am I just saying all this to get it out of my system, as you said, or am I telling the truth at last?"

"You're skipping chapters. Chapter one was meeting him. Chapter two was falling in love. After that, the plot has to get weaving. In chapter three, you've got over the initial excitement and you've got to do some reassessing."

"That is exactly what I'm doing: reassessing. And the result of it is that if I met Alexander again on the ferry, I would fall in love – but if there had been no ferry, if I had met him, for instance, in England and listened to him talking on and on about his rugby clubs, then – then it might have been different. There are two Alexanders, just as that grandmother of his said. I saw one of them for a short time, and then he disappeared. Now I'm left with a not so nice substitute. I don't like the substitute very much – and the substitute won't ever change his way of living. That's what I've got to come to terms with."

"How can you tell?" Ross asked. "I remember sitting on the sands at some seaside resort at the age of six or seven, looking at what must have been one of the last performances ever given by a beach concert party. A man sang a song that ended:

'I've got to look after the baby,
    So I can't come out tonight.'

I appreciated, even at that tender age, the sacrifice he'd made. I understood that he'd changed, fallen in love, become a father. It was, I thought, a splendid performance. I wanted to wait for him to come and do it all over again, but I had a nanny who tried to direct my mind to higher forms of music, and she hurried me away. Alexander *will* change – if you wait."

"Do you remember much about your mother?"

"Nothing consecutive. Brief impressions like being in a train and sitting on her knee and gazing out of the window. Ices in a teashop somewhere in London. Watching her buying a pair of gloves – that sort of thing. I might not have remembered her at all if my father hadn't made a point of mentioning her frequently in a natural sort of way – I suppose to keep her memory alive. Laura used to talk about her, too."

"You're so lucky to have Laura. My mother must have been very beautiful, very attractive to have made my father let her go."

"I'm glad he did. If you're not dining with Alexander tonight, how about making me an omelette plus at my flat?"

"You won't have all the things I need to make one."

"Then make me an omelette minus. After that, I'll drive you to Simone's, or back to Downpass if you'd prefer. I'm going there for the weekend anyway."

"I'll go with you. But I'll have to drop in at Simone's first to get some things to wear."

"Don't you leave things down there, as I do?"

"No. When I left to go to London, I cleared away all my possessions. My aunt was very pleased to see me go. Now she'll be happy because there will be no more parties in the house."

"Pity. It could do with some brightening up. So could she."

"My father thinks she is going to start a youth club or something of that kind. I hope she does. She needs something she can do by herself. She can't work with other people without quarrelling with them, but on her own, I think she's got the – the capacity to take on some big project, and make a success of it." She paused and added reluctantly: "We ought to go back."

He admitted that they should, and started the engine. He drove slowly; he did not want to return to a world filled with other people. He was happy in this warm, comfortable shelter, close to her, safe from intruders, talking or not talking . . . and letting himself imagine that she was his.

163

They arrived at his flat thirsty, but not yet hungry enough to make dinner. Ross remarked that after the Evans' high tea, he would never feel really hungry again. All he wanted – and to his surprise and pleasure all she seemed to want – was to sit in semi-darkness with the curtains open to the night, in comfortable chairs, listening to music playing softly.

Breaking a long, contented silence, Gianna made what he thought was the first personal remark she had ever addressed to him.

"You've been very good to me," she said quietly.

"Have I? How, exactly?"

"You know how. Aren't there any other girls who want some of the time you've given to me?"

"At the moment, no."

"Who was the last one?"

"Not, according to Laura, a nice girl. She chain-smoked and she came out with some rather startling swear words – sort of peppered them into the conversation. The free-and-easy type."

"Does Laura always meet your girlfriends?"

"Don't make it sound as though there's a steady procession of them. If I like a girl enough to take her to Downpass, we stay in the chalet but I take her across the garden and show her to Laura, because Laura's opinions are objective and sensible."

"Do you need objective and sensible advice in your love affairs?"

"They haven't usually developed into love affairs when Laura sees them. They're still on the fringe."

"And if she says 'No, don't', you don't?"

"It depends. I remember a Greek girl. Laura had some harsh things to say about her, but then she hadn't seen her on a beach and so wasn't aware that she had a body that . . . well, it was streamlined. She went back to Greece and I didn't forget her for . . . oh, weeks. She married someone whose surname ended in 'oupoulis'. She now lives with him on Mykonis."

"You could go there for a holiday."

"I'll wait until her children are older. They're still in prams."

"How many little oupoulises?"

"To date, three. One single, the other two came into the world together. They're twins."

They drove to Downpass dinnerless. Laura gave them coffee and biscuits and then Ross drove Gianna to Hargreaves House. He returned to his chalet and went to bed, but for the first time since meeting her, his last thoughts on the verge of sleep were not solely of her; they were now divided between Gianna and the animal shelter he was already building in his mind between the Evans' farmhouse and the village of Shepland.

10

The repairs to the roof of Alexander's house seemed to drag interminably and Ross invited him to move into his flat until they were completed. The two men discussed the matter over drinks one evening, but Alexander finally decided that it would be unwise to risk offending his grandmother by cutting short his time with her.

"She wouldn't like it," he explained, watching Ross mixing drinks at the miniature bar in the flat. "She takes the line that she's a lonely old widow, neglected by all her relations and grateful to have me as company – in other words, she's glad to have a captive listener. I couldn't have stood it if I hadn't had these interviews to give me an excuse for being out most of the time." He took the drink Ross handed him. "What I'll do, if you've no objection, is use this flat as a refuge, a sort of retreat for Gianna and myself. You're not far from this college she's studying at, and with you, we can both relax. I'm not saying anything against Pierre's sisters, but sitting on the floor of the ten–by–ten living room talking Franglais isn't my idea of an ideal evening. Nor yours, I presume; you've only been to see them once since you came back after Christmas."

"I've been busy with other things."

"Things?"

"Well, people."

"People, plural?"

"All right. One person. You know all about it."

"Yes, I do. She tells all, that girl. You hadn't got your latchkey out before she was ringing you to say welcome back." He got up and helped himself to more ice. "But let me warn you, Ross my friend, Daphne Maxwellton isn't the woolly-wit some people mistake her for."

166

"I don't need warning. I never underestimated her intelligence."

"Well, I did at first. I was convinced her father had used me as a daughter-dump. Another misleading sign was that I thought she'd been thrown out of those three previous jobs he'd found for her. They didn't throw her out; she threw herself out and came to roost in my office."

"Does she do any work?"

"She doesn't overwork. If she needs to do any typing, she hands it over to one of the juniors. She's got one quality I envy; she can assess what's important and what isn't, after one glance. So can I, but not at her speed. When I give her anything to do, she riffles through the papers the way a bank cashier shuffles banknotes, and gets straight to the core of the problem. How often have you seen her since you got back?"

"She's dropped in now and then for a drink."

"And what else?"

"Nothing else." He went to a cupboard, took out and opened a jar of Spanish stuffed olives and emptied them into a bowl. "She asked me to help her buy a car. My God, have you any idea of the amount of money some of these girls get through?"

"Yes. And I make sure to keep out of their way. When I was young and green, and first put a tentative toe into the social pool, I met one or two of them."

"Were you ever left to pick up the bill after one of their shopping expeditions?"

"Never."

"You're lucky. I've been taken for many an expensive ride. My brief experience as a husband taught me not only to limit my intake of drink but also to keep an eye on the outgoings of cash."

"You're getting your divorce?"

"Yes."

"And then what? If Daphne's after you, you'll have to chain yourself to some railings."

Ross did not say that he suspected Daphne of merely filling in time. She was as frank as Alexander had said she

167

was, but he had already learned that what she said was very often a cover for what she did not say.

"How many more of these interviews have you still got to do?" he asked.

"Four. There were five, but the skiing champion I was to interview came to grief on a ski jump. Gianna was upset when I told her about it – I'm still trying to get her to understand that a reporter, like a priest or a doctor, has to be, to a great extent, objective."

"How much is she going to see of you after you're married?"

"As much as the job permits."

"Or the sport permits."

Alexander came as near to looking worried as his cast of countenance would allow.

"Has she said anything to you? I mean, has she made any complaints?"

"If she made them, she'd make them to you. Go slow with those olives. Gianna likes them, and that's the last of my supply."

Alexander looked at his watch, gave a startled exclamation and finished his drink at a gulp.

"Time to go and fetch her," he said. "How about making a threesome for dinner?"

"Thanks, but no."

"Pity. I could have taken you to Crespins and then pretended I'd left my wallet behind. Shan't be long."

He returned half an hour later with Gianna. Ross had refilled the ice-bucket and put out cheese biscuits and nuts. She threw her coat carelessly on to a chair and stood by the bar watching him as he poured out drinks. She seemed to him either tired or out of spirits.

"There." He handed her her drink. "Alexander, come and get yours."

"I need it. We've just had our first quarrel," said Alexander. "It lasted four minutes and then we made it up."

"No, we didn't." Gianna walked to an armchair and seated herself. "You're still making excuses."

168

"Not excuses, love," Alexander protested. "All I'm saying is that recitals aren't really my favourite leisure pursuit." He appealed to Ross. "It's this affair of Pierre's the week after next," he explained. "I told Gianna I'd go, but – "

"You told Pierre you'd go," Gianna reminded him. "You also told him you were looking forward to it, which obviously wasn't true."

"I said it to please him. You can hardly tell a chap who's been practising his fingers to the bone for weeks that you're going to dodge out on the day. I've told you how it is, love; my mother got all the musical know-how that was doled out to our family. My father didn't know a sharp from a flat and several of my great-aunts were tone-deaf."

"You're not tone-deaf," Gianna said. "When you sing, you can keep in tune."

"Only if it's one of those tunes you can recognise, like that . . . can't remember the name. Anyway, it goes like this: pom, pom, pomety pom, diddy dum."

"We can dispense with the encore," Ross said.

"But that's not the kind of music Pierre's going to play, is it?" Alexander pointed out. "I heard some of the strains floating down from his room at Downpass. Virtuoso stuff, admittedly, but nothing you could hold on to."

Gianna spoke to Ross in a tone of despair.

"The Cervin Variations – nothing to hold on to. Does he think they're a rugby ball?"

"No, he doesn't," said Alexander. "The Cervin Variations may be the highest peak of ecstasy for the aficionados, but to me, they sound a bit limited, like taking an egg and serving it up in a dozen different ways, but in the end, it's still only an egg. Must I really go and sit through that, love?" he pleaded.

"Yes." Gianna spoke firmly. "To please me – but I wouldn't make you go for that. It's to please Pierre. Look how hard he's worked – the least his friends can do is go to his recital. When it's over, we're all going out to dinner, ten of us. If you're not there, he'll know you weren't at the recital and he'll feel hurt."

Alexander, filling his mouth with nuts, was understood to enquire why Pierre's feelings should be given more consideration than his own.

"Don't argue any more. You're coming with me," Gianna said. "And one more thing: Laura has invited us to lunch on Sunday, and this time, you've got to be there, even if your car breaks down." She put down her glass, shook her head at Ross' offer of a refill, and gave a long, unabashed yawn. "I'd better go. I'm so sleepy. The classes aren't easy to understand, and at the end of the day, my eyes won't stay open."

"You coming to the match tomorrow?" Alexander asked Ross.

"Only if you want me to take Gianna."

"Thanks, no. It's on home ground – I'll be able to get her there and back."

"We'll meet at the cottage on Sunday," Gianna said. "Thanks for the drink."

She went to the door with Alexander. He opened it and spoke over his shoulder to Ross.

"Lady to see you."

Coming towards them was Daphne, elegant in a wide-fitting coat and a trailing scarf.

"You two just off?" she enquired. "Good. I saw Alexander's car outside, and I was afraid I wouldn't have Ross to myself. How's the flat-hunting?" she asked Gianna.

"Nothing yet," Gianna said. "We don't have much time to go round looking, and what we've seen so far has been terrible."

"Keep trying." Daphne walked past them, slipped off her coat and handed it to Ross. "Rum and orange, please. My favourite new drink." Then she turned to address Alexander. "I'm going to those music publishers tomorrow, to get those papers you wanted."

"Tomorrow's Saturday," he pointed out. "There won't be anybody there."

"Yes, there will. Some man or other is going in specially to give them to me. If I don't go and get them, they'll go back into the archives. The firm was founded in 1800 and they haven't changed their business methods at all since then." She closed the door. "How's their romance proceeding?" she asked Ross.

"You could have asked them, instead of shutting them out before they'd even got as far as the lift. And you'll have to drink something else with orange – I've no rum."

"I'll bring some with me next time I drop in. I came to tell you that I've found the car I want."

"Good. Did you have your cheque-book with you?"

"No. Before I finally decide, I want you to take me for what the salesman calls a spin. She's beautiful, she really is. Only holds two. When you're at the wheel, the bonnet looks as long as a runway. Will you come?"

"What's the make?"

She told him. She also told him the price.

"Gold-plated?" he enquired.

"Sober black. I could meet you tomorrow morning and we could drive out of town and you could drop me at the music publishers on the way back."

He hesitated, and then nodded. It was a car well outside his financial range and so would be interesting and novel to try out. But he wished he could have had Gianna with him instead of Daphne.

"What time?" he asked.

"Ten?"

"All right. What's your second choice in drinks?"

"Same as yours."

"What's taking you to a music publisher?"

"Winding up that abortive mission Alexander was sent on. Pity my father gave him the job. If he hadn't gone, he wouldn't have had to come back overland and then he wouldn't have crossed the Channel with that girl and fallen for her. That's what always happens if I let my father in on one of my plots: they misfire."

"What was the plot?"

"To become Alexander's so-called assistant, of course. How did I know he was going to be snatched?"

"He wasn't snatched."

His tone was cold. She gave him a speculative glance.

171

"Have I said something to offend you?" she asked sardonically.

"No. I merely said he wasn't snatched."

"Meaning that only nasty girls like me go round man-snatching?"

"Exactly."

"That's one of the things I like about you, Ross. You're so refreshingly frank. It was clever of me, wasn't it, to suggest this new project to my father?"

He looked at her, wondering how much truth there was in this.

"You mean it was your idea?" he asked.

"It was. I convinced him that interviewing sports personalities would be an assignment exactly suited to Alexander. So now he has to go travelling and leave that girl behind."

"Does your father always do what you suggest?"

"He's beginning to. He's already regretting that he didn't sack his secretary and give me the job, instead of handing me over to Alexander. On the other hand, he's seeing more and more possibilities in that situation."

"What situation?"

"Getting Alexander and me joined in holy matrimony. It would have to be holy matrimony; they're both the type of rigid Scot who wouldn't settle for anything less. The idea didn't come to my father all at once, of course. Initially he just wanted to get me out of his hair. He didn't really appreciate my intelligence – he thought living with my mother had made me grow like her. It's only lately that he's come round to understanding that we wouldn't make a bad team."

"You and Alexander?"

"And him. But my opinion is that Father will never make a good newspaper proprietor. It's not his . . . his métier, as that girl would say. He bought *Newshound* to give him an excuse for getting away from my mother, but there was another reason, too – he fancied himself as one of those press barons, poking his nose into politics and ending up with a print empire. But the dream's already beginning to fade;

172

he's only been in the driving seat for two years, and he's already heading for the ditch. He's no fool, though; he's got something to offer, but not to journalism. It's Alexander who's going to end up running *Newshound* – one day."

"With you as the power behind the swivel chair?"

"Exactly."

"Weren't Alexander's parents neighbours of yours at one time?"

"Geographically, yes, though not socially."

"What does that mean?"

"They were only six miles away, but it might just as well have been sixty. My mother and father both loathed Alexander's mother – for quite different reasons. My father thought she was a whatsit of Babylon."

"Stroma?"

"Oh, you've heard about her?"

"Laura and Gianna went to see – "

" – that Belgrave Towers exhibit. So they did; I'd forgotten. She could have told them all about Stroma, but I suppose she didn't like to let herself go in case it got back to Alexander. He knows most of what there is to know about his mother, but he doesn't let anybody mention her if he can help it. Have you noticed my empty glass?"

"Yes. Wait until mine's empty, too, and I'll provide refills. Do you remember Stroma?"

"Don't be silly. I was only four – same age as Alexander – when she died. But my mother told me most of the history."

"Tell me some of it."

"You could only understand it if you'd met my mother. She's not exactly certifiable; let's just call her weird. She's convinced she's a repository of all the arts. She dresses in long, floating robes and writes awful verse and conducts scratch choirs – you know the sort of thing. She used to invite artists – painters, musicians – to stay, and because she paid their fares and they fancied being housed in a castle, they came. Stroma used to drop in, select one she fancied, and carry him off. My mother used to go frantic. The Rolls was always being sent to fetch the errant guest back. It was

173

always a musician – Stroma only collected musicians. It must have been hard on my mother, who'd gone to all the trouble and expense of getting them up to the castle. She thought of herself as their Egeria. Incidentally, who was this Egeria?"

"Legendary."

"You mean she never existed?"

"Only in classical myth. She was a nymph. A king of Rome named Numa Pompilius – "

"Who?"

"Numa Pompilius."

"I shall call my first son Numa Pompilius. Egeria wouldn't be a bad name for one of the girls Did Numa Pompilius love Egeria?"

"She loved him. She wept so much when he died that she dissolved in her tears and the goddess Diana turned her into a fountain."

"That doesn't explain why people like my mother call themselves Egeria."

"Egeria had a great intellectual influence over the king. She handed out advice and made prophecies. And so the Egerias are women who stimulate, or think they stimulate men's intellectual development."

"I see. Well, Stroma didn't claim to be Egeria. She just liked music with her men in bed, that's all. The reason my mother took it so hard was because she at least had the honesty to realise that she was just a dabbler in music, whereas Stroma was a genuine, almost a professional, performer. Funny she didn't pass any of it on to Alexander. He takes after his unmusical father. I remember meeting Rannoch senior in Edinburgh once when I was about nine, and thinking he looked like a pirate – dark skin, black eyes, what's called swarthy. My mother said he knew all about Stroma's goings-on, but pretended not to. I don't wonder the old grandmother hated her."

"Your father doesn't seem to worry about Alexander's Babylonian ancestry."

"I'm the one who'll have to do the worrying. But can you see Alexander lusting after women?"

"No. He hasn't the time, for one thing."

"I'm just waiting to see how long that girl can stand it."

"If you mean Gianna, why don't you call her by her name?"

"Because I think of her as That Girl. She's soon going to get tired of hanging around waiting for him to arrive long past the time when he's expected. Then I can have him."

"And take over the hanging about?"

"Of course not. You don't *understand*. I *want* an absentee husband – the sort you were. I say 'were' because my spies tell me the divorce is going ahead. True?"

"Yes."

"So you'll soon be a free man. But too late for me. I've got Alexander in my system."

"That's just the result of propinquity."

"Explain."

"Propinquity. To be near in time or place. You see Alexander every day. You work for him. You – "

"I work *with* him, not for him."

"All right. You work with him, you get to know him, and you end by imagining you're in love with him."

"I'm not imagining anything." She waited for her glass to be refilled, picked it up and paused with it halfway to her lips to give him a long, intent look. "You seem to have adopted a very protective attitude towards the romance. So why? I ask myself. Is he – meaning you – protecting Alexander, or is he – still meaning you – worrying about that girl, meaning Gianna. Which?"

"Work it out. But not now."

"Why not now? I was hoping you'd take me out to dinner."

"I can't take you anywhere. I'm going down to a birthday party at Ascot."

She gave a sigh of resignation.

"Well, if you can't you can't. Do you know what I'd really like out of life?"

"Yes."

"But not only that. I'd like to catch Alexander, and then I'd like to find a series of escorts who'd take me to places

175

like Samarkand and Srinagar and Siberia. Long, leisurely journeys, with you beside me watching the sensational sunsets."

"Not me. I've got my living to earn."

She looked at him with a puzzled frown.

"I don't understand you, Ross. You *like* me, don't you?"

"Now and then."

"But you won't look this situation in the face. Here we are, you and I, both of us stuck – for the moment. We're waiting for two ends of the same pole. I'm waiting until I can get Alexander away from that girl, and you're waiting to catch her as she falls."

Ross found nothing to say. He stood listening to the echo of what he knew to be the truth. Waiting. Yes, he was waiting. And he had begun by waiting without hope, without any expectation that Alexander's place would ever fall vacant. But lately he had watched – with a mixture of pity, regret and hope – the change in the picture. Gianna was fighting what for the first time, looking at the calm, confident face of Daphne Maxwellton, he knew would be a losing battle. Alexander would go on his self-absorbed way and expect her to be satisfied with the small crumbs of his company he deigned to offer her. She would not blind herself to facts; she was in love, but she was clear-seeing. And she would recognise defeat when it came in sight.

He saw Daphne watching him.

"I knew you were trying not to see the warning lights," she said. "Your trouble is that you overestimate our friend Alexander. He's really only a bundle of muscle wrapped in a sports shirt."

"He loves her."

"Did I say he didn't? There was only one gap in his life, and she filled it. But this isn't the sexy season for athletes. I know, because I've experienced more than once their so-to-speak closed season. When they're not in training, they'll chase you round the bed panting for cooperation. But whisper a word about sex on the eve of a game, and they lock themselves in the bathroom screeching for their team-mates to come and rescue them. I don't know what that

176

girl's idea of intimate relations is, but she must have learned by now that Alexander is too busy worrying about the next scrum to think about sex. It's a girl like me he needs – a girl who'll find her own amusements in between sports events. And here you are, free for the moment, but impervious to all my hints."

"I haven't heard any hints. All I've heard is propositions."

"Good. Then you've been paying attention."

"But *you* haven't. I told you the very first time we met that I liked curves. If you put on a few pounds, we could reconsider the matter."

"I've got a figure that every woman – every elegant woman – would give her all to achieve."

"No doubt. But as I said, I like curves. I am not going to risk being impaled on your hip bones."

"Then you're very ungrateful. Look what you owe me: I may be manoeuvring to get Alexander for myself, but you stand to gain in the end. You could at least give me another drink."

"No, I'm sorry. I'm due at the party."

She sighed.

"Oh, all right. Did we say ten tomorrow morning?"

"Yes."

"Make it nine thirty."

He put her into the lift and then, feeling tired and depressed, went back to his room and carried the glasses to his kitchen. He walked to the telephone and picked up the receiver to ring Dave Forrest and say he was unable after all to go to the party; then he put it down, pulled himself together, had a shower, changed and went down to his car. On the way to Ascot, he replayed in his mind tonight's scene, but with a different cast: send Alexander away with Daphne, keep Gianna to himself.

But she didn't want him. She wanted Alexander.

11

On Sunday morning, Ross rose early, made himself a cup of coffee and was on the road to Downpass by eight o'clock.

It was a morning borrowed from spring; by the time he reached the outskirts of the village, the sun was shining steadily and almost warmly. The windows of Laura's cottage were open. He entered the hall, opened the kitchen door and paused to savour appreciatively the breakfast awaiting him.

"Good morning. Nice welcome," he said, and bent to kiss Laura's cheek.

"You ordered it. Now sit down and enjoy the food. How did David's party go?"

"He was in good form. I thought it was a birthday celebration, but it turned out to be an engagement party."

"They've decided to get married?"

"Yes. About time." He put a package on the dresser. "Present for you."

"Chocolate peppermints?"

"As usual."

"Bless you. I'd eaten my last box."

"Now you can stop eating boxes and start on the contents." He drew a chair up to the table. "I'm starving. Is that an omelette you're preparing to make?"

"An omelette plus. I've been trying out Gianna's mixture, and I think I've got it right. Is skiing for this year definitely off?"

"Yes."

She waited until the milk came to the boil before turning to study his expression.

"You're disappointed?"

"Not really. Once I got that hook in my shin, I knew I'd be off the slopes for some time."

"Anything else on your mind?"

"Yes and no. Alexander's behaving a shade too casually and it's beginning to get on my nerves."

"So long as it doesn't get on Gianna's . . . "

"There are signs that it might. Somebody ought to warn him – he's pushing his luck." He poured himself a cup of coffee. "It's one thing for a girl to have to hang about waiting for a man if he's about his business, but my feeling is that he doesn't see her nearly as often as he could."

"He doesn't have much free time, does he? Rugby, those interviews, writing reports. It isn't as though he could keep regular office hours." She paused. "You don't think he's being got at by Daphne Maxwellton, do you?"

"She's certainly after him, though she hasn't made any impression – so far. But if she really goes after him, she'll get him. Gianna isn't a girl who'll put up a fight."

They sat in silence for a time, and Laura found herself speculating on what the situation would be if Alexander was removed from the scene. Gianna and Ross? She thought it unlikely. They got on well, they saw each other frequently, but if Gianna decided to break with Alexander, she was not a girl who would forget him and switch her affections to another man. Of the extent of Ross' feelings for her she could make no assessment; where women were concerned, she had always found him elusive. He told her as much as he thought was good for her, and kept the rest to himself.

He carried his second cup of coffee into the living room and stood by the fire.

"Leave the clearing-up," he said. "We'll do it together afterwards. Sit down and tell me the local news."

"There's not much. The vicar's two sisters came for a week and caused a stir by genuflecting in church. The doctor has become a grandfather."

"Perhaps that'll put a check on his pursuit of the nurses over at Upleigh Hospital."

"Perhaps."

179

"Any news of Beatrice?"

"Yes. She's trying to form a committee to work with, for, or among, juvenile delinquents. Somehow, I think she's on to something that she'll stick to."

"Has she been to see you?"

"No. James has dropped in once or twice. I think he's happier now that Beatrice spends so much time up in London. Incidentally, he's coming to lunch today. He rang up to ask if I could feed one more, and I said I could. He – Oh heavens, my cake!"

She went hastily to the kitchen, opened the oven door and gave a sigh of relief.

"Just in time." She drew out the cake and turned it on to a wire rack. "Walnut, made specially for Alexander."

He helped her to clear away the breakfast things and then strolled across to his chalet to look for some books he wanted to take back to town. He was still selecting them when he heard Gianna's voice at the open door.

"May I come inside?"

He turned and looked at her. As fresh as the morning, he thought. A woollen suit in a soft shade of green. Hair blowing in the breeze.

"You're early," he said.

"I came round to help Laura to make the lunch. But she sent me away."

"Come in and sit down. I'm sorting books."

She was about to mount the steps of the chalet when she stopped, gave an exclamation of delight and stooped to look at a tiny white flower half-hidden in the grass. Then she sank on her knees and put out a finger to stroke the delicate petals.

"Ross, look. *Perce-neige*. Have you ever seen anything so lovely?"

He thought he had. And now, looking down at her, watching her as she knelt before the little flower, he ceased to delude himself. He was not a friend, an older man anxious to see her happy with Alexander. He was a man in love, a man whose envy of Alexander at this moment was something he could scarcely bear. He loved her. Hopeless though it might prove, he loved her.

180

She rose and entered the room and sat on a low stool watching him as he arranged books in piles.

"Did Laura tell you my father bought a car at last?" she asked him.

"No. Not a racing model, I suppose?"

"No. It's only people like Daphne Maxwellton who buy those." She was silent for a moment. "Do you like her?"

"Like – ?"

"Daphne Maxwellton."

"Oh, her. Yes and no. I don't like her type, but I admire the way she deals with her handicaps."

"What handicaps?"

"Her mother for one. Her father for another. And she's amusing, up to a point."

"Shall I tell you something? She's in love with Alexander."

After the first moment of surprise, he smiled.

"You're quite safe. You got him first."

"Nothing is safe when girls like her want something. At first, I thought it was you she liked. But no, it's Alexander."

"Are you guessing?"

"No. You can see. I mean, I can see."

"Are you worried?"

"No. At least, I don't think so. But – "

"But what?"

She was frowning.

"It's only that Alexander is so . . . so uncomplicated, that he doesn't see what other people are really like. In some ways he's easy to lead, and in other ways impossible. A girl like Daphne Maxwellton could get round him, could . . . entangle him before he knew what was happening. She doesn't like me; she could . . . "

Gianna stopped abruptly. Ross was about to tell her that she was worrying unnecessarily, when he saw that she was weeping quietly. He dropped to his knees beside the stool, took her hands in his and spoke in a soothing tone.

"Snowdrops," he said, "are a sign that spring's on the way. They shouldn't make you cry. Honestly, Gianna, a girl like Daphne mustn't worry you like this."

181

She shook her head and groped for a handkerchief. He shook out his, handed it to her, and she wiped the tears away.

"It isn't her," she said. "It's Alexander. I'm beginning to feel he isn't really in love with me."

"That's nonsense, and you know it."

"Not any more. If he loved me, wouldn't he want to be with me as much as possible? Wouldn't he? Ross, I'm frightened."

"Then don't be." He rose, drew a chair close to her, and sat. "You've nothing to worry about. You and he started off in too much of a rush, that's all. You were bound to come to a cooling-off stage. Alexander is – "

"I said it was Alexander, but it isn't. It's me. At first, I thought I understood how everything was – he liked playing games at weekends, and he had to go away a lot. I was sure I could be the kind of girl who didn't try to stop him from doing what he wanted to do. I was sure I could be happy because he was happy. But I'm not silly, Ross. Even if I love him, I can see things I didn't see at first. More and more I can see that he is just going on with his life as it was before he met me. He hasn't made any room at all for me in his life. I'm on the outside."

She stopped talking and wiped away more tears. Watching her helplessly, he wished Alexander would appear at the door, so that he could manhandle him back to his car, put him into it and send him straight to hell. Pushing his luck? Yes. This looked as though he had pushed it too far. She was intelligent and she was clear-sighted. But she was also in love with someone else, groping for a response in him that would reassure her, and finding nothing.

"I'm sorry, Ross." She dried the last tears angrily. "I'm very sorry to have been so silly."

"If you want to go on crying, I can lend you a shoulder. Any time."

She gave an unsteady laugh.

"I'm all right now. I've just got to stop blaming him when he chooses to do something else instead of being with me. I've got to stop myself from being angry with him. I've been angry with him lately, more and more. I've got to go on seeing him as I first saw him."

"No, you haven't. You've got to see him as he really is. You've got to come to terms with the hard fact that life isn't one long ferry ride with an attractive man who feeds you croissants and honey. You fell in love with the wrappings. Now you've got to look inside and see what's there."

"And if I don't like what's inside?"

"You will. You do."

"Sometimes I don't."

"Every man's got some faults."

"I know. But what I *don't* know is how to get from the outside of his life to the inside."

Ross had no advice to offer. He did not believe that Alexander would change his ways or make room in his life for this new element. And in spite of the anger he was feeling against him, he could not brand the man as totally selfish or insensitive. He had known many of Alexander's type, men who in childhood had found themselves without a secure family background and who, thrown back on themselves, had developed along lines of their own, asking little from others and giving little in return. Alexander could not be likened to Thursday's child; however loving, he was not much disposed to giving. He was in love, but his formative years had been spent at schools in which prowess on the playing fields was regarded as paramount, and any manifestations of love were seen as suspect.

When Gianna said she would go to the crossroads and look out for Alexander, he walked to the gate with her and stood watching until she was out of sight. Then he went back to the chalet, tidied the books he had left lying about and sauntered moodily across to the cottage. Laura was in the kitchen, putting the finishing touches to an appetising-smelling lunch. He glanced round in search of the Sunday newspapers.

"No papers today?" he asked.

"Not yet. They're late. Perhaps the van has broken down again, like Alexander's car. I thought Gianna was with you."

183

"She went to look for Alexander. She's not happy."

"Beginning to have second thoughts?"

"I think so."

"Would it do any good if you said a word to him?"

"My God, no. This is their affair."

She put lettuce into the water-extractor and spun it abstractedly. Taking it out, she spoke casually.

"You don't look as though it was entirely their affair."

"I'm sorry for her, that's all. Damn sorry."

"Is that really all?"

"Yes. Well, no. I feel I'd like to settle the thing in my own mind by writing him off as a self-centred swine. But he isn't. I'd like to think she's one of those women who take whatever their men dish out. But she isn't."

Laura smiled.

"You never liked complicated situations. You always wanted everybody to read the script and stick to it."

"What's wrong with that?"

"Nothing – except that it isn't real life. As far as I know, this is the first check Gianna has ever come up against. She and Alexander are rather alike, in a way: they act first and think afterwards."

"Only he doesn't think."

"She might force him to. Eventually. But in the meantime, there's nothing we can do about it."

"I know. Why the hell did he have to be on that ferry?"

"Fate." She stirred the contents of a saucepan and then turned to glance out of the window. "What's happened to the sun?"

It had vanished, and now the sky, this morning so clear and blue, was obscured by black clouds.

"There's rain on the way," Ross said. "There's James on the way, too."

James was locking the doors of his new car. Holding a mackintosh over his head, he hurried up the path and through the front door Ross was keeping open as the first heavy drops of rain began.

"Just missed the downpour," he said thankfully. "It's hail – just look."

184

Ross, about to shut out the sudden storm, paused to allow Gianna and Alexander to enter. They were taking off their coats when Laura came into the hall to see Jass struggling with the garden gate. She opened the front door at the same moment that Jass, breathless, arrived on the doorstep.

"For heaven's sake!" Laura drew her inside and closed the door. "Look at you – soaking. Give me that mackintosh. The papers could have waited."

"The van was late," Jass panted. "I said I'd bring you the papers, and then it started to hail."

Hailstones were dashing against the windows, falling on to the path and bouncing off again. The wind died down, but the downpour continued. Laura sent Jass into the living room.

"Sit on the hearth-rug and dry off," she directed. "No, don't. Before you do that, ring your mother and tell her I'll give you lunch. You can't go back in this storm."

Jass, overcome by a mixture of joy, pride and the dread of forgetting her table manners, went to the telephone, falling over the cat on the way and missing by inches its vicious scratch of reprisal. In the living room, Alexander was explaining why he had arrived a little later than he had hoped to.

"It was such a grand morning that I got up early and went for a jog," he said. "I went back for what I hoped would be a nice refreshing shower, but no, grandmother in bathroom, grandson locked out. I've discovered why she spends so long in there – she does all the repair work I thought women did in their bedrooms. Hair treatment, facial; generally make yourself beautiful without giving a thought to the queue lined up outside the door. Then I had what passed for breakfast and was about to turn my nose in the direction of Downpass, but halt! Grandmother in trouble. Residents' car not available, kind grandson begged to deposit her for the day with friends in Guildford, only a few miles out of his way – in actual count, twenty-two. Grandson could also pick her up again at seven p.m. How kind, how very kind."

"But you promised to take me out to dinner!" Gianna protested.

185

"I know, love, I know. Did you think I could have forgotten? But telling my grandmother was a fatal move, because she invited herself to join us."

Gianna spoke calmly.

"Then you can leave me out."

He took her hand.

"She won't be a thorn in our flesh much longer, love," he pointed out. "I went along and took a peek at my roof, and apart from the place looking as though it was scheduled for demolition, I ought to be back there in a couple of weeks."

Gianna said nothing. She sat beside Jass on the hearth-rug and stared at the fire, while Ross simply marvelled at how Alexander could hold a treasure in his hands and value it so little. Alexander's eyes at this moment were not on Gianna but on the morning papers, which he was clearly longing to open at the sports page. Laura, interpreting the look, put them out of his reach.

"Lunch is ready," she announced, "but there's time for a quick drink if anyone wants one."

James and Alexander asked for beer, Laura and Gianna had sherry, Jass was given a lemonade and Ross thought the weather a good pretext for giving himself a whisky and soda.

When they were seated round the table, it was Jass and Alexander who contributed most of the conversation. James, as usual, said little. Gianna was almost as silent, but Jass, recovering from the unexpected elevation to the status of guest, regaled the company with highly embroidered tales of her prowess in school, after which it was Alexander's turn to give his usual monologue on the wonders of rugby. Laura felt that Ross should have made an effort to introduce a subject of more general interest, but he was absorbed in wondering what effect Alexander's latest lapse would have on Gianna.

The meal over, they gathered round the fire for coffee. Laura leaned back and relaxed. James sat beside her, quiet and content. Jass, finishing a cup of hot milk laced with a teaspoonful of coffee, sighed with contentment and spoke reluctantly.

"I gotta go," she said. "My Mum's going to make a cake, and she said I had to help her. We're going to put a crib on it – the same one we put on the Christmas cake – because she's Mum's cousin and she's going to have a baby at Easter. A girl, it's going to be."

"That's nice," said Laura lazily.

"It's going to come on Easter Monday, the doctor said, and if it does, you know what they're going to call it?"

Nobody had any idea.

"They're going to call it Easter. Don't you think that's silly?"

"It's unusual," Gianna commented. "What happens if it doesn't come on Easter Monday?"

"Then it's going to be called Lily. Lily's all right, but Easter! When she goes to school, all the other girls will laugh at her."

"Some girls are called April or May or June," Laura pointed out. "I suppose it's the same sort of thing."

"Not quite," said Gianna. "My birthday's in September, but my parents didn't call me Harvest."

"But if they had, Harvest Hargreaves would've sounded nice," Jass said. "I'm September, too – the fourth. What are you?"

"The first. We're practically twins."

This mild joke had the effect of sending Jass into a fit of giggles so prolonged that Ross judged it time to give her her almost-dry mackintosh and send her home. The weather had cleared. Alexander asked Gianna if she felt like going for a walk.

"All right," she said.

There was no noticeable enthusiasm in her tone, but Alexander had succeeded in getting hold of the newspapers and was glancing through the pages that interested him. Then he folded them and joined Gianna in the hall.

"If we don't come back to eat my walnut cake" – he kissed Laura's cheek – "thank you for the lovely lunch and the drinks and the welcome and the fire." He waved a hand at Ross. "So long."

Ross waited until they had gone out of sight and then

187

returned to the living room expecting to find James ready to depart. But though he had risen, James was showing no signs of leaving. He was standing with his back to the room, staring out at the drenched lawn. Something about his stillness puzzled Ross, and he turned to look enquiringly at Laura.

But her attitude, he found, was even stranger than James'. She was standing staring at the fire, and he saw that she was very pale. Looking at her, he felt stirring within him the familiar stab of apprehension that since his boyhood had always gripped him whenever he sensed that something was troubling her. He had become aware of his affection for Laura through the fear that rose in him whenever he saw her physically or emotionally upset. And this tendency to worry about her had persisted through the years.

"Anything wrong?" he asked her.

She came out of her abstraction and looked at him for a moment as though wondering who he was. Then she shook her head.

"No. Nothing," she answered.

James turned slowly from the window, and his face looked grey.

"What's the matter, James?" Ross' voice was sharp with anxiety. "Is there anything I can do?"

"No." James cleared his throat. "No, thank you. This is . . . this is something between Laura and myself."

Ross went towards the door.

"If you need me," he said, "I'll be over at – "

"No, Ross." Laura put out a hand to stop him. "Please don't go." She addressed James. "Anything you say to me," she told him, "can be said to Ross too. But there's no need for you to say anything."

"Yes," James said. "There is. Laura," he told Ross, "is puzzled about a discrepancy in dates. Some chance remarks spoken after lunch made her realise . . . The matter can't be left there."

"Yes," said Laura. "It can."

"No, Laura." It was the first time Ross had heard him speak firmly. "No," he repeated. "I was watching you

188

when Gianna spoke of dates, and I saw your expression change from being merely puzzled to . . . " He turned to Ross. "My last letter to Laura, written from Nice twenty-three years ago," he said, "informed her that I was married in April. She heard Gianna say a few moments ago that her birthday is on the first of September. She is owed an explanation."

"Why can't we leave things where they are – in the past?" Laura asked.

"For two reasons," James replied, and once again Ross noted the unusual authority in his tone. "First, as I have just said, I owe you an explanation. Second, it will be more than a relief, it will be a godsend to be able to speak frankly at last. You must believe me when I say that carrying the secret all these years has been an almost insupportable burden. There has never been anyone to whom I could mention it, nobody who – at the time – could give me advice, and nobody, afterwards, to whom I could explain, or try to explain what had taken place. Now that it has come into the open, you must let me tell you the truth. You must let me explain – if I can find an explanation."

He broke off and gazed for some moments out of the window, as though seeking words. Then he continued.

"I know very little of what lay behind the circumstances of my marriage. Much of it was far from clear to me at the time, and hasn't become much clearer as the years have gone by. I was told certain facts, and I made myself believe them. I could have – should have – demanded to know more, but I found it impossible. I hadn't the courage to voice my doubts. I . . ."

His voice faltered. He was trembling. Ross drew up a chair, guided him into it, poured out a small measure of brandy and handed the glass to him. "One sip at a time," he said. "And if Laura wants to leave the past in the past, why get yourself into this state by recalling it now?"

Laura came to sit beside him.

"If it'll make you feel better to talk, James, then do. But twenty-three years ago you told me all I needed to know. You told me you were married."

"To tell you, to write and tell you, was a mistake. But when I wrote that letter, I hardly knew what I was writing. I felt a compulsion – an obligation – to be honest and send you the news at once – but I should have waited. By the time I wrote to Beatrice, I had had time to think, and so I told her nothing about my marriage. But you had my letter, you knew what I had said in it, and when Gianna spoke just now of her birthday, you knew that there was something wrong, something missing, something I hadn't told you. Explaining it all to you now is like lifting a weight from my heart."

His heart, or his conscience? Ross wondered. He was standing in the archway, and he had begun to guess what James was about to reveal. He wondered if Laura had any inkling.

James was looking down at his untouched drink, turning the glass slowly in his hands.

"You know the beginning," he said. "She was enchanting, as a child and as a young woman. I was disappointed to find she was still away from home when I got to Nice on that last journey, but her father told me she would soon be back, because her musical ability had proved to be less than she had at first hoped. She had lost heart and decided to give up her studies. She came home. I was shocked, stunned – as was everyone else – by the change in her. She was no longer the laughing, carefree girl she had been when she went away.

"It was her father who told me that she was pregnant. She had fallen in love, something had gone wrong, and she had come home to have her child. Those facts would mean little or nothing in a present-day household. Parents have grown used to unmarried girls living free and unrestricted lives. In today's world, babies born out of wedlock present nothing approaching the problem, the scandal, and the misery they used to cause. But I am speaking of a time and a place in which concealment was considered necessary. In those days . . ."

He stopped, and seemed to lose himself in a dream.

"You asked her to marry you?" Laura asked at last.

"No. It never once occurred to me to do that. I felt

190

bitterly sorry for her: I would have helped her if I could have thought of any way of doing so – but marriage to her didn't cross my mind. Not then."

"Her father?"

"Yes. I said nothing to anyone of my engagement to you. He regarded me as a free man. He pointed out that I had known and been fond of his daughter almost all her life, that if I married her, I could take her to England and make her happy. So after thinking about it for a week or so, I asked her if she would marry me. She agreed – but she wouldn't consider living in England. I was relieved when she made this one condition, because by that time, I was beginning to think more clearly and realised that in the circumstances I wouldn't, or couldn't, return home. Her uncle Philippe – her father's brother – said that his wedding present to us would be a house in Biarritz. I was reluctant to accept it, partly because I could afford to buy a house of my own, but chiefly because I didn't like him. He worked in a Government office, and was the only prosperous member of the family. But he was devoted to his niece and she accepted his offer. She placed far more reliance on him than on her father – or on me. She asked me to leave everything in Philippe's hands, and I did. He saw to every detail connected with the marriage. And he did more: knowing his niece's wish that her child should never know the circumstances of the birth, he promised that she need have no fears on the matter. He would attend to it. The papers were forwarded to me at Biarritz. When I looked at them, I found that the date of the marriage was not given as April, but January."

There was an awkward silence. Ross longed to ask what he felt to be the obvious question – but this was not his affair. He said nothing. It was Laura who asked it at last.

"The baby's father?"

James shook his head.

"You must believe this: I never asked, and I was never told. Perhaps Philippe knew. Her father, I'm almost certain, did not. Nobody but you, Laura, would believe that I could never bring myself to find out who the man was. Nobody but you, who knew me well, would believe that I preferred not to know. To know – so I reasoned – would bring him close, bring him into what might in time become a happy trio, a close-knit little family. I preferred to ask nothing and to say nothing. Can you understand that?"

"Yes," Laura said gently. "I can understand."

"When the baby was born, we were happy, though my wife was never again the light-hearted girl I had first known. She was fond of me, she loved our daughter and she knew that I regarded Gianna as my own child."

Once more, James fell into a reverie. His drink was untouched. Presently he lifted the glass and slowly drained it. He put it on the table beside him, and rose slowly to his feet.

"I'm sorry," he told Laura, "for being what I am. I'm sorry for my weakness, for my cowardice, for my secrecy. I'm grateful to you, more grateful than I can say, for your kindness and patience and forgiveness. You and Ross are the only people in the world to whom I have told any of this, and I know that it will remain, as it has all these years, a secret."

"Did you never think of telling Gianna?" Laura asked.

"Never. What could I say? That she was the child of an unknown father? No. I couldn't bear to lose what I have now – the love of a daughter. If I ceased to be her father, what would I be? Her mother never wanted Gianna to be told, and I will never tell her."

He said nothing more. He held Laura's hand in his for some moments and then allowed Ross to help him on with his coat and see him to his car.

When Ross returned to Laura, he found to his surprise that she was preparing tea. She spoke in a voice of desperation.

"I know it's too early," she said, "but I must do *something*. My head's going round. I thought a cup of tea might clear it."

He sat at the kitchen table.

"Do you want to swallow the story whole," he asked, "or do you want to examine some of the holes in it?"

She turned to look at him with a frown.

"Has it got holes?" she asked.

"Several." He got up and put cups and saucers on to a tray. "Do you believe he would have been as easily manipulated as he made out?"

Her answer was unhesitating.

"Yes, I do. And if you knew him as well as I do, you'd believe it too."

"Do you think she failed to make the grade as a pianist, or was that an excuse to account to the neighbours for her sudden return?"

"I don't know. According to Gianna, her mother never resumed her piano-playing, so perhaps it was true that her talent had at first been exaggerated. It couldn't have been pleasant to go all that way to study, only to find that you hadn't got the makings."

"You agree that while she was away, she didn't spend all her time playing scales and arpeggios?"

"Yes. But just think: a lovely young girl, all those handsome Italian men, and music, music, music. Remember that she came from what seems to have been a pretty narrow family circle in Nice."

"You agree that her uncle Philippe fiddled the date of the marriage?"

"That's where my head starts going round. How could he have done that? It would have been a criminal act."

"It would and it was."

"Wouldn't James have had to register the marriage at the British Consulate in Nice?"

"Not necessarily. What he was bound to do was register it at the civil registry in Nice. Would you like to bet that Uncle Philippe was the head of the department? He registered the marriage under a false date, or he altered the date after James made the registration."

"That's only guesswork."

"Most of it is guesswork. Weak and woolly though James is, all he had to say when approached by the father with the marriage proposal was : 'Sorry, I've just become engaged to a girl in England.' So why didn't he?"

"Because he is – and was – as you said: weak and woolly."

"You really believe that he could marry a woman and

193

take on her illegitimate child and never make a move to find out who the father was?"

"People who adopt very often aren't told the identity of their child's natural parents. Do you think he was in love with Gianna's mother?"

"God knows. And speaking of God, let's give thanks that you didn't marry James Hargreaves."

"I did that twenty-three years ago."

"Not that I think you would have married him, anyway. If he'd come back as planned, you would have had time to think, and if you're given time to think, you're not bad at it."

"Thank you. But there's a flaw in that argument: he married her because he felt sorry for her, and how do you know I wouldn't have married him for the same reason?"

"I've just told you – you would have had time to think. From what my father told me, you needed time to think before you married him. Every time you mention him, you stress his gentle nature. But that was only his manner, not his true character. You married him when you found that he had reliability, horse sense, humour and moral strength – all the things you wouldn't have found in James."

"Poor James."

"Poor James? Money, a lovely step-daughter, discreet friends like you and me to share his burdens, a sister to save him from himself . . . poor James?"

"Do you think he's right in keeping the secret from Gianna?"

"Yes. He's nowhere near perfect as a father, but he's better than a randy music student who seduces innocent girls under Italian skies."

She handed him the tray to carry to the living room.

"Perhaps you're sorry," she suggested, "that you didn't take up the study of music?"

12

Laura passed a restless night worrying about the events of that afternoon. Before falling asleep, she had come to the conclusion that notwithstanding Ross' opinion of the unknown Uncle Philippe, there was no sound reason for labelling him a crook. And there was even less reason to imagine that pressure had been put on James; very little pressure, she thought, would have been needed to persuade him to marry a lovely young girl he had known and liked since her childhood. Had he fallen in love with her? It was hard to imagine him carried away by passion, but it was equally difficult to account for the speed with which he had acted – James, who throughout his life had been incapable of any impulsive action, who had needed time before making any decision, however trivial. He had arrived in Nice, abruptly broken a previous engagement, married, left Nice and settled in Biarritz. It sounded almost impetuous, and was certainly out of character. Perhaps Uncle Philippe had, after all, engineered the whole deception, changing the date of the marriage and posting the papers to James, leaving him with no alternative but to accept an accomplished fact.

But it was all surmise and speculation. Only one person – James – knew all the details, and nobody would ever ask him to disclose them. He had unveiled the past; he had disinterred a long-buried secret. Now he felt safe, secure and relieved. Let him remain so.

As the days went by, Laura could believe that things were as they had been. James came and went, and they talked – of everything but the past. Gianna bought a car, found an apartment but attended no more games of rugby. Beatrice inspected a number of youth clubs and pronounced them all incompetently organised. Walter and the vicar met and discoursed on Buddha. Life flowed on, leaving the past still farther behind, and bringing nearer the evening of Pierre's recital.

This took place in a central London concert hall. Ross drove Laura up from Downpass, and on entering the auditorium found that it was still half-empty. Perhaps Pierre's claim to have sold all the tickets had been exaggerated. But before the time came for the lights to be dimmed, the hall was filled to capacity, only one or two seats here and there left vacant by probable latecomers.

Ross was seated beside Laura, and one by one he managed to locate the scattered members of their party. Pierre's sisters were in the second row, with two vacant places behind them. These, he guessed, must be reserved for Gianna and Alexander, of whom there was as yet no sign. As the minutes went by, he became increasingly anxious, for the doors would be closed to those who came late, and would not open until the interval.

Laura drew his attention to an elderly woman in a black lace dress seated a few rows in front of them.

"Alexander's grandmother," she said.

He took in the impeccable grooming of the aged gentlemen seated on either side of her.

"A credit to Belgrave Towers," he commented. "And look who's in the third row, on the right-hand side of the gangway."

It was Daphne Maxwellton who, like Mrs Rannoch, was accompanied by two male escorts. Their voices could be heard raised in argument as they arranged and rearranged their order of seating.

Laura, looking round at the members of the audience, thought they could not, on the whole, be considered a well-dressed assembly. She guessed the majority to be students; they wore jeans and crumpled shirts and had long, wild-looking locks. Deciding their sex was sometimes difficult, too, but occasionally a few bushy beards gave a clue. She envied the informal appearance of the girls, comparing their casual outfits to the staid and constricting suits in which at their age she had accompanied her father to concerts.

It was almost time for the lights to be lowered. The noise in the auditorium gradually lessened and then ceased, giving way to an expectant hush. All eyes were on the dark green curtain hiding the platform. But there was still no sign of Gianna or Alexander.

"They're cutting it fine," he whispered uneasily to Laura.

It could not be transport trouble, he thought. Alexander was to have lunched at Simone and Denise's flat and was then to be driven to the concert in Gianna's new car. There had been a party at the flat last night, which Ross had not attended, preferring instead to drive down to stay with Laura for the night.

"Here they are," Laura said.

As she spoke, they saw Gianna and Alexander enter and go hurriedly along the aisle to the vacant seats behind Pierre's sisters. The doors were closed, the lights dimmed; the curtain parted, revealing a stage empty save for an imposing black grand piano. Moments later, Pierre and his accompanist entered. There was a prolonged burst of applause and then sudden silence. Pierre bowed to his accompanist and raised his violin.

It was, Ross acknowledged, playing of the highest order. Pierre, eyes half-closed, his thin, tall form swaying slightly, was lost to everything but the music. The audience, intent, unmoving, was held by the brilliance of his execution. But though Ross realised he was listening to a master, he also knew that the music itself had no meaning for him. He found himself responding to it as he did to orchestras playing complex works: with admiration but without emotion. Though Laura, beside him, had a still, rapt look.

There were two works before the interval; there were to be three after it. Pierre returned to the stage several times to acknowledge the enthusiastic applause, but played no encores. The curtain fell, the lights went up and the audience streamed slowly out to the bar. Ross, steering Laura through the throng, felt a tap on his shoulder and turned to find Gianna and Alexander standing behind them.

197

"Don't go through there," Alexander said. "That's the bar for the hoi polloi. We're the privileged section of this audience. Lead the way, Gianna love."

She took them to a quiet room off the foyer. Here on a large central table were drinks to which they could help themselves. Alexander was in his usual exuberant mood, but Ross thought that Gianna looked pale and strained, and hated Alexander for showing no sign of having noticed.

"You nearly got shut out," Ross said to her. "What made you so late?"

"Alexander," she answered.

"Well yes, it was my fault in a way," Alexander admitted. "I – Oh hello, Simone. Aren't you going backstage to see Pierre?"

"Never during a concert," Simone explained. "He won't see anybody until the end. Tell me, Alexander, is the music critic from your paper here? I saw several from the other – "

"I'm standing in for him," Alexander said.

"But – "

"I know what you're going to say – that I'm not capable of doing it. You're right; I'm not even going to attempt it. Gianna's going to tell me what to write, and I'll send in the report accordingly."

"Your grandmother is here – did you see her?"

"I pretended not to. What would you like to drink?"

The room had become rather crowded. All those present were friends of Pierre and his sisters, or friends of friends. The talk was solely about the recital and this kept Alexander silent for almost five minutes; but then he saw, over intervening heads, a man he recognised.

"Look – there's Roger Conyers," he said to Gianna.

"Who's Roger Conyers?"

"He's a rugby international. What's he doing here?"

Simone supplied the answer.

"He loves music, that's why he's here. He's not like you – he can find room in his life for more than rugby. He plays the oboe."

"He didn't play the oboe when we were at school

198

together," Alexander said. "He played scrum-half. I must go and have a word with him."

Drink in hand, he elbowed his way through the crowd and joined Roger Conyers. The meeting between the two was loud and cheerful, Alexander making it clear to all that he considered playing the oboe a less meritorious pursuit than playing for England.

"How's the Mayfleet going?" Roger asked.

"Fine, fine. Why don't you come down someday?"

"I will. You've never won that shield."

"No. But this year, with luck, we will."

Gianna had come to join them. Alexander took her hand and drew her closer.

"Meet a real player, love," he said. "I'll take you to see him on the field one day." He turned back to Roger. "I saw that match you played in Tonbridge. I was on my way back from a job and I took time off to watch."

"It was a scratch team. We did our best, but we weren't good enough."

"There were some good moments, though. You – Yes, love. I'm coming."

"The bell has gone," Gianna said. "We should go back to our seats."

"Just one second," Alexander begged. He addressed Roger. "Remember that scrum on the halfway line, fifteen yards in, when – "

" – when it was our put-in? Yes. The ball was whipped out to the fly-half and he got going like a machine. My God, he moved! For a few beautiful moments there was the kind of line-up you dream about but seldom see. Then the damned fool of a centre kicked straight into touch, and after that, it was the beginning of the end."

"I wondered why you didn't – Yes, love; I'm ready. You go ahead and I'll follow you in twenty seconds."

She turned and walked back to Ross and Laura. With them, she entered the auditorium. They could hear Alexander's voice as he and Roger Conyers made their way slowly towards the hall.

"I thought it would have been a good idea if you'd made

199

one change in the lineout. If you'd put your jumper at number seven, it might have – "

"It wouldn't have made much difference to the final score."

"I suppose not. Well, I suppose we'd better get back to the music."

"You're still hanging on to your drink," Roger pointed out.

"So I am. Go ahead; I'll get rid of the glass."

He walked to the bar and put down the glass. When he returned, there was no sign of Roger or of anybody else. The doors were closed. He knocked softly, and then with more force.

"Hey, let me in," he demanded.

There was no response. He stood in indecision for some moments, and then with a philosophic shrug went back to the bar and asked for another drink.

"A strong one," he requested. "I'm in trouble. Deep trouble."

When the concert ended, Ross found him hunched over the counter of the bar, which had closed shortly after the interval. People were shuffling slowly towards the exit, step by step, shoulder to shoulder. Soon the hall had emptied; only a few attendants remained, clearing debris, closing up.

Alexander looked up and spoke.

"I suppose she's angry?"

"What d'you expect?"

"Where is she?"

"With the others in Pierre's room. They're all going on to this celebration dinner. I've got orders to get you there."

Alexander did not move. This was the first time Ross had seen him deflated, but he was too angry to feel any sympathy. He had seen Gianna's face as she returned to her seat, leaving Alexander and Roger Conyers together, and the expression on it – helpless, defeated – was still clear in his mind.

"I don't want to go to the dinner," Alexander said. "She'll be surrounded by that French lot. I won't be able to see her alone."

200

"I don't think she wants to see you alone."

"I suppose not." He stared at Ross. "I suppose you think I'm a damned fool."

"To a mere spectator like myself, you appear to be off your head. You're unbalanced; nine-tenths of you is dedicated to the Mayfleet Club; the remaining tenth is parcelled out between your job, your interviews and your reports. God knows where you fitted falling in love."

"Ross, I swear to you – "

"Save it. Are you coming?"

"No. Not yet. I've been sitting here trying to sort it all out. And all that's emerged is that I'm what I am, and I don't see what the hell I can do about *that*."

"You could try thinking of Gianna instead of concentrating on yourself."

"Do you imagine that I *don't* think of her? I love her. I thought we could get married and settle down happily together. But now . . . I'm not so sure, and I've a feeling she's not so sure either. Loving each other, that's fine. All that's wrong is that I can't see any way of changing myself from what I am into what she – and everybody else – thinks I ought to become. I'm not making excuses for myself. All I'm saying is that somewhere, at some time, I was poured into a mould and I set – hard. I thought I was normal enough; a good rugby player who worked to get the game going round the county. I never, before meeting Gianna, saw a girl I wanted. I did my share of sleeping around, usually when I was a bit high after a team dinner, but the next morning, I'd forgotten all about it and slotted back into what I thought of as my regular life. And now I'm faced with a choice: to change myself into someone else, God knows how, or to let Gianna send me to hell, which she's undoubtedly ready to do."

"It needn't be a radical change. All you need to do is put her in the forefront and not the background of your mind. Have you any idea of the way you treat her? What other man would have left her to go back to her seat alone tonight while he stayed behind rehashing the history of a game? My God, isn't there any other theme you can discourse on?

201

Don't you ever feel the need to get off a games field and look at what's going on in the world? In a few years, you're going to be a monumental bore, droning on non-stop about long-forgotten matches. You're as blind as a bat not to see that Gianna's running out of excuses for you. Do you think I enjoyed this recital any more than you did? Do you think I enjoy being dragged to concerts by Laura? I go because it pleases her, and I stick it as well as I can and feel happy because she's happy."

"That's all very well." Alexander pushed his fingers through his hair in a gesture of desperation. "That's all very fine. But it isn't only the music. There are other things I find hard to take."

"Such as?"

"Well, this attitude they've all got – Gianna and Simone and company – towards food. When I go to their flat, hungry and hoping for a quick bite, I have to sit and watch them go through a series of complicated arrangements to produce a meal which might win prizes in a chefs' competition, but which, for all that, isn't really up my gastronomic street. When I'm by myself, my idea of a meal is some ham or cheese between a couple of hunks of brown bread, washed down with a pint of beer. That's what I give myself in my own flat and that's what satisfies me. If I want a blow-out, I go round the corner to a restaurant and order a steak and kidney pie. And then there's the matter of language. I speak good French, but it isn't equal to the idiomatic exchanges I have to listen to at Simone's. It wears me down. When you're with a girl you love, you want to relax, be yourself, be at ease, be happy, and not exist on your toes all the time. And something else again: the difference in nationality, which didn't strike me at first, but is beginning to. With a girl brought up in this country, I can make references, bring up ideas, talk, as it were, the same language, share the same background. With Gianna, I have to go back and explain what I've been saying. It sounds trivial, but it tends to emphasise more and more the gap between us. So how do I deal with that?"

"All you have to do – "

Ross stopped, certain that nothing he could say would alter or improve the situation. But it was some time before he could get Alexander away, as the thought of facing Gianna was filling him with foreboding.

"She won't look at me. She won't speak to me. I'll have to sit there listening to Pierre's praises being sung in French."

But when the two latecomers arrived at the restaurant and joined the rest of the party, they received a greeting from Gianna that seemed cordial enough. On their arrival, she was seated at a small table in the bar with Pierre and his sisters. She raised a hand in greeting.

"You're late," she called. "But you've time for one drink if you're quick."

She spoke in French. At the neighbouring tables, round which the rest of the company were seated, no English could be heard. Laura, hemmed in by the accompanist and his friends, was doing her best to contribute to the conversation, but Ross saw a slight look of strain on her face. His glance met Gianna's and he felt certain that she was going to be graciousness itself. However, she was obviously not going to give Alexander a chance to get near her.

This was confirmed when they went into dinner; he was certain she had made a last-minute change in the seating, for she was at the head of the table with Pierre, while he and Alexander were relegated to places at the other end, separated from one another by Daniel Rekovitch's stout Swiss wife. Laura was opposite, but the noise of conversation and the clashing of crockery and cutlery prevented them from speaking to her.

When the toast to Pierre had been drunk, and he had made a brief speech in reply, the company rose. Alexander joined Ross and spoke gloomily.

"D'you suppose she'll let me take her home?"

"You've nothing to take her home in. You haven't got your car and you can't borrow mine because I'm taking Laura back to Downpass."

"I've got to talk to Gianna."

"You won't get a chance tonight. She'll go back to the flat with Simone and – "

"I've got to talk to her. Tell her that, Ross, will you? Just one word."

When Ross had an opportunity to get near Gianna, he did his best.

"No. No, Ross. There's nothing I could say that would do any good. Tomorrow – perhaps."

"All this needs is patience, Gianna."

"No." Her tone was quiet, but firm. "Patience isn't enough. You can tell him, if you want to, that when the concert was over, Daphne Maxwellton came up to me and said I wasn't to worry; she would send a review to Alexander's newspaper herself. It wasn't said in kindness. I wanted to say to her that she could have him, that she was welcome to him – but I didn't say anything. Take him away, Ross. And tomorrow . . . I don't know."

"Will you meet him early, before you go to your classes?"

"No."

"Will you have lunch with him?"

"No. But I would like to have lunch with you. I only have an hour, but it would be enough for me to tell you how I feel and what I'm going to do. But take him away now."

Ross gave a toned-down version of this exchange to Alexander, and then offered him a lift to Belgrave Towers.

It was uncanny to drive with a totally silent Alexander. He said nothing whatsoever until they arrived at the Towers, and then he got out of the car and with a muttered word of thanks, walked away.

"I wish I could feel sorry for him," Laura said. "But all I can think is that it serves him right. He's been asking for this for a long time." She sat pondering for a few moments. "A suitable punishment for him would be to marry him off to that Maxwellton girl."

"He's hardly in her financial bracket."

"He will be, when he gets his inheritance. He's good at his job, and she'd see that he got to the top."

"She won't be able to do that if he gets that sports complex job in Scotland."

"Oh yes, she will. She wants him, so she'll go after him. Wait and see. Did you enjoy your evening?"

"It was a good dinner."

"The recital wasn't bad, either – but you wouldn't have noticed that. Didn't you like the pieces Pierre played?"

"Not much."

"I give up. You're a . . . What's a Philistine?"

"Among other things, a person of no culture."

"Then you're a Philistine."

"Thank you. I've got a lunch-hour meeting with Gianna tomorrow."

"Did you tell Alexander that?"

"No. If there's anything to tell him, I'll get in touch with him tomorrow evening."

Ross left Downpass early on the following morning and drove to his flat. Before leaving for his office, he ordered a cold lunch from the kitchens.

Shortly before one o'clock, he called for Gianna at her college. He took her back to his flat and carried the food from the service hatch to a table in the living room.

"Hungry?" he asked.

"No. I think I'm going to cry. Will you mind much?"

"I won't mind at all, so long as you eat, too. They charge extra for sending food up to the flats."

She managed a smile, but tears were beginning to flow. Her voice, however, remained steady.

She helped herself to cold chicken and salad, but made no move to eat.

"Talk," he urged. "All I have to say is that Alexander's figuring out how he can make himself into some other kind of man."

She shook her head.

"He can't. And I can't change myself into any other kind of woman. And that's the trouble, Ross. That's what has gone wrong. We haven't" – her voice faltered and she paused until she had it under control – "we haven't one ideal, one subject, one idea in common. There *is* something between us – we both recognised that on the way over from

205

France. It didn't happen in the way you think it did. We weren't being childish or romantic. We didn't really have to begin to know each other – there was something there already, and we responded to it. But after that, everything began to change. Slowly, since then, we've been finding out that we haven't any common ground to meet on. He wants, he needs . . . well, you know him. I need books, music, study – I like to study. I need friends who are . . . I don't want to say cultured, because that would sound like making too much claim for them or for myself, but people who want their minds to go on developing, people who look on games only as good exercise to be enjoyed in moderation." She paused, took a forkful of food and stared at it unseeingly. "For weeks, I've tried to find somewhere in Alexander's life where I can make a place for myself, but it's been no use. Half the time, he doesn't listen to what I'm saying, and the other half, he doesn't understand what I'm talking about. All these weeks, I've been realising slowly and very painfully that you can't make a life with someone unless you have something besides love to keep you together. They say love is everything, don't they? It isn't. It's the base, but there has to be, for life day after day, year after year, something besides love. Do you agree with that?"

"Yes. Will you please eat something?"

"I will in a minute." She dried her tears, and more began to fall. "I'm telling you this for two reasons. First, because I lay awake last night thinking about it, and I wanted to say it out loud to clear my mind. Next, because you were the only person I wanted to talk to. You saw the beginning, now you can see the end."

She stopped, unable to go on.

"Look, Gianna." He spoke pleadingly. "You're tired, you're – "

He was about to use the word overwrought, but nothing could have been more controlled than her manner, nothing clearer than her reasoning.

"I said the end, Ross." She spoke gently. "I know how much you like him. I know how much you've tried to help us both – but it's no use. I know it, and I think Alexander knows it too."

"You could see him, talk to him."

"I'm going to do both, this evening. But it's the end. Please believe that. This is the answer to weeks of trying to make myself believe that everything would be all right. I love him. He'll always be a . . . a special person. I believe that in his way he loves me; but I'm certain he has realised what I've come to know – that we'll never make what he would call a team." She gave a long, relieved sigh. "Now I've told you. Now I can have some lunch."

She did not eat much, but she did not go away hungry. She spent a few moments in his bathroom removing the marks of tears from her cheeks, and then he drove her back to her college. He got out to open the door on her side; she took a step towards the building, paused, came back, slipped her arms round him and kissed him fleetingly on the cheek.

"Thank you for everything." She released him. "You know something? Perhaps, after all, the best way to know a man is to push an iron hook into his leg."

Ross stood watching her go up the steps and disappear into the groups of returning students; then he went back to his office. His mind was filled with conflicting and confusing thoughts. He was sure that she would not alter her decision to bring the affair to an end. He believed that Alexander would accept it. It was over, and he was sorry, because the beginning had had a certain beauty; a young man and a young woman seen in the light of love.

He wanted to telephone Laura, but on reaching his office, his secretary, the bony, straight-backed Miss Streetham, told him that a lady was waiting in his room.

"A Miss Maxwellton, Mr Mirren. I asked her to come with me to the waiting room, but she – "

"That's all right, Miss Streetham."

He opened his door and Daphne greeted him from the depths of an armchair.

"Had a nice lunch?"

"Yes, thank you. That chair you're sitting on is for clients only."

207

"Which is just what I am. This visit is strictly business. But before we get down to business, how did things go at the celebration dinner last night?"

"It was extremely successful."

"Did that girl really talk to Alexander after he skipped the second half of the act?"

"Yes, she did. Now I can ask what brings you here."

"I told you – business."

"Kindly state it."

"Certainly, sir. You must have heard that the *Newshound* offices are to be altered. My father even moved some of the occupants out of their rooms in preparation for the changes, but that's as far as he got. Now he's made up his mind – or I've made it up for him. The project is going ahead, and we need an architect. No change to the exterior is planned, but the interior is to be brought into the twentieth century. Lower ceilings, more modern stairs, not so many useless corridors – you know the kind of thing. My father left the choice of architect to me, so I chose you."

"Thank you. But we're pretty busy at the moment."

"I daresay. But think of the publicity: Morris and Mirren chosen to redesign the offices of *Newshound*. Nice big head-lines."

"Is this another plot?"

"How did you guess? It means that you have to come into my parlour, but apart from that, it's a job I'd be keen to do if I were an architect. You'd have a free hand."

He walked slowly to his desk and sat. A job was a job, and he enjoyed transforming the interior of old buildings. The money would be useful, and a project of this kind brought in plenty.

"I'd have to put it to – "

" – your partners or seniors or colleagues. Having done that, when can you come round and do a preliminary survey, so to speak?"

He pressed a bell for his secretary, asked her for his list of engagements and studied it.

"How about today week?" he asked Daphne.

"For the survey, yes, if you like. But what's the matter

with dropping in and taking a look at what I'd like done in Alexander's room?"

The secretary withdrew, and Daphne stared after her retreating back.

"How old is she?" she asked when the door closed.

"Between forty and forty-five. She worked for my father."

"And for your grandfather, from the look of her."

"She's extremely efficient, and we're all very fond of her."

"No, you're not. If you were, you'd do something to improve her terrible dress sense."

"She's always very neat."

"Send her outfit to Oxfam and I'll take her out shopping and refit her."

"Sorry. We like her as she is."

"I don't. Every time I see a woman dressed like that, I get militant. Perhaps you're too stingy with her salary."

"Her salary is more than adequate."

"God, you're in a pompous mood today. I bet something's happened, something you won't tell me about."

"Will you please go away and let me get on with my work?"

"You don't know what you're sending me back to. Alexander only looked in for an hour, but he managed to cast a general gloom all the same. Are you sure that girl forgave him?"

"Ask him. Do you want to be shown out, or thrown out?"

She rose reluctantly.

"I can take a hint. Will you do the job or won't you?"

"I will."

"Good. That's one plot that didn't misfire. Goodbye – for now."

13

Laura was neither surprised nor sad to learn that Gianna had given up Alexander. She had always felt, she told Ross, that there had been something not quite real about the affair from the outset.

"That's what's called being wise after the event," he answered.

"I know – but it's true. Love and commitment sprang up too quickly, before they had a chance to get to know each other. And they were so different in every way. Do you think he'll take it hard?"

"He won't have time to brood. He's been short-listed for that Edinburgh post, and he's been asked to go up for an interview with the promoters."

"Do you think he'll get the job?"

"He stands a good chance. He's a Scot, he comes from a well-known family, and you only have to look at him to see 'Sport' written all over him. He'll be all right. It's Gianna who's taken a knock."

But how hard a knock, he was unable to judge. He saw her almost daily. He waited outside her college every evening and drove her to his flat for tea or a drink, whichever she chose. They talked, but she could not as yet mention Alexander without losing some of her self-control. It was not, she explained, just a matter of missing him.

"It's looking back and realising what a fool I made of myself. To arrive in England and say to everyone: 'I'm in love with this man after one hour' – how could I have done that?"

"It was true. You loved him."

"But to lose one's heart is one thing. To lose one's head . . . and that's exactly what I did. It wasn't like me. If you knew me better, if you had known me before I met him, you would have thought I was sensible, what my father called level-headed. I told you I was always in love, but that only meant that there were men who danced well, or played good tennis, or were nice escorts, and so for a time one pretended to be in love – it was nothing. So with Alexander, I was unprepared."

"I suppose you know he's up in Edinburgh and is likely to get the job there?"

"Yes, I know. Daphne Maxwellton telephoned to tell me. She was angry – she wants him here in London. She said, speaking very frankly as usual, that she would like him back in London and me back in France."

"You're not going back, are you?" He heard but could not disguise the note of anxiety in his voice.

"Not until my classes finish – there is a break for Easter, and I plan to go back to Paris then."

"But you'll come back?"

"For a time, yes. I like the flat I've just found. Would you like to come with me to see it?"

"Of course."

"It is rather a long way out – Roehampton. But I can see the river from my windows, and I like that. And there is a balcony with a small, a very small, garden at the back."

He drove her out and they inspected the flat together. It was in a block overlooking the river; there were only four storeys, which she found a relief after the number of high-rise blocks she had been shown. Ross thought that the rent of this flat was excessive, but she seemed to have given up her original idea to buy. The knowledge depressed him; it seemed to him that she was leaving herself a kind of escape route.

"I'd like you to bring Laura out to see it," she said. "Perhaps she would help me choose the furniture."

"She'll tell you to buy a few comfortable chairs, and leave it at that."

"Then we'll begin with those."

They had dinner at a small roadhouse. She looked tired,

but seemed calm and at ease. He felt that she had accepted him as an older brother; she needed him, she sought his advice, she was content to be in his company – but that was all. And perhaps for the moment, he decided, it was enough.

"You're doing the alterations to the *Newshound* offices, aren't you?" she asked over coffee.

"Yes. I haven't been round yet to do a survey – I'm going tomorrow. Daphne's already got a number of ideas worked out, and most of them will need unworking."

"Will she interfere with what you want to do?"

"No. Because she knows that if she does, I'll drop the whole thing."

"She likes you."

"She likes men."

"She wants Alexander. Will she get him, do you think?"

"She might. She's been trying hard enough, but you were in the way."

"It would be a strange marriage, wouldn't it?"

"So strange, in fact, that it might work. At least, it might have worked if he'd stayed in London. I can't see her going back to Scotland and settling down on a kind of campus. But if she did marry him, she'd get something she wants very much, something my wife wanted when she put off our divorce. Freedom."

"And Alexander wouldn't mind?"

"He wouldn't be told much, and he'd be too busy to try and find out what she'd been up to."

Ross went to the *Newshound* offices on the following afternoon. Daphne received him in what she called her cell, a small room leading off the one Alexander had occupied. In it was a large, empty desk. Ross glanced at it and raised his eyebrows.

"Busy?" he enquired.

"I don't do desk work – especially when my colleague has taken himself off with a view to giving up this job. I think he's crazy. And I told him so."

"If he goes, will you go too?"

212

For once, Daphne hesitated before replying.

"As it's you who asked," she said at last, "I'll admit that I don't know. While he was here, I *had* him – almost. With that girl out of the way, I could have filled the gap nicely. I could have crept up on him slowly and he wouldn't have seen me coming and I would have got him. But now . . . Just think. You haven't seen that spread up there in Edinburgh. I have. I drove up to take a look last week. It's a mixture of tracks for field sports, grounds and pitches and spectator stands, and pavilions and halls for indoor games. To find Alexander, I'd have to hire a helicopter. It's even got a restaurant and countless cafés, so I wouldn't even necessarily see him for meals. Added to which, it's Scotland, and it may be the land of my fathers, but it's also the land of my mother, and once she knows I'm north of the Border, what's to stop her from appearing and even planting herself on me for a visit? Can you imagine? I'm at least safe from her in England; England is the place where my father lives, so she avoided it up till now. But if I go back north, I'm taking an awfully big risk. And I doubt if even Alexander is worth it. If I stayed down here, I could go back to my original intention, which was to catch you. But you wouldn't be interested. Right from the start, you and I had the same end in view: to wait until that brief romance fell apart. I wanted him, and you wanted her. Let's see, now, if we each get what we've waited for."

"And in the meantime, could we come down to business and discuss these alterations to the interior of the building? Or do I have to see your father about them?"

'You needn't see him until you send in your estimate. Then you'll see him and hear him, both. He'll probably tear it up before your eyes, but you don't have to worry; that's routine. You just draw up another estimate, doubling the amount, and I'll see it gets passed by his so-called advisers. You're going to make a lot of money out of this – do you realise that?"

"How much interfering are you going to do?"

"None. But there's nothing to prevent me from seeing you while you're on the job, is there?"

213

"Nothing, unfortunately. I just hope that Alexander will return soon and get you back to work."

Alexander duly reappeared, but only to work out the short period that remained of his contract with *Newshound*; thereafter, he would take up the job he had been awarded in Edinburgh. He gave up his flat, but made no attempt to get in touch with Gianna. To Ross, he explained in a telephone call that he would like to see him, but not yet.

"You'll remind me of what's happened," he said. "I'm all right, but I don't want to look back. In a way, I'm happier than I've been since I got on to that ferry. I'm lonely and I'm miserable, but – if you follow me – there's no more of that gnawing feeling I had of not measuring up to what Gianna expected. I'm free. Free to work."

"I never noticed any gnawing," Ross remarked.

"It was there, all the same. My conscience was never entirely quiet. Now all I've got to contend with is Daphne Maxwellton."

"Good luck."

"Thanks. I'll get in touch with you before I go north. So long."

That was all. He was never in the *Newshound* office when Ross had occasion to go there; whether he had been told of his coming, and arranged to be out, he did not know.

Ross left his office one dull, windy day and drove to another of the projects he had in hand; a row of mean terrace houses near the Tower of London, which had been bought by a patient and astute speculator over the last few years, and were now to be given a new – and very expensive – look. Ross liked going to inspect the progress of the work, because the district fascinated him. It was full of history, with almost every street recalling long-dead figures about whom he had written essays when he was at school. It was a congested area, an overspill from the city proper, and he had always had difficulty in finding a place to park his car until he discovered a dusty patch of waste ground with a car park sign and a down-at-heel attendant down a hidden side-street. After he had left his car there a few times, the

214

man got on to friendly terms and always kept a corner for his car.

This afternoon, as Ross walked to the row of little houses, he could see police being drafted into an area near the river. He heard shouts and saw a number of people running, but went on his way. As he returned to the car park, however, he saw down a narrow street that a small shop was on fire. He asked the attendant how the fire had started.

"Same lot as looted an off-licence last week." The man spoke in a tone of weary disgust. "Hooligans. One gang of these no-good kids meets another gang, and that's all it takes to start trouble. My brother got a couple of bricks thrown at his car a couple of hours ago as he passed the end of a street they were in, but it wasn't damaged – just a scratch or two. He wanted to get out and tackle the young devils who threw them, but a copper got there first."

"I might go and take a look at what's burning."

"You keep away, that's my advice. When those kids go on the rampage, they don't stop at much. In a mob, they suddenly become brave as lions. If you can prise 'em out of their group, they run. There was a few oldies got mixed up with this lot. The last my brother saw, the ladies were getting the worst of it."

Ross drove out of the car park, reached the main road and found himself seized by an impulse to go to the trouble area. At a red traffic-light, however, a policeman stepped from the kerb to the side of the car and addressed him.

"I wouldn't go that way if I were you, sir. You can keep straight on and turn at the junction."

It sounded like friendly advice, but Ross knew well that it was an order; he saw that all cars were being diverted from the area. He drove on. When he reached the junction, he saw a crowd of youths converging on a row of shops a little way down a street to his left. He could hear shouts, yells, an occasional scream. Half a dozen policemen appeared from a street opposite. Moments later, the battle began and moved in Ross' direction. This was the point, he decided, at which non-combatants should remove themselves.

But the sounds of strife pursued him as he drove away.

He passed running figures and saw people hurrying into houses or shops for shelter, yelling teenagers hard on their heels.

And then one person in the mêlée – a running figure – caught his eye. He recognised something familiar – the clothes, or perhaps the hat. Uncertainty lasted only a few moments. His next movements were instinctive. He slowed the car to the pace of the awkward, shambling figure; then he leaned across, swung open the car door and shouted. "Get in. Mrs Risdon, get in!"

She hesitated and glanced over to him. He stopped the car and in a moment she had clawed her way into it, tearing her skirt from the grasp of a shock-headed youth who had caught up with her. Ross leaned across her, seized the door, banged it almost on the nose of the youth, and put his foot down hard on the accelerator.

She sat fighting for breath, drawing in harsh, noisy gasps of air and expelling them with a kind of moan. He could see her hands clenched tightly together on her lap to stop them from trembling. He said nothing; he drove in the direction of his flat, waiting for her to recover.

After several minutes she was able to utter a few words.

"Where are . . . where are you taking me?"

"To my flat. You can clean up and rest, and then I'll see that you get home. Don't try to talk; just take it easy."

Beatrice was silent until they reached his flat. He helped her out of the car and into the lift. Opening his door, he took her straight through to the bathroom, got out clean towels and left her. When she emerged, he had coffee ready. Into her cup he also poured a generous measure of brandy, and she drank it without protest.

"How did you get caught up with the trouble-makers?" he asked at last.

"I was with a group of women; we had met in committee and were on our way home. We met a . . . gang of youths at the end of a narrow street, and they . . they walked through us. The police did what they could, but it wasn't much. Then some of the youths saw that we were a some- what elderly group, and they began to ridicule us. We stood our ground as long as we could, but things got . . . it seemed wiser to try and get away."

He made no comment, but he watched her with growing admiration. Under his eyes, the panting, fleeing, dishevelled wreck he had picked up was reverting to the woman he knew. Part of the recovery, he conceded, was no doubt due to the brandy, but she had another kind of spirit, and it was showing now. He did not find it hard to picture what she had just been through; the scratches on her hands and face, the blood now washed away from her temples; all this was evidence enough. She had pinned her torn skirt together.

"The police were there," she told him, "to deal with a gang of youths who had set a small shop alight. Perhaps they were hampered by having to protect a number of elderly women, but there certainly weren't enough of them to be effective. It was as well that the end of the street wasn't blocked. If we had been trapped there I don't know what would have happened."

Her voice was dragging. Fatigue, shock and the brandy were all combining to make her head nod. In a few moments she was in a heavy sleep. Ross went to the telephone and rang Gianna. At the sound of her voice his heart-beat quickened momentarily.

"Hello, it's Ross. I need some advice." He told her what had occurred. "I could take her back to Downpass," he continued, "but I thought it would be better if your father came up and drove her back. A nice brotherly gesture. What do you think?"

"Certainly. I'll telephone and tell him to come at once. Is she really all right?"

"Yes, though she might well have a bad hangover when she wakes up. Do you know what spunk is?"

"No."

"Well, she's got it."

"Can I come and see her?"

"I was about to suggest it."

"I'll come as soon as I've telephoned my father."

When she arrived, Beatrice was still asleep, slumped in a corner of the sofa, breathing noisily. Gianna stood looking

217

down at her, noting the marks of battle. A little while later, Beatrice started, opened her eyes, took in her surroundings and sat upright. She was alert and showed no signs of what she had recently been through. Indeed her eyes narrowed in disapproval as she took in the large room and its contents.

"Far too large for a single man," she snapped. "You could fit dozens of people in here."

"I frequently do," said Ross. "How do you feel?"

"I've got a headache, that's all. What I feel most is disgust. There was not the slightest need for the violence that broke out today or any other day. It's the fault of the authorities. In an area where there are large numbers of unemployed youths, young people who want jobs but can't get them, what do the authorities do to help? I've been asking them that question for weeks, and I've also supplied them with the answer: they do nothing. They draw their salaries but do nothing whatsoever to earn them. For weeks, months, I've been looking into the problem, and all I've met with is excuses, evasions and, in some cases, insults. They referred me to the youth clubs. How many youth clubs do you think there are in this district? Tell me that," she demanded, glaring at Ross. "How many?"

"I don't know."

"Of course you don't. You're not a man who concerns himself with the underprivileged. I don't know how you can live in this luxurious manner and reconcile it with your conscience. A few miles away, there are youths roaming the streets day after day, night after night, with nothing to do but make trouble, and you close your eyes, like all the so-called authorities I've been round interviewing." Her eyes went to Gianna. "And what are you doing here?"

"I came round to see how you were feeling."

"If you listen, you'll learn how I'm feeling. Today, I've learned something. I've learned that the people who ought to fight the problem do nothing. Action is needed, and it's action that I'm going to institute. If the authorities can't do anything, then I'll have to tackle the problem myself. I am

218

going to do something practical in an effort to put things right. I shall do it alone, because I've found nobody willing to help me with my schemes."

"What schemes?" Gianna asked.

"I am going to gather together some of these potential criminals and I'm going to give them a chance to do some work. I can't provide jobs, but I can see to it that some of them have somewhere they can occupy their time usefully – and if they have any skills or talents – gainfully, too. May I have some tea?"

"Sorry. I should have asked you before," Ross said apologetically.

He went into the kitchen and was about to fill a kettle when he decided to give Beatrice another proof of his decadence. He returned to the lounge and telephoned the kitchens for tea and toast for four.

"If I'd known that neither of you could make a cup of tea," Beatrice said wrathfully, "I wouldn't have asked for one. Why did you order tea for four? Can't you count?"

"Your brother James is coming to drive you back to Downpass."

"Who asked him to?"

"As a matter of fact, I asked Gianna to ask him to. I could have taken you myself, but I thought you'd prefer to go home with your brother."

However, when James duly arrived, Beatrice gave him a frosty reception. Heavy traffic had delayed him by thirty minutes and she was unable to prevent Ross from ordering fresh tea – perhaps because her voice lacked its usual bullying tone. Her mind seemed to be on other matters, but as she recounted to James the afternoon's adventures her manner grew more animated.

"What those young hooligans need," she concluded, "is employment. The devil, we all know, finds mischief for idle hands. These youths are jobless. They live in rabbit hutches without room even to swing a cat, so what can they do with their energy but take it out into the streets? Where else can they go?"

James, surreptitiously helping himself to a forbidden lump

219

of sugar, was heard to mutter the words youth clubs. His sister snorted.

"I've been into all that," she told him. "Some of them, I grant you, have the right approach, but they're in the minority. We need places – houses, buildings – in which tools are provided for those who have skills and want to use them."

To this James, with an unexpected upsurge of spirit that brought his daughter's eyes to rest admiringly on him, replied that half the tools would then be stolen and the other half rapidly put out of action.

"They're extremely violent, some of those youths," he ended. "They can be dangerous."

"Of course they can. They're animals without care or responsibility, and most of them are wild. But they weren't born in the jungle; they just grew up in one, that's all. People talk too much about the problem of delinquency – I've been listening to them for the past months – but nobody is prepared to do anything practical to deal with it. The thing to do is get hold of the teenagers before they embark on their road to the juvenile courts. In that street this afternoon, jostled, jeered at and pursued though I was, I learned a lot. If I were to go through it again, I wouldn't run away."

"It was as well you ran today," Ross said. "I agree with what you're saying, but – "

"You needn't agree with what I'm saying. You can wait a little while and watch what I'm doing," Beatrice responded belligerently. "Things have to start somewhere, in however small a way. I'm not claiming that I can make any impact on this problem. I'm not such a fool as to suppose that anything I do will result in any significant amelioration of the situation – but I intend to try an experiment. I've had it in mind for too long; now I'm determined to act. If it succeeds – and it will – other people will follow my lead."

James, about to pour himself out a third cup of tea, paused and regarded her apprehensively.

"You mean you've got some kind of plan?" he asked.

"I have. It's this. I am going to provide a place where there are large rooms for any young men who have the urge

220

to work at something they're good at, or would like to be good at. There will be rooms for those who want to paint, or do woodwork; walls for those attempting murals, libraries and studies with reference books for those who need to research; grounds for games, a gymnasium for building healthy bodies. No girls. I can deal with young men, but I am not prepared to mix the sexes. If I get the right type of youth – I shall of course do the choosing myself – all will go well. And if there are trouble-makers, I shall weed them out, root them out, throw them out."

The explanations of weeding and rooting and throwing out were accompanied by gestures of such ferocity that James quailed.

"I hope," he quavered, "you're not going to do anything in a hurry."

"I am sixty-one years old. How long do you expect me to wait before putting my plans into effect?"

"But . . . but you must first find a building in which – "

"Ah, but I've already got one," Beatrice replied triumphantly. "Or, more accurately, you have."

James gazed at her in horror.

"A . . . a building? You can't mean – "

"You own a house, a large house, a house which for far too long has been wasted on three people – yourself, our brother Walter and myself. It is ideal for my purpose. It has enough rooms, enough bathrooms; there are ample grounds, there are kitchens and pantries and outhouses. In short, everything we need."

"We?"

"I shall need your assistance, of course. Most of the youths will come to Downpass daily from London, but certain of them – the more civilised – will be residents. I will not turn you out of your rooms – don't be afraid of that. I shall offer Walter the choice of staying, or going to live at the vicarage, where he will be both welcome and comfortable."

"W-what do you want me to do?"

"The paper work. The accounts. You are, or you once were, a competent businessman. I shall count on you to attend to the financial side. I'm well aware that this scheme will take money. I am not poor, as you know. I am not asking you to contribute financially, but this is the first time in my life that I have seen and recognised a need, and I shan't hesitate in setting up my plan." She raised a hand and seemed to write a sign in the air. "Hargreaves House. I shall provide whatever is necessary for the workers in it, and they can sell the results of their work and donate one-third of the proceeds to a central fund. If you are going to argue that it is your house and I have no right to, as it were, annex it, I shall ask you if you propose to live the rest of your life with the knowledge that you turned your back on a scheme which might – which will – do good to your fellow creatures."

She turned to address Gianna.

"I am going to ask your help, too," she told her.

Gianna smiled. "You want me to help in putting the wild animals to work?"

"No. I would just like to enlist your support in over-coming your father's objections."

"Objections? I have no objections," James said. "All I feel is that the project needs time. Time to plan."

"The plan is made," Gianna told him. "Do you remember the Bible story about St Paul going to Damascus?"

"Yes."

"Aunt Beatrice has just been through a similar experience. Ross would say that she has found a cause, but I would say that she has found her métier. She is the only woman I know who could do what she says she is going to do, and make it work. If you find taking over the financial side too much for you, or if the new life is not congenial, you can escape to my Roehampton apartment – or if I decide to go back to France, you can come out and live with me there. Aunt Beatrice is right about Uncle Walter; he will be very happy with the vicar and Buddha."

There was silence. Then James addressed his sister in a tone of resignation.

"For fifty years or so," he said, "I've done what you told me to do. I suppose it's too late to change."

222

"That's the most sensible remark I've ever heard you make." Beatrice rose. "And now take me back to Hargreaves House."

Left with Ross, Gianna spoke with relief.

"At last," she said, "she has found what she wants to do. Now she will be happy."

"You think it will work?"

"I am sure it will. She will choose the boys; and some of them will undoubtedly make trouble, but that's when they will begin to see what she's made of."

"She'll need a bodyguard."

"No. You still underestimate her. The *boys* will need bodyguards."

"When you came to Downpass, she was in charge, and you quickly displaced her. Would you call that being strong enough to take on what she's about to take on?"

"That was only a small domestic crisis. This thing is different; bigger, and much more important to her. She'll make a success of it. You wait and see."

That was one thing he had shown he could do well, Ross thought bitterly. Waiting.

"Did you mean what you said about going back to France?" he asked.

"I am going over for Easter."

"You'll come back?"

"Of course. I told you. I have an apartment to furnish. Certainly I'll come back."

He said no more. It was not a promise, but it was a hope. And that, he supposed, was enough for the present.

14

Beatrice wasted no time in setting up what she decided to call the Hargreaves Work Centre. Walter was ejected, and the first teenage residents quickly installed. Her days were now divided between London and the Centre; she still argued and bullied, but there was now a new quality present in her manner that worked to disarm most of her opponents: an authority, a certainty that what she had set out to do was practical, and of great potential value to future planners in this field. Every day, a twenty-seater bus brought non-residents to the Centre, and visitors and residents alike settled down to a routine of work and leisure activities. No one – for the moment – gave any trouble.

James was the only person who was not surprised at the amount of money Beatrice had at her disposal to put into the scheme; having for most of his life been the victim of her parsimony, he had guessed correctly that there had to be a great accumulation of funds in her bank account. His own interest in the project was only superficial until he began to study the financial aspects; then his business sense, always keen, asserted itself and he became more and more absorbed in details which, though totally unrelated to tea importing or silk importing, had a human, a personal angle, to which he responded. And working with his sister did not prove, as he had feared, difficult; it turned out that Beatrice had so much to supervise in other departments that she was obliged to let him do his work in his own way.

"It would have been useful," she said one morning while organising some sports activities, "to have had someone like . . . what was the name of that man who hung round Gianna for a time?"

"Alexander Rannoch," James answered.

"Yes. Him. He could have given some of his time to coaching the boys in football. Where can I get hold of him?"

"You can't, I'm afraid. He's been given a job up in Scotland – running a big sports complex near Edinburgh. There were some pictures of it in *The Times* the other day."

"I thought someone said he was a journalist."

"He was, for a time." And I, he added to himself, was an importer of tea and silk. It seemed a long, long time ago. He marvelled to think that this scheme was proving to be a change for the better for all three members of the family concerned. Beatrice had found an outlet; he himself was content to juggle with figures and Walter was certainly happier than he had ever been in his life: while the vicar went about the affairs of Christ, Walter now spent his days writing the long-awaited book on Buddha. The vicar joined him in the evening and they revised the chapters together. The congregation frowned, but it was not so much a frown of disapproval as an expression of collective bewilderment.

Alexander had come to say goodbye to Ross before leaving for Scotland. He was not, he said, going to see Gianna.

"Why not?" Ross asked. "She'd like to see you."

"And I'd like to see her – but I think it's wise to leave things as they are: finished. Is she happy?"

"She seems so."

"You know what I think? She'll decide to go back to France, and she'll end by marrying a Frenchman."

Ross said nothing, but he began to wonder if this – Alexander's complete lack of intuition – had been at the root of all that had gone wrong. He was intelligent, but in some crucial ways he was also blind.

"What's Daphne going to do when you've gone?" he asked.

"God knows. She talked of joining me up there. But I quickly put the lid on that little proposal."

"She won't stay on at *Newshound* though, will she?"

"No. I can't see her ever holding down a regular job. And it's a pity, because she's got a brain – of a kind. She might

225

even have made a good architect; some of those ideas she had for the office alterations weren't at all bad."

"Not bad at all. Just completely impracticable." And those were Ross' final words on the subject of Daphne Maxwellton.

He gave Alexander a last drink, saw him to the lift and went back to his living room deep in thought. An encounter, a sea crossing, a brief flaring of love . . .

He rang Laura to tell her he would see her during the Easter weekend.

"I'll come down when I've seen Gianna off to Paris," he said.

"I don't think she should go until she's got herself settled in her flat."

"She's asked us to do the preliminary settling-in."

"What happens if she decides to live in Paris permanently?"

"If she does," Ross said evenly, "I'll go and fetch her back."

There was a pause.

"You said that as though you meant it."

"I did mean it," he told her.

This time, the pause was longer.

"Ross, I've never liked to ask you this – to your face, I mean. It seemed, it sounded too soon after . . . But you *do* like her, don't you?"

"I've been in love with her ever since that day we met just before Christmas. Do you want it in writing?"

He had to wait some time for a reply; he was certain she was fumbling for her handkerchief.

"Are you still there?" he asked, "or have you fainted with joy?"

"Almost. Oh Ross, how can I make you realise how happy I am?"

"You'll have to wait and see what Gianna says when I tell her."

"Haven't you said anything to her?"

"Not yet. Not out loud."

He said goodbye and rang off. After a long interval, he picked up the receiver and dialled Simone's flat. He had no

226

idea what Gianna felt about him, but was convinced that it was time he found out. He was tired of being an older brother. Moreover, she was going away, going back to what she thought of as her own country, and there was no guarantee that she would return. She would leave in his hands the disposal of her flat and furniture, and that would be the end.

He heard her voice.

"Ready to leave?" he asked.

"Practically. But I've got another two hours, haven't I?"

"Yes. Could I drop round now? There's a small matter I'd like to talk to you about."

"Yes, of course you can come."

When he arrived at the flat, he found her alone. She took him to her room, which was difficult to enter because of the number of large cases ranged along the floor, packed ready to be sent to Roehampton.

"Pity you couldn't have moved before leaving for France," he said.

"There was hitch after hitch, so I gave up. I'm leaving these cases to be sent by Simone, and I'd like you to ask Laura if she'd mind seeing the furniture in. What did you want to talk to me about?"

"I wanted to tell you what I told Laura a short while ago: that I've been in love with you since I met you."

He spoke with so little emphasis that she did not at first take in the meaning of what he had said. Then she turned away, walked to the window and turned again to face him. Her eyes were on him, but he could not interpret their expression.

"Did you have any idea?" he asked.

She shook her head. Her face was in shadow.

"I knew you liked me, but I thought . . . I thought what you liked was Alexander and me together."

"I did my best to make it stick."

"I know. Thank you."

"So now I've told you. I don't want you to say anything. I just wanted you to know – before you left. You're not ready to make any decisions yet, but I wanted you to keep

227

what I've said in mind while you're away. I'm sorry you're going."

"Ross, I *have* to go. I have to think, to start again . . . "

"I'm still frightened that you might decide to stay there."

"I won't. I promise."

"You might meet some man who – "

She cut into the sentence.

"Please don't say it. There has been enough of that, for me."

"Do you like me at all?"

"I . . . May I answer that when I come back?"

"Yes. Could I make one stipulation?"

"What is a stipulation?"

"I want you to promise you won't come back by sea."

She stared at him, and then he heard her laugh. Still laughing, she left the window, made a space for him on the luggage-laden bed, and told him to sit down.

"You can watch me finishing off my packing," she said.

"You're not doing it very well. Want me to take over?"

She moved aside. He began by removing most of the things from her suitcase and putting them back in again in better order, explaining as he did so the difference between packing a suitcase and merely filling a suitcase.

"And now," she said admiringly at the end, "I've got room to put in all those things I thought I hadn't space for."

She made coffee before they left. At the airport, she kissed him goodbye – a kiss that might mean anything or nothing, he thought. Watching her plane taxi out of sight, he discovered that he had lost his fear of her not returning. She would come back.

Ross did not go back to his flat; he wanted to check the progress of the work being done at the *Newshound* offices. On entering the building, he saw Daphne emerge from one of the lifts. She joined him and they picked their way through the workmen's debris until they reached her office.

"I took another quick trip up to Scotland," she told him.

"With Alexander?"

"No. Alone. I wanted to see if I could stand it."

"And can you?"

"I think so. As I told you, it's impressive. So is the salary they're paying him and the house they've given him. But I didn't like the location, so I went round looking for a small hideout for myself – and found one. Now I'll be able to see him on the job and off the job."

"Does Alexander know all this?"

"Not yet."

"Why don't you give him time to get on his feet up there before joining him?"

"He'll be lonely. Losing that girl was a jolt, though he hasn't realised it yet. I don't know whether he'll ever fall in love again, deep in love, as he did with her. But I don't want that kind of relationship with him anyway, thank you very much. I want . . . well, you know already. I suppose you've come to see what the workmen have done today. When you're through, come back here and you can give me a lift home."

But when he entered the room some time later, he found she was not ready to leave.

"D'you mind waiting a few minutes?" she asked. "I'm just clearing up something with Mr Shelway." She waved a careless hand towards a thin, meek-looking man standing by the window. "He's from the music publishers and he wants to take back the papers they let me look at, the ones about the composer Kleinhart. He won't take them without a covering letter – it's being typed now. I'll go and hurry them up."

She swept out of the room, leaving the two men to make polite conversation. After a brief silence, Mr Shelway gave a nervous cough and spoke.

"Changeable weather, isn't it?"

"Yes, very. You're Mr Shelway? My name's Mirren."

"Mirren . . . Ah. Is it your firm which is carrying out these alterations to the building?"

"Yes."

"I've come from Petwing's – the music publishers. I'm one of the partners of the firm."

229

"I think I dropped Miss Maxwellton at your office some time ago – she was to pick up some papers."

"Yes. But she . . . er . . . she omitted to send them back to us. The matter must have slipped her mind. I wasn't dealing with the enquiry at that time. It was in the hands of Mr Petwing, but I'm sorry to say he's no longer with us."

"Retired?"

"Dead. The result of an accident back in February. He was a keen cyclist, but on a treacherous piece of road, his machine skidded and he never recovered from his injuries. His assistant got in touch with Miss Maxwellton to request the return of the papers we had lent her, but he had so much difficulty in, one might say, getting her attention, that he appealed to me and I agreed to come here and ask for them personally." He indicated a bulky envelope that lay on the desk. "They're all there, but I thought it necessary to ask Miss Maxwellton to let us have a covering letter stating that they were of no further use to this newspaper." He paused and lowered his voice. "Frankly, Mr . . . er . . ."

"Mirren."

"Frankly, Mr Mirren, I have never understood why we were asked for the papers in the first place. I was surprised to learn that anybody was showing any interest in Kleinhart. One hears his music now and then, very infrequently, and in my opinion, it hasn't a great deal of merit."

"Didn't your firm buy the copyright of the symphonies he wrote?"

Ross put the question absently. His mind was not on Mr Shelway but on his first meeting with Alexander. It had all really begun, he mused, with this composer. A mission that had proved abortive . . .

"Yes, you're right," Mr Shelway was saying. "They were bought by Mr Petwing himself, when he met the composer in Lausanne many years ago. It was one of the few occasions on which he – Mr Petwing – could be said to have acted impulsively, I could even say unwisely. He was on holiday in Lausanne, and . . . But perhaps this is of no interest to you?"

"I'd like to hear about it."

"As I said, Mr Petwing was on holiday, and he went to a concert and heard one of the symphonies performed. Afterwards, he was introduced to the composer, and during the remaining two weeks of his holiday saw a good deal of him. They were about the same age, they were both interested in music, and from what Mr Petwing told me on his return, Kleinhart was a likeable man – in rather poor health, but mentally active and very good company. He told Mr Petwing very little about himself, but one fact did emerge: that he had been for a time a teacher in a music school in Italy – Milan, to be exact. He had been sorry to leave it. He did not state his reason for leaving, but Mr Petwing guessed that there had been some – er – indiscretion, some trouble in connection with the young English girls attending the school. Kleinhart hinted more than once that he had been on what one might call intimate terms with some of them. Mr Petwing concluded that this had led to his dismissal and his decision to leave Milan altogether. He did not begin composing until he settled in Lausanne."

"He died there, didn't he?"

"Yes. He didn't leave a Will, but he had written to Mr Petwing asking him to deal with any papers he might leave outstanding at his death. There were not very many, and certainly none of any general interest; bills, half-finished compositions, that sort of thing. Everything fitted into this envelope." He picked it up and drew out a sheaf of papers. "They're all here. I explained all that to Mr Rannoch – perhaps you have heard of him? He was the reporter who first – "

"Yes. I know him."

"He was the one who first approached us to see if we knew anything of Kleinhart. After that, it was Miss Maxwellton who asked to see anything we had in our possession regarding the composer. She came to fetch the papers; after a great deal of difficulty, I have now got them back. The covering letter is necessary because" – he lowered his voice – "I have not found Miss Maxwellton very professional. I need an assurance that she has seen the papers and has no further use for them."

231

He stopped, looked at his watch and made clicking sounds of irritation.

"I ought to be going. I wonder how long they're going to be?" He went to the door, peered out into the corridor and addressed Ross over his shoulder. "I can hear typewriters. I'm going to find out what the delay is. I can't wait much longer."

Ross heard his footsteps retreating down the corridor. Left alone, he gazed idly out of the window for a time and then examined the pictures on the walls. Finally he went to stand by the desk on which lay the sheaf of papers and the large envelope addressed to the music publishers. Glancing at the papers, he saw protruding from the bottom sheets something that looked like a snapshot. Without pausing to reflect, he pulled it out.

It was not one snapshot, but three. He was about to replace them when something in the topmost photograph caught his attention.

A building. A villa. Not large; white-painted, set among pine-woods; a villa like hundreds of others which could have been in any country where the sun shone with an intensity that could almost be felt even in a snapshot. Just a villa.

But he had seen this particular villa before. He had seen it in the photograph he had seen on Christmas Eve at Gianna's party – the photograph in which her mother had been standing on the steps.

But in the snapshot he was looking at now, it was the figure of a man who stood on the steps – a man who for a few astounded seconds Ross took to be Alexander.

Alexander? No. He was several years older than Alexander. A man in his thirties – but with Alexander's features and build all the same. The squarish face, the eyes, the nose, the mouth – even the figure; sturdy, and somewhat stocky. Alexander. Alexander to the life.

He turned the snapshot over. On the back were written four words: "Kleinhart. Villa Rosina. Milan."

With a dazed feeling, he looked at the second snapshot. Kleinhart again – and standing beside him, her hand in his, a

232

figure Ross had no difficulty in recognising. She was the girl who had been standing on the steps in the photograph at Hargreaves House. Gianna's mother.

His head spinning, he stared at the two figures. Then he looked at the last snapshot. Kleinhart – this time standing on the steps beside a girl Ross did not recognise. One arm was round her shoulders; the other shaded his face from the sun.

Through his bewilderment, he heard Daphne and Mr Shelway returning. Acting purely on instinct, he slipped the snapshots into his pocket.

When they came in, Mr Shelway had the covering letter in his hand. He straightened the sheaf of papers, clipped the letter to them and put the bundle into the envelope. Then he sealed it, bowed to Daphne, nodded to Ross and left. Ross put out a hand to detain him – and withdrew it. He attempted to speak, to produce the snapshots – but he seemed unable to move or to utter any words.

"Well, that's that, thank God." Daphne spoke briskly. "A complete waste of everybody's time."

He turned his gaze from the empty doorway.

"Did you look through all those papers?" he asked.

"No. I didn't even take them out of the envelope. The entire business, from start to finish was – as I've just said – a waste of time. Alexander saw there was nothing in Kleinhart to get excited about, my father had lost interest, and I had more pressing things on my mind."

"Were those music publishers the only people who had any information about Kleinhart?"

"Yes. When you come to think of it, how many untold thousands of composers have written symphonies and sunk into oblivion? Kleinhart was just one of them. We said in the covering letter that we had no further interest in the matter."

No further interest. No further interest. No further interest. The words seemed to him to reverberate from the very walls. No further interest in the matter. But in his pocket were three . . .

Ross longed desperately to get away, to go back to his flat, to study the snapshots, to clear his brain.

"Are you taking me home," Daphne asked, "or will you buy me a drink first?"

"I'm sorry. I've got to get back."

She gave a shrug.

"Perhaps you're good for me," she remarked. "You deflate my ego, if that's the right expression. I don't know any other man who lets opportunities slip as often as you do."

He scarcely heard her. Ideas, preposterous, impossible, were beginning to stir in his brain. He needed to be alone.

But when he left her, Ross did not go back to his flat. He drove straight down to Laura's cottage.

She was surprised to see him, but her pleasure at the unexpected visit was greater still. He refused her offer of tea, said that drinks could wait, and when they were in the living room, took from his pocket the three snapshots. He handed the first one to her.

"Recognise anyone in that?" he asked.

She glanced at it and spoke unhesitatingly.

"Yes, of course. Alexander."

"Look again."

"It's Alexander," she repeated.

"It isn't."

She stared at the snapshot.

"Well . . . yes, I see now. He's older. Alexander's father, perhaps. He must have been about thirty when this was taken. Where's the house?"

"Take another look."

"It's . . . wait a minute. I've seen it before somewhere."

"Can you remember where?"

"No. Yes. It's . . . isn't it the same villa we saw in that photograph of Gianna's mother?"

"Yes, it is. And now" – he handed her another snapshot – "will you take a look at that?"

This time, she stared at the picture for some time in silence. Then she looked at Ross with a frown.

"I don't understand," she said. "It's Gianna's mother – that's clear enough – but . . . but with . . . Will you please explain?"

234

"I can't. Read the back of that first snap."

She turned it over and read the words aloud.

"Kleinhart. Villa Rosina. Milan."

"Do you happen to know whereabouts in Italy Gianna's mother went for piano lessons?"

"No. All I know is that Alexander's mother – she was called Stroma – went to Milan to study music."

He handed her the last snapshot. She gave it only one glance before identifying the figure in it.

"Stroma," she said.

A tremor went through Ross. He tried to find something to say, but no words would come. Laura spoke in a dazed tone.

"Ross, I'm . . . I'm at sea. Say something."

He pulled himself together.

"It wants working out, that's all," he said.

"Who is this man Kleinhart?" she asked.

"He's the composer Alexander went to Lausanne to . . ." He stopped and began again. "Alexander was sent to Lausanne to see if he could find out anything about a composer who died there some years ago. He came back without having found out anything. He handed the job over to his assistant, Daphne Maxwellton, but interest in Kleinhart had died down and all she did was collect a few papers the music publishers had in their possession. She was returning them when I went to the *Newshound* offices today. She left them on the desk, and I saw these snapshots, picked them up and glanced at them. And when I saw who was . . . when I saw someone I thought was Alexander, and recognised that villa, and Gianna's mother, I came down here to show the snaps to you and see if we could . . . well, make some sort of sense between us."

He stopped; she was very pale, and looked so shaken that he went to the cupboard and poured a drink for her, and for himself. But she put hers aside, untouched.

"These snaps were among the papers you mentioned?"

"Yes."

"Why hadn't Daphne seen them?"

"Because she hadn't bothered to look through the papers.

235

Alexander had lost interest in Kleinhart; her father had also lost interest and had no further interest in the composer. When Daphne had taken the trouble to go to the music publishers to – "

"What music publishers?"

"A firm called Petwings. A member of the firm had been in Lausanne on holiday and had met Kleinhart and became friendly with him. Kleinhart sold him the copyright of four symphonies and also asked him to see to any papers he left in Lausanne after his death. There weren't many – they fitted into a big envelope – and these were of no general interest. Daphne went to fetch the papers but never even troubled to look through them. The firm got impatient and a man, one of the partners, came to get them back. He was there when I arrived to take a look at the workmen. He asked for a covering letter. Daphne went out to get it done, and he got impatient and followed her to speed things up. I was left with nothing to do but wait for them, and I picked up these snaps merely to pass the time. I thought – as you thought – I recognised Alexander. But it wasn't Alexander. It was Kleinhart. He'd told his friend the music publisher in Lausanne that he once taught at a music school in Milan, and admitted he was on more than friendly terms with some of his young foreign girl students. Given a music school filled with immature and probably temperamental girls, he'd have had a lot of scope. We know that Alexander's mother was in Milan. We know from the snapshot that Gianna's mother was there too – though not, I imagine, at the same time. One hopes not."

"But Ross – "

"I didn't think of all this when I first looked at the snaps. I didn't think of anything – I was in a state of what I suppose you could call shock. I worked some of it out when I was driving down here. You recognising Stroma gives us a pretty complete picture." He picked up her glass and handed it to her. "Take some of that. You look as though you need it."

She held the glass, but drank nothing. She was staring at Ross with something like fear in her eyes.

236

"Have you thought what this means?" she asked.

"Of course I have. God knows why you and I have got caught up in this tangle of which parents were whose, and when, and why. I wish, and I know you wish, we hadn't got involved. For the second time, the past – Gianna's parents' past – has come up and hit us. It was bad enough to try and guess the circumstances surrounding James' marriage. This is worse, because we don't have to guess. I don't know what you feel about it all – all I know is that I must believe my eyes, and looking at that snap of Kleinhart with Gianna's mother gives me a clear idea of the situation as it was. What do you know about Stroma?"

"She left Milan, went back to Scotland, married Alexander's father and had Alexander the same year."

"It fits. She produced a replica of Kleinhart. Gianna's mother didn't, but it's a hundred to one that he was the father of the child."

"I wish, oh Ross, how I wish you hadn't picked up – "

" – those snaps? Once I'd looked at them, I had a peculiar, undefined feeling that they shouldn't be left in that envelope. While they were there, the evidence was there for anybody to see, and examine. On the way down here, my mind went round and round all the near-misses: suppose the music publisher who had known Kleinhart in Lausanne had met Alexander? The only reason he didn't meet him was because he'd died in an accident. If they'd come face to face . . . But they didn't."

"Do you remember . . . "

"Do I remember what?"

"The way Gianna and Alexander insisted that when they met, they felt a kind of . . . affinity. Do you think it's too fantastic to believe that they – "

"Nothing's too fantastic to believe, after this."

"This is another secret we've got to carry to the grave, isn't it?"

"Yes. Finish that drink and I'll give you and myself another. We need them."

He refilled the glasses. She was still very pale and he wondered whether she felt as shaken as he did.

237

"The awful part of this, to me," she said after a time, "is that we can never tell any of them anything. Not James, not Gianna, not Alexander."

"As there's no longer any likelihood of Gianna and Alexander marrying, there's no need for them to be told."

"Suppose they hadn't called it off?"

"They did call it off, and it was final."

"My father would have said that the hand of God had separated them."

"Perhaps he could have explained why God brought them together in the first place."

"What are you going to do with the pictures?"

"Burn them."

"But if, years ahead, anything happens to make it necessary to tell the truth about this, won't you feel that you should have kept them?"

"No. They're only proof as far as Kleinhart and Stroma are concerned. Nothing can brush off that resemblance between father and son. But in the other case – Gianna's mother – we're still left in the region of guesswork."

"Like the facts about Gianna's date of birth."

"Yes." He studied her expression. "You're upset. I'm sorry I sprang this on you."

"I'm all right. Or I will be. But I have a feeling that I won't be able to get this out of my mind."

"Don't brood on it. What you need is a counter-interest. What would you say to getting away for a long weekend?"

"When?"

"Now."

She looked surprised, and then she laughed.

"Oh Ross, what a wonderful idea! Just to get this . . . this bombshell . . . to give us time to . . . Where would we go?"

"Up to Windermere. I want to look at a boat someone's selling."

"I'll go over to the Craigs and ask their maid to look after the dog and the cat."

"And then start packing."

He picked up his drink and stared thoughtfully into the

glass. He was silent for so long that Laura looked at him anxiously.

"Brooding?" she asked.

"No. Just wondering what would have happened if there had been any physical resemblance between Gianna and Alexander. What would have happened then, d'you suppose?"

She could not tell him.

The airport was crowded with passengers returning from a prolonged Easter vacation. She was one of the last off the plane. She disappeared into the luggage hall and he did not see her until she came out to the exit pushing a trolley. They met without words, and she followed him out to his car. Her first remark, as they drove away, was to tell him she had brought him some duty-free brandy.

"Good girl. Did you enjoy yourself?"

"Yes. I saw hardly anybody. I walked, and walked, and walked. What did you do?"

"Waited."

She smiled.

"And what else?"

"Laura and I took a trip to Windermere. I bought a boat. Then we went to Roehampton and fixed up your flat, Laura arranged the furniture and sent me out to buy flowers Now she's waiting to show you patterns of covers and curtains. As she's about it, you might manage to persuade her to choose some for her cottage. Are you glad to be in London again?"

"I'm glad to be seeing you again."

"I'm glad to have you with me again."

He drove her to St James's Park, stopped the car and turned to look at her.

"Happy?" he asked.

"Very, very happy."

"Before you left, I asked you a question."

"Do you want an answer now? You said you loved me, and you wanted to know if I liked you. Well, I do."

"Is that all?"

"No."

He turned towards her and took her in his arms. When he kissed her, he felt in her a passion equal to his own. When he released her, he was content.

"Do you want me to say it?" she asked.

"No."

"I would like to, just to hear how it sounds. Ross, I love you very much."

c.2

CAD   Cadell, Elizabeth.
       The waiting game

       12/9/0

DATE			

© THE BAKER & TAYLOR CO